D0927402

Cassian

THE IMMORTAL HIGHLAND CENTURIONS
BOOK TWO

JAYNE
CASTEL

WINTER MIST PRESS

A wounded warrior who vows never to love again. The shy lady's maid who adores him from afar. An adventure that will bind them. Unrequited love in Medieval Scotland.

Cassian Gaius is over one thousand years old and cursed to live forever. After watching his lover grow old and die, he vowed to remain alone until the curse is broken. But three hundred years later, his acquaintance with a lady's maid blossoms into something beyond his control.

Aila De Keith has been in love with Cassian ever since he took up the role of Captain of the Dunnottar Guard. Unfortunately, the enigmatic warrior remains polite yet distant with her.

But when Cassian and Aila accompany their laird and his wife on a mission to occupied Stirling, their relationship changes. The man they serve makes dangerous enemies, and Cassian and Aila are thrown into an adventure that risks revealing both their secrets: his immortality and her love for him.

Book #2 in The Immortal Highland Centurion series, CASSIAN is a tale of friendship, loyalty—and the courage to love.

Historical Romances by Jayne Castel

DARK AGES BRITAIN

The Kingdom of the East Angles series
Night Shadows (prequel novella)
Dark Under the Cover of Night (Book One)
Nightfall till Daybreak (Book Two)
The Deepening Night (Book Three)
The Kingdom of the East Angles: The Complete Series

The Kingdom of Mercia series
The Breaking Dawn (Book One)
Darkest before Dawn (Book Two)
Dawn of Wolves (Book Three)
The Kingdom of Mercia: The Complete Series

The Kingdom of Northumbria series
The Whispering Wind (Book One)
Wind Song (Book Two)
Lord of the North Wind (Book Three)
The Kingdom of Northumbria: The Complete Series

DARK AGES SCOTLAND

The Warrior Brothers of Skye series
Blood Feud (Book One)
Barbarian Slave (Book Two)
Battle Eagle (Book Three)
The Warrior Brothers of Skye: The Complete Series

The Pict Wars series
Warrior's Heart (Book One)
Warrior's Secret (Book Two)
Warrior's Wrath (Book Three)
The Pict Wars: The Complete Series

Novellas
Winter's Promise

MEDIEVAL SCOTLAND

The Brides of Skye series
The Beast's Bride (Book One)
The Outlaw's Bride (Book Two)
The Rogue's Bride (Book Three)
The Brides of Skye: The Complete Series

The Sisters of Kilbride series
Unforgotten (Book One)
Awoken (Book Two)
Fallen (Book Three)
Claimed (Epilogue novella)

The Immortal Highland Centurions series
Maximus (Book One)
Cassian (Book Two)

Epic Fantasy Romances by Jayne Castel

Light and Darkness series
Ruled by Shadows (Book One)
The Lost Swallow (Book Two)
Path of the Dark (Book Three)
Light and Darkness: The Complete Series

ISBN: 978-0-473-54679-3 (Paperback)

Published by Winter Mist Press

Edited by Tim Burton
Cover design by Winter Mist Press
Cover photography courtesy of www.shutterstock.com
Roman Imperial image courtesy of www.shutterstock.com

Visit Jayne's website: www.jaynecastel.com

***

For Tim.

***

"Why love if losing hurts so much? I have no answers anymore, only the life I have lived. Twice in that life I have been given the choice. As a boy and as a man. The boy choose safety, the man chooses suffering. The pain now is part of the happiness then. That's the deal."
—Quote from *Shadowland (1993 film)*

PROLOGUE

ETCHED IN MY HEART

Lothian
Alba (Scotland)

Spring, 1001 AD

THE TIME HAD come to say goodbye.

Like a doomed man awaiting his execution, Cassian had dreaded this moment.

But now it was before him, and there was no hiding from it.

Lilla was dying.

It was dark and smoky inside the cottage, despite that bright spring sunshine bathed the world outdoors. The glow of the hearth a few yards away cast a ruddy light over Lilla's face, softening the lines of sickness and age. Her grey hair, once the color of ripe wheat, fanned out around her upon the pillows.

Staring down at Lilla, Cassian could still see the lass he'd swept away to live with him in the hills of Lothian. Despite that she was now aged and gravely ill, to Cassian, she was as bonny as she'd been the first day he laid eyes upon her.

Lilla had been barely twenty when they met. She hadn't cared who he was, or that they could never have a normal life like other people.

"Cass, mo chridhe … don't look so sad." Lilla's voice, weak and raspy, filled the gentle silence.

"I can't help it, love," he whispered back, his fingers tightening around hers. Her hands were so thin and frail these days, the skin papery. "I wish I could have given you the life you deserved."

"Ye have," she replied, offering him a weak smile. The expression pained her, and she sank deeper into the nest of pillows supporting her head and shoulders.

Cassian shook his head. His throat was now so tight it was difficult to swallow, to speak, to breathe. Yet he forced himself on. "I couldn't give you children."

His voice choked off then. He wanted to say more—that she should have left him while she was still young, should have returned to her kin and found herself a man who could give her a normal life.

But instead, she'd remained with him.

"Fifty years," she whispered, her sunken gaze fixing him with a surprisingly fierce look. "All this time together and ye still think that matters to me?"

"But doesn't it?"

Her thin fingers clutched at his hand. "Ye have given me everything, Cass. I only wish that I too could live forever." Her chest rattled now, making it hard for her to finish the sentence, yet she managed. "So that we may never be parted."

Tears blurred Cassian's vision.

The Lord of Light strike him down. He'd known this moment would come, yet he was utterly unprepared for how awful it felt. The agony of impending loss crushed his chest with a pain that was hard to bear.

Lilla had remained youthful and vibrant for so long, he'd almost believed that nothing would change. Even when the first signs of age came upon her—stiff joints in the morning and the appearance of lines around her large blue eyes—he still denied it. But time marched on, relentless and cruel, and when she became bent and frail, he could no longer lie to himself.

The Grim Reaper was coming for his wife, and he was powerless to stop it.

The other two who'd been cursed along with him all those years ago—Maximus and Draco—knew that it was foolish to give your heart to a mortal woman, or to live with one as long as he had. They'd warned him this day would come. But he'd shrugged off their concerns.

Neither of them had met a woman like Lilla MacKenzie.

"I wish that too," he whispered back, his voice breaking. "I'd give anything to make it so."

"Tell me a story, mo ghràdh," she murmured, her eyes flickering shut. "My favorite one ... about how ye became immortal."

Cassian swallowed hard. She'd always enjoyed that tale, despite that it wasn't a happy one. In the past, he'd tease her by refusing to tell it, until she tickled him under his arms and he finally relented.

He wouldn't refuse this morning, even if he wasn't in the mood for storytelling. Lilla liked hearing about his past, and he wouldn't deny her, especially now.

"I was once part of the Imperial Roman army's Ninth legion," he began softly, one hand clasping hers while the other gently stroked her face. "'The Hispana' it was called, for the bulk of its force was made up of men from Spain ... like me."

He sucked in a breath, digging deep to remember those days. "We were once a proud legion, but centuries of campaigning in Britain had weakened us, and when I found myself stationed at Eboracum, near the northern frontier, morale was at its lowest point. Emperor Trajan wanted the uprisings in Caledonia quashed. He demanded that we take back the northern fort of Pinnata Castra, which Agricola had built many years earlier."

Cassian paused there, bitterness spiking through him even after all these years. They'd been offered up like sacrificial lambs. No one cared what happened to the

Ninth—the once great legion had become an embarrassment.

"And so ye marched north," Lilla continued the story for him. Her voice was weak, and her eyes remained closed, yet her words were clear. "And the Picts picked ye off, one by one, until the last men stood before the crumbling walls of that old fort and made their final stand."

Despite the heavy stone in his gut, Cassian smiled. "Yes, flower. That's what happened. A druidess then captured me and two others ... and she cursed us to an immortal life. She told us also that we could never father children or leave the boundaries of this land."

"But ye didn't believe her at first," Lilla reminded him.

Cassian squeezed his wife's hand softly. "Would ye?" Cassian paused then, his voice low as he continued. "The next day, the bandruì set us free and sent hunters after us. They stuck me full of arrows, but the following dawn, I awoke to find the arrows had disappeared and my flesh whole and healthy. I knew then the witch was indeed powerful."

"She gave ye a way to break the curse." Lilla's eyes flickered open, and she fixed Cassian with an unnervingly direct stare. "Only of late, ye don't seem to care."

Cassian's faint smile faded. She was right. His years with Lilla had turned his focus away from solving the riddle that had the power to set him, Maximus, and Draco free. "It doesn't matter," he said huskily. He didn't want to discuss the curse or that infernal riddle now.

But Lilla wasn't prepared to let the matter drop. Her thin fingers tightened around his, her throat bobbing. "It does, Cass," she whispered. "And once I go, it'll matter more than ever. Please promise me that ye will dedicate yerself to solving it."

Cassian stared down at her, his vision blurring. He hated this conversation; it made everything seem so final.

Swallowing hard, he reached out and stroked his wife's cheek. It was so cold; death's shadow already touched her. Right now, he'd agree to anything, if only he could bring her back from the brink. "I promise," he whispered.

Lilla died at noon.

Cassian wrapped her body gently in furs and then lifted her into his arms. She weighed nothing these days, so different to the robust woman of her youth. He then carried her outdoors, stepping into brilliant sunshine. Sunlight filtered across the hills, bringing with it the scent of heather.

Bitterness knotted deep in his chest. How dare the sun shine so gaily when the woman he loved lay dead in his arms?

How dare the world continue on? The wind still rustled through the pines, the birds still sang, and the burn bubbled merrily down the hillside.

Lilla was dead, and everything should stop.

And yet it didn't.

Cassian carried his wife up to the crest of the hill behind the cottage where they'd lived for the past fifty years.

He preferred an isolated life. The nearest village was half a day's ride on horseback, and with the passing of the years, few people had traveled this way—mostly to stop and refill their water bladders or to ask directions. Those who did assumed that Lilla was Cassian's mother. Cassian had simmered with fury at their presumption, yet Lilla hadn't minded.

She'd often teased him about it afterward, but for Cassian, it always took a while for the sting to fade.

It was a reminder that the outside world saw them as an unnatural coupling: she was a crone and he a man who looked barely older than thirty winters, a man still in his prime.

At the top of the hill, Cassian lay Lilla down and prepared to dig a grave for her. He knew he should have done this before now, yet he'd put the task off. It had seemed so final.

However, there was no getting around it now.

Cassian got to work, and all the while, the sun beat down on his back—and upon the shrouded figure that lay a few feet away, awaiting her burial.

Eventually, Cassian heaved himself out of the hole he'd dug. His body ached, and sweat poured off him, yet he paid his exhaustion no mind.

It wouldn't do any lasting damage. Nothing would. He could dig until his back literally broke, yet he'd awake the following morning whole and healed.

That Pictish bandruì had made sure of that.

Breathing hard, Cassian picked up his wife's body and gently carried it over to the grave. He then climbed down and laid her upon a bed of rushes. Hauling himself out of the grave once more, he began to fill it, shovel by shovel, with dark peaty dirt.

The shadows were growing long, pink streaking across the eastern sky, when Cassian finally completed his task. After filling in all the dirt, he placed a cairn of stones over the grave—a tradition that didn't belong to his homeland, but to Lilla's.

He'd made the green glens and rugged mountains of Alba his home, and had even come to love this land. Meeting Lilla had given him a sense of belonging he'd never known previously. He'd been so happy with her; there had been times he'd almost forgotten the curse upon him.

Almost.

Lowering himself to his knees before the cairn, Cassian stared at it. His temples pounded from exhaustion and too many hours working under the sun, and his limbs were leaden. Yet the physical discomfort was nothing compared to the pain deep in his chest.

She's gone.

Lilla MacKenzie had been his light, his hope. She was his shield from the darkness of eternity.

"Goodbye, my love," he rasped, hot tears burning his eyelids. "Thank you for everything." He paused there. His throat constricted. Grief rose within him like a spring tide. He wouldn't be able to hold it back for much longer. "I'll never forget you, Lilla. No matter how many years I live on … you will always remain etched in my heart." His voice caught, but he continued. "I will remember how you looked with the wind in your hair, how you laughed at my attempts to impress you." He tried to smile then, but his lips wouldn't curve. "You were always a terrible cook, but that didn't matter to me."

Images of the long years they'd spent together flooded over him then: the harsh winters huddled under furs, him gathering her posies of the first spring flowers every year, and Lilla's lovely voice as she sang to him in the evenings.

"The world is so dark now, my love," he whispered. "How can you leave and not take me with you?"

The storm hit him then, like a mallet slamming into the center of his chest. Cassian had heard tales of what it felt to be truly broken-hearted, but he was unprepared for the agony of it. Deep inside him something shattered—something that could never be pieced back together.

Lilla was gone.

Cassian bowed his head, and placed his trembling hands upon the cairn before him. Then he began to weep.

300 years later ...

I

CORNERED

Dunnottar Castle
Scotland

Beltaine, 1301 AD

AILA PLACED THE posies before the altar and then stepped back to admire them. A smile curved her lips; she adored flowers. Pale pink roses, daisies, and gillyflowers were her favorites.

"Thank ye for bringing the posies down, lass," Father Finlay's low voice rumbled across the incense-scented interior of the chapel. "They certainly brighten this place up."

Aila glanced over her shoulder, at where the chaplain stood a few feet away. Around him, stone arches reached up to a high ceiling. Despite that over five years had passed since William Wallace had locked the English garrison in here and torched the lot of them, the chapel still bore signs of that day—dark scorch marks around the high slit windows and the nave.

"The keep's garden is blooming beautifully this year," she replied with a smile. "Lady Gavina wanted ye to benefit from its bounty."

Beltaine was upon them, and Aila had spent the morning hanging garlands of lilac in the hall. Her mistress was planning a banquet and dance for the occasion. After dusk, folk would light a great bonfire on a hill near the fortress and dance around it. Although Beltaine—which heralded the beginning of summer—came from the old ways, Father Finlay wasn't a man to take offense.

The chaplain favored her with a kindly smile. "Please thank Lady De Keith for me, lass."

"I will. Good day, Father." Aila picked up her empty wicker basket, turned, and made her way from the chapel.

Stepping outdoors into a windy morning, she angled her face up to the bright sky. They'd endured a week of chill weather, but fortunately the sun had reappeared for Beltaine.

Aila closed her eyes, letting the warmth soak into her—and as she stood there, an uneasy sensation stole away the sense of well-being.

The fine hair on the back of her neck prickled. She lowered her face and shifted her gaze left, to where a man dressed in sooty leathers stood outside the smith's forge, legs akimbo.

Blair Galbraith was staring at her.

Big and bulky, with a thick auburn beard and long hair of the same color that he'd tied back with a leather thong, the smith wore a formidable expression this morning. He stood there, brawny arms folded before him, glaring at her as if she'd done him some personal offense.

Aila swallowed, her gentle mood evaporating as tension knotted in her belly.

She hadn't—but her sister had.

Aila's fingers tightened around the basket's handle. She shouldn't have come down to this area of the lower ward alone. She should have asked one of the other maids to accompany her, but she'd been so excited at the prospect of making posies for the church, she'd forgotten that the forge lay adjacent to the chapel.

Heather had warned her younger sister to stay away from this corner of the keep.

Aila remained frozen at the top of the steps and considered whether or not to attempt a greeting. Deciding against it, for she didn't want to encourage any interaction, she continued down the steps and then turned right, heading for the postern door and the stairs that led up to the upper ward.

Galbraith's stare drilled into her back, but Aila did her best to ignore it.

She wished she and her kin didn't have an enemy within the castle, but the events of just over a month earlier weren't Heather's fault.

Her elder sister had once been wed to Galbraith's brother, Iain. However, when Iain never came home from war, Heather had eventually returned to live at Dunnottar. And the very day of her arrival, her husband had risen from the dead.

Things were never going to end well after that— especially since Heather had fallen in love with Maximus, the man who'd accompanied her north to Dunnottar.

One evening, Iain cornered Heather and tried to kill her. He'd have succeeded too if Maximus hadn't interceded. Iain Galbraith 'disappeared' that night. Never to be seen again.

Few besides his brother had mourned him. Heather's husband had been a bully, and his brother was cut of the same cloth.

Aila couldn't get away from Blair's stare fast enough. Flinging open the postern door, she fled up the stairs. But she'd only gotten halfway up when a large hand clamped around her arm and hauled her backward.

Aila's cry of surprise echoed up the stairwell. Turning, she shrank back against the damp stone to see the smithy looming over her.

"I was wondering how long I'd have to wait," he growled. His grip on her arm increased, and Aila gave a gasp of pain. She tried to wriggle out of his grip, but he was a man of formidable strength.

"Let me go," she pleaded, her heart fluttering like a caged bird against her ribs.

"I don't think so. I've been waiting to see yer whore of a sister ... but ye will do well enough."

Aila winced at his crudity, even as indignation rose within her. How dare he speak of Heather in such a fashion? Raising her chin, Aila forced herself to meet his belligerent green gaze without cowering. "Heather isn't to blame for yer brother's disappearance, Blair."

"Aye, she is." He gripped her by the other arm and shook her, his gaze narrowing. "She and that cèin devil. I don't know how they managed it ... but they somehow did away with Iain, so they could be together."

A chill settled over Aila, dousing the indignation that had given her courage. His fury scared her, and she started to sweat.

"That murderer is now part of William Wallace's band." His voice lowered to a growl. A vein pulsed in his neck, and his fingers now bit into her flesh. "He kills my brother and gets rewarded for it. De Keith and Wallace both pretended his death didn't matter ... and they'll pay. Ye *all* shall pay!"

Aila stared back at him, fear clenching in the pit of her belly. Menace crackled in the air between them.

Blair leaned in closer, bracketing Aila against the wall. "I've recently received disturbing news," he continued. "My cousin's rotting corpse has been found north of Stirling. He and his men were butchered like dogs ... Maximus are Heather are to blame!"

Aila's breathing quickened, panic roiling in her belly. "I don't know anything about this." She tried to twist out of his grip, yet he held her fast. It was the truth; this was the first she'd heard of it. "My sister had nothing to do with such brutality."

"She has *everything* to do with this," Blair countered, biting out the words. "The messenger told me that my cousin Cory had an altercation with both Heather and that foreigner before leaving Fintry. Cory tracked them north, but was never heard from again. Eventually, my uncle sent out men to search for him."

"That's not proof."

Blair's mouth twisted into a sneer. "It's all the evidence I need."

He then grasped one of her breasts and squeezed hard.

Crying out in outrage, Aila raised a hand and struck him across the face.

Blair didn't even reel back in shock. He just stood there, immovable as a boulder. Something dark and frightening shifted in his eyes. "Ye shall regret that, Aila De Keith," he murmured.

"Will she?"

A man's voice rang out across the stairwell.

Aila craned her neck to the right, peering over the barrier of Blair's muscular frame, to see a tall man clad in chainmail and leather standing above them. A plaid cloak in cross-hatchings of blue, turquoise and green— her clan's colors—hung from his broad shoulders.

Aila's breathing caught, her limbs weakening as relief flooded through her.

"Let the girl go," Cassian Gaius, Captain of the Dunnottar Guard, continued. "Before you do something you regret."

Blair Galbraith spat out a curse. "Walk away, *Captain*. This is none of yer business."

Cassian inclined his head. His gaze was hooded, his expression cold. "Step away and go back to your forge." He moved, descending the stairwell toward them.

Blair's face twisted. However, the captain didn't utter another threat. He just waited for the smith to do as bid.

Aila's pulse quickened once more. She wasn't sure Galbraith would heed him.

Tense moments stretched out, and then, surprisingly, Blair released Aila and stepped back.

Aila drew in a shaky breath. Her legs wobbled under her, although she remained where she was, frozen against the wall.

"This isn't over," the smith growled, pinning Aila under his stare, the captain forgotten. "Ye and I shall continue this later."

"Enough, Galbraith," Cassian cut in, a harsh edge to his voice. "If I ever catch you intimidating Aila De Keith again, I'll shove your teeth down your throat."

Blair snorted and cast the captain a malevolent look before turning his back on him. "All ye *cèin* are the same," he muttered. The smith then moved off down the stairwell. Moments later, the postern door thumped closed behind him.

Wordlessly, Cassian descended the stairs so that he stood level with Aila. Like Blair, the captain was tall. Aila had to crane her neck up to meet his eye.

But when she did, the knot in her belly dissolved. Transfixed, she stared up at him.

Never, in the three years that Cassian had been at Dunnottar, had he given her his full attention like this. She knew he had hazel eyes, but this close, she saw his irises were flecked with brown, gold, and green. He had a strong jaw, an aquiline nose, and tanned skin that she longed to trace her fingertips along.

Cassian Gaius wasn't a Scot, but a Spaniard. Unlike most men at Dunnottar, who sported long hair and beards, he was clean shaven and wore his brown hair short.

How many nights had Aila lain in bed imagining what it would be like to run her hands through his hair? What would it feel like? Soft like thistle-down, or coarser like a pony's mane?

Staring down at her, his brow furrowed, concern clouded Cassian's eyes. "Did he hurt you, Aila?"

Aila's breathing caught. Twice now, he'd used her name. She loved the way he said it too; his slight accent made her name sound beautiful. Cassian was a man of principle and honor. Her father, who was steward here, often spoke highly of him. Folk here admired his calm, stoic manner.

And over the years, Aila had grown increasingly desperate to catch glimpses of Dunnottar's enigmatic captain, desperate to gain a moment of his attention.

Aila swallowed, forcing herself to focus. She then rubbed the spots upon her upper arms where Galbraith had grabbed her. "I'll likely bear some bruises," she admitted. "The smith has a fierce grip ... but apart from that, I am well."

Cassian's mouth thinned. "You faced him bravely."

Warmth flowered within Aila at his praise. "I did?"

"I'd just entered the stairwell when I heard the slap you gave him."

"Aye, but it was like striking a boulder. He didn't even flinch."

The captain's gaze glinted. "He'll do more than flinch if I ever catch him cornering you like that again."

II

DAYDREAMS

"WHAT HAPPENED ON the road to Dunnottar?"

Heather glanced up from the flowers she was arranging in a vase in their parents solar. She'd likely just come from spending time with Lady Gavina. Shortly, Aila would have to wait on her mistress. However, she wanted answers from Heather first.

Aila had been relieved to find her sister alone. This wasn't a conversation their parents needed to hear.

Heather's face tensed. "Excuse me?"

"Don't act as if ye don't know what I'm speaking about," Aila countered, folding her arms across her chest. "Ye didn't tell me that ye fell foul of the Galbraith laird's eldest son ... or that he tracked ye north after ye left Fintry."

Aila's belly tightened then. *There used to be a time when ye told me everything.* Aye, once. But all that changed when Heather left Dunnottar on Iain Galbraith's arm five years earlier.

Heather's grey-green eyes widened, alarm flickering in their depths. "Where did ye hear this?"

"From the smith. He just cornered me on the stairs and told me that Cory Galbraith and his men's bodies have been found north of Stirling."

A guilty look passed across her sister's pretty face; Aila had always been able to read her easily. Folk said that the two sisters looked very much alike, but Heather was taller, curvier, and more confident. She had an ample bosom that Aila had always envied, and a feisty nature that her husband, Maximus, adored. Aila sometimes felt mousy and meek in her shadow.

Right now though, anger made her bold. Aila placed her hands on her hips. "Did ye and Maximus kill them?"

Heather's throat bobbed before she nodded.

Aila frowned. "I can't believe ye hid this from me!"

"It was better ye didn't know," Heather replied, stubbornness lacing her voice. "Cory and his men attacked us, and we fought them off. It was 'kill or be killed'. Afterward we hid the corpses and continued north."

Aila's frown deepened to a scowl. "What? Two of ye against a group of armed men ... and ye arrive in Dunnottar without even a scratch? *Ye* don't even know how to fight."

Heather's mouth thinned. Aila knew she was pushing it, yet hurt still boiled within her. She was tired of being the last to discover things. Her parents still wrapped her in wool like she was a five-year-old. Often they'd be discussing politics when she entered the room, and then they'd abruptly change topic. It was as if they thought she'd shatter if she came in contact with the world outside the fortress.

Aila wasn't a fool; she knew things were bad for the Scots at the moment. After a few years of uneasy truce, the English had attacked once more. King Edward of England had just taken Stirling Castle, while a second fork of his army was rampaging up the south-western coast of Scotland. If the English took Dunnottar again, her parents wouldn't be able to protect her, yet they seemed intent on keeping her cosseted.

"I know how to wield a dirk ... Maximus showed me," Heather replied stiffly. "And Maximus is a formidable swordsman. He defeated them."

Aila stared back at her sister, torn between disbelief and admiration. "Well," she said, a little deflated now. "Ye should know that Blair Galbraith is intent on avenging not just Iain, but Cory too."

Heather's gaze shadowed, and she took a step closer to Aila. "Did that bastard harm ye?"

The concern on her sister's face was real, yet Aila clenched her jaw as irritation surged. She would not let Heather change the subject. "He grabbed me ... and would have done worse ... if Captain Gaius hadn't intervened."

Heat flowered across Aila's chest when she said these last words. Moments later, a blush crept up her neck. Ever since her sister's return to Dunnottar, she'd done her best to avoid Heather's questions about her feelings for the handsome captain.

Heather's eyes gleamed, her expression turning sly. "Really?"

Aila stiffened, her face flaming. "Aye," she replied. "But that's not important ... what matters is—"

"Ye have gone as red as a poppy, dear sister."

Curling her fingers into fists, Aila clenched her jaw. "No, I haven't."

"Aye, ye have ... and if I had a looking glass to hand, I'd show ye."

Aila glared back, aware that her cheeks now burned. Curse her sister and her knowing looks. Heaving in a deep breath, she decided to use Heather's own trick and brazen the situation out. Maybe, her sister would back off if she thought Aila didn't care what she thought.

Aila gave Heather a haughty look she'd learned from their mother. "Well ... I'll have ye know that he was very gallant. Captain Gaius sent Galbraith slinking away like a beaten dog, and he was *very* concerned about me."

That made Heather's smile slip. "He was?"

"Aye ... it's not that strange." Aila drew herself up, chin tilting. "Perhaps he will dance with me this eve ... it is Beltaine after all."

Heather drew in a slow breath, her expression growing serious. "I do hope ye aren't pining for him, Aila ... it won't do ye any good."

Aila's breathing hitched.

Her sister had no idea how she pined for him. He was the first thing she thought about each morning when she awoke, and her last thought before she drifted off to sleep at night. She looked forward to those times, to the quiet moments of the day, for they allowed her to daydream of what life would be like as Cassian Gaius's wife.

"Why won't it?" she replied, her tone sharpening. "Ye speak as if he'd never be interested in the likes of me."

Heather shook her head. "That's not what I meant. Ye are lovely, Aila ... and one day a man will sweep ye off yer feet and make ye his wife. But Cassian has never shown any interest in taking things further. It's unwise to give yer heart to someone who doesn't want ye in return."

Aila drew back. "What makes ye think he doesn't want me?"

"Has he ever encouraged ye?" Heather's tone was gentle now, her eyes shadowed.

However, her concern merely angered Aila. She was tired of being patronized. "He takes his role as captain seriously," she shot back. "And I respect that. But ye should have seen him today ... he was protective and concerned about my welfare."

Heather huffed. "He's a decent man ... but that doesn't mean he has any interest in ye. If he had, he would have courted ye."

Once again, her sister's words cut deep. Aila stared back at Heather, her throat thickening.

Damn her, I won't cry.

"I don't know why ye say such things," Aila finally managed, hurt squeezing her ribs like a mailed fist. "I've only ever championed yer cause ... but ye cut me down before I have a chance to go after my own."

Heather's eyes widened, red spots flaring on her cheeks. "Of course, I want ye to be happy. It's just that—"

"Lady Gavina will be awaiting me," Aila cut her sister off. Her tone was cold, yet it was merely a shield to hide the hurt that burned underneath. Heather was no different to her parents. Everyone treated her as if she was some fragile, goose-witted lass who needed to be shielded from life's harsh realities.

She'd had enough of it.

Without another word, Aila turned on her heel and stormed from the solar.

When the door thudded shut behind Aila, Heather loosed a heavy sigh.

She wanted to go after her sister, to explain the reason for her caution. But she couldn't betray Maximus, Cassian, and Draco's secret to another soul—not even to her sister.

Aila was clearly besotted.

Heather had noted the signs from the first day she'd returned here. She'd caught Aila staring at Cassian when they joined the laird and his kin in the hall for meals.

But until today, her sister had always denied Heather's teasing accusations.

"God's teeth," Heather muttered, twisting her hands together. "She's about to get her heart broken."

Heather knew Cassian Gaius couldn't love her sweet-natured sister. Like Maximus, he was immortal—but unlike her husband, Cassian had walled off his heart.

Maximus had told Heather that Cassian once loved a woman deeply. He'd lived with her for many years, and the pain of losing her had nearly driven him mad. He'd sworn then and there that he'd never bind himself to another again.

It was a lonely choice—and not so different from the one Maximus had made.

But Cassian and Maximus were different men. Unlike his friend, Cassian's past still drove him. She'd noted how aloof the man was, how little he gave of himself to others. Maximus said that when he, Cassian, and Draco spent time alone, the shield came down a little—but Heather had never seen it.

Heather's belly tightened. What a cruel fate that druidess had given them. It had been a risk to give herself to an immortal, and to wed him, yet Heather had known that whatever happened, she would always love Maximus. It sometimes worried her that if they didn't break the curse, he would one day suffer the same fate as Cassian. She didn't want him to watch her age and wither while he stayed forever young. She didn't want to see such grief in his eyes.

Shivering, Heather banished the chilling thought. It cast a shadow over the bright day. She turned to the window, and her gaze traveled south, over the walls of the upper ward and across the glittering North Sea. Today was Beltaine, a time for revelry and good cheer, not for morbid thoughts that might never come to pass.

All the same, she worried for her sister.

III

MATTERS OF THE HEART

AILA HAD ALMOST finished putting up Lady Gavina's hair, when the laird burst into the bed-chamber.

"David!" Gavina gasped, jumping as the door slammed back against the wall. Meanwhile, Aila only just managed not to stab the pin she was holding into her mistress's scalp. "Please knock before entering my chamber. I could have been in the midst of dressing."

In response, the De Keith laird curled his lip, making it clear how little he cared for his wife's propriety. "Ye have organized a bonfire outside our keep's walls," he accused.

"Aye," Gavina replied, her tone serene. "What of it, husband?"

Aila went still, rapidly blinking at the laird's show of temper and his wife's stoic response to it. David De Keith usually wore an urbane smile. He possessed a serpent's charm, which Heather had warned Aila about before she left Dunnottar.

Over the years, many a tale had circulated the keep about De Keith's infidelities. Everyone knew about the servants the laird took to his bed in favor of his beautiful Irvine wife. The laird and lady seemed to have very little to do with each other. In fact, this was the first time De Keith had ever entered Lady Gavina's bed-chamber while Aila was attending her.

As if realizing this, David's gaze flicked to Aila. Tall and handsome, with brown eyes and a neatly trimmed beard, De Keith had often favored Aila with melting looks—looks she'd studiously ignored. And as Heather had warned, she'd been careful never to find herself alone with him.

However, today his expression was fierce. "Send yer maid away," David growled.

Gavina drew herself up. "Anything ye have to say to me, ye can say in Aila's presence."

The laird drew in a harsh breath, his hands fisting by his sides.

Aila's breathing quickened. Was he going to lash out at his wife?

Long moments passed, yet De Keith didn't move. In the years that Aila had waited on Lady Gavina, she'd never seen her mistress sport the tell-tale bruises that came from a violent husband.

The laird wasn't going to strike the lady. However, his dark eyes blazed. He ignored Aila now, his attention entirely focused on Gavina. "Have ye lost yer wits, woman? Yer traitorous brother is breathing down our necks, and ye decide to build a bonfire outside our walls … to open our gates, and empty the fortress after dark."

Gavina made a small noise in the back of her throat. "It's Beltaine. The folk of Dunnottar and Stonehaven always dance around the bonfire together."

"Witless woman," De Keith snarled back. "Perhaps this is all part of ye and Shaw's master plan. No need to bring the 'Battle Hammer' to our gates … not if we leave them wide open." He paused there, breathing hard. "Or maybe, ye are in league with the English? I wouldn't be surprised if ye wrote Longshanks himself a missive, inviting him to the festivities. Ye have no idea the danger we're all in!"

Gavina went still. Standing behind her, Aila couldn't see the expression on her face. Yet the rigidity of her mistress's shoulders told her all.

"I would never betray ye, David," she replied softly. "Not to the English ... or to my kin."

"Words are easy ... just like the promises yer clan made and then broke."

"But surely the castle is well defended? Especially now we have the Wallace and his men here."

David De Keith's lip curled once more. "Wallace could easily bring doom down upon us," he spat. "He's using Dunnottar as his hide-out ... and using *us* to further his own ambitions." He took a threatening step toward her. "In future, ye will speak to me before ye make any preparations like these."

"Ye have always said ye don't like to be bothered," Gavina snapped. "Has that changed?"

The laird's eyebrows drew together, while his beard narrowed to a point as he pursed his lips. "Ye know full well that I care not what cloth ye purchase for yer gowns," he replied, his voice dripping with scorn. "But if ye put this keep at risk again with yer empty-headed wish for frivolity, I shall lock ye in this chamber for the rest of the summer. Is that clear?"

The threat hung in the room, heavy and cold.

Silence drew out, and when Gavina replied, her voice shook slightly. "Aye, husband. Very."

"We shall celebrate Beltaine *inside* the hall tonight," De Keith replied. He still held his wife in a gimlet stare. "I'll leave it to ye to inform those within the castle of the change of plans."

And with that, the De Keith laird swiveled on his heel and strode from the chamber without a backward glance.

Another silence followed him.

Gently, Aila inserted the last pin into Gavina's hair and stepped back to admire her crowning glory. Her mistress had the most beautiful hair: it was as pale as sea-foam, and when loose, it fell over her slender shoulders in heavy waves. But it was also just as lovely braided and pinned atop the crown of her head.

Many folk said that David De Keith had wed the bonniest woman in Scotland, yet Aila had rarely seen him glance at his wife with anything but disdain.

"My Lady," Aila ventured finally when the pained hush drew out. "Are ye well?" She moved around to look at Gavina's face, her heart constricting when she saw that the lady's cornflower-blue eyes glittered with tears. Her heart-shaped face was pinched.

With a jolt, Aila realized that Gavina wasn't upset as much as infuriated. "My Lady?"

"Aye, I'm as well as to be expected, Aila," Gavina replied tightly. "I'm torn between wishing my husband would choke on his nooning meal, and chastising myself for giving him another opportunity to humiliate me."

"But ye weren't to know that—"

"I should have realized that holding a bonfire this year wasn't wise," Gavina cut her off.

"But everyone looks forward to it." Aila certainly had been. She'd hoped that Captain Gaius would attend, and that they'd dance around the fire together, hand in hand.

"Aye, but as much as it pains me to admit it, David is right. My brother's threats are worrying indeed. We can't leave the keep vulnerable to attack ... even for one night."

Aila went silent at this, lowering her head as disappointment settled upon her. "So, there will be no dancing?"

Lady Gavina favored her with a brittle smile. "Of course, there will be, Aila. Once the banquet is done, we shall push back the tables and let the dancers take the floor in the hall." A groove etched itself between her brows then as she studied her maid properly for the first time since David De Keith's stormy exit. "Are ye hoping a certain man will ask ye to dance?"

Aila stiffened, cursing the blush that rose to her cheeks at her mistress's penetrating look. However, unlike Heather, Lady Gavina wouldn't push her to reveal the name of her wished-for suitor. Aila's throat tightened. Heather's lack of support still stung.

"Aye," Aila admitted, dropping her gaze to the woven rug on which she stood. "Can I ask ye something, My Lady?"

"Of course," Gavina replied. Aila noted the edge of reserve in the woman's voice. She never had to worry about Lady Gavina prying, for her mistress was an intensely private person herself. Despite that she'd served Gavina for years now, her mistress had shared very little of her thoughts and feelings with her.

Perhaps it was their relationship that prevented her. Maybe she confided more in Heather, whom she often spent afternoons with, or in Lady Elizabeth—the wife of Robert, Dunnottar's former laird. Robert De Keith was now an English prisoner, and his brother had taken his place until his return. If he ever returned.

"What would ye suggest, if a lass is in love with a man who hasn't yet noticed her?" Aila asked, gathering her courage. "Is there a way to ... encourage him?"

She glanced up then, meeting Lady Gavina's eye. Her mistress surveyed her for a long moment before a rare smile curved her lips. "I'm probably not the best person to ask such a question," she said after a pause. "As ye know, my marriage was an arranged one."

Aila inclined her head, her interest piqued by Gavina's response. "Were ye pleased when yer father organized the match?"

The faint smile remained upon Gavina's lips, although her eyes shadowed when she nodded. "I was never rebellious ... and as the only daughter, I was expected to marry advantageously. When the younger De Keith son sought my hand, it was an opportunity to forge peace between our clans ... and I was eager to please my father."

Aila fought the urge to frown, questions bubbling up inside her. This was an opportunity to learn more about the woman she served. However, before she could ask anything else, Gavina spoke up once more. "Like I said, I know little about such matters ... but I would suggest that sometimes men do need a little encouragement."

Aila's pulse quickened. *Finally, someone is willing to help me.* "Such as?"

"Well … if this man is to be at tonight's banquet, I suggest that ye make an effort to look yer best." Gavina cast a critical gaze over the simple blue kirtle that Aila wore. "Do ye have a pretty gown for this evening?"

"I have a nice silver-grey kirtle that matches my eyes … I was going to wear that."

Gavina shook her head. "Grey is no shade for Beltaine. Ye need to shine like the sun tonight, if ye wish the man ye desire to notice ye." A real smile flowered across Gavina's face then, and she rose to her feet, brushing off her skirts. It seemed that focusing on Aila's predicament had made her forget her own. "Come … let's see if one of my kirtles and surcoats can be adjusted. Ye are a little taller than me, but we are of a similar size."

"But, My Lady … the laird insisted that—"

"Telling the servants that we're no longer holding a bonfire can wait," Gavina replied with an airy wave of her hand. She caught Aila's eye once more and winked. "We have more important matters of the heart to deal with first."

IV

OLD FEUDS AND NEW

"I'M NOT BENDING the knee to Longshanks!" David De Keith's voice cut through the solar, causing the three other men gathered there to grow still. "And I'm not traveling to Stirling ... not with Irvine sharpening his dirk at my back!"

Cassian lowered the cup he'd been about to take a sip of wine from, catching Draco Vulcan's eye. His friend stared back at him, his expression veiled. Cassian's gaze then flicked to where William Wallace stood by the open window.

Both Draco and Cassian had joined the men they served in the solar for this important meeting.

A few yards away, the De Keith laird stood before the glowing hearth—not that a fire was needed in the solar this afternoon, for the sun streamed in through the open window, pooling like honey upon the deerskins spread across the stone floor.

Wallace was watching De Keith, his bearded face shuttered. "There are worse wolves in the woods than Shaw Irvine," he rumbled. "Not only that, but we have the men here to deal with the likes of him." Wallace paused then. "We need to stop fighting with our fellow

Scots and face the real enemy ... the English. This is a unique opportunity ... Longshanks has invited all the northern lairds to visit him in Stirling ... to pledge their fealty."

De Keith snorted, before reaching for the clay bottle of wine on the mantelpiece beside him and refilling his cup. He then took a large gulp. "I told ye ... I'm not kneeling to him."

"No one is suggesting ye do it in earnest," Wallace replied. "Make the sign of the devil's horns behind yer back if ye must, when ye pledge yer troth, but it's Edward ye should be focusing on ... not yer brother-by-marriage. We must know what Edward intends, and our best chance of finding out is if ye go to Stirling and bend the knee."

De Keith scowled. "That's easy for ye to say, Wallace. Ye left yer clan years ago ... ye have forgotten how dangerous old feuds can be."

Wallace's dark gaze narrowed. Across the room, Cassian grew still. He'd only known William Wallace a little over a month, but had already noted that he wasn't a man to cross. Usually, De Keith minded him—but this afternoon, the laird wore a disgusted expression, as if someone had over-salted his porridge.

"Old feuds are meaningless," Wallace answered. "Especially if we all end up under the English yoke." He paused there, his heavy brow furrowing. "That's how they'll defeat us in the end ... they'll use the fact that we squabble like brats amongst ourselves instead of uniting against them."

The laird's brown eyes glinted. "Why don't *ye* go to Stirling, William? I'm sure Longshanks would be delighted if ye bent the knee to him."

Wallace huffed a laugh. "Things have gone too far between me and Edward for that. He'd have me strung up." The big man's expression sobered then. "Besides, it's vital that my presence in Dunnottar remains a secret. The English can never know I'm here."

De Keith's mouth puckered. While there were benefits to hiding Wallace and his men at Dunnottar, the outlaw had also just reminded him of the danger his presence here put them all in.

Cassian took a sip of spicy plum wine and shared another look with Draco. Wallace spoke true about the feuding. Both Cassian and Draco had lived long enough to watch the tribes of Caledonia war amongst themselves before eventually forming the kingdoms of Pictland and Alba. The fighting still continued, even after the clans were eventually united under the kings of Scotland. Feuding was a constant, and Cassian and Draco had been involved in a number of them over the years. The clans of this land had never gotten on. And to make matters worse, these days Scotland no longer had a king, a void that Edward of England helped create—and one he was keen to fill.

"Ye forget that Irvine wrote to me recently, bragging about that twenty-foot battering ram he's had built," De Keith pressed on. "A traveler from Drum Castle a few days ago confirmed it's true ... apparently it can bring down any gate, no matter how strong."

Wallace raised a heavy eyebrow. "Don't tell me ye have been losing sleep over this 'Battle Hammer'?"

De Keith's face screwed up before he threw back another deep draft of wine. The laird had been drinking heavily of late, Cassian noted. He wondered if the pressure of ruling Dunnottar was taking its toll on him. The man had been delighted to take over his brother's mantle. Yet, ever since the English had resumed their campaigning, he'd grown twitchy and paranoid. And now, he spoke incessantly about the weapon his brother-by-marriage had threatened him with.

"Irvine wants Dunnottar," the laird growled, glaring at Wallace, his fingers clenched around his cup. "He hated that his father tried to weave peace with us ... that he *sacrificed* his sister to a De Keith."

The laird's face twisted at these last words, reminding Cassian of just how much contempt he held his wife in. The relationship between them was wintry these days; Cassian rarely observed De Keith show Lady Gavina any warmth on the many occasions he'd seen them together.

But, ever since Shaw Irvine's threat, he treated her with open scorn.

"Ye are like a dog with a bone," William Wallace spoke up once more. He was watching the laird with a faint look of distaste upon his rugged features. "Not only that, but many men would be happy to have Lady Gavina as their wife ... ye are a fool to treat her as yer enemy."

De Keith drew himself up at that, slamming the now empty cup upon the mantelpiece. His brown eyes gleamed as he stared Wallace down.

Cassian tensed. Ever since the Wallace's arrival, the relationship between these two men had been strained.

Unlike his elder brother, Robert, David didn't welcome the freedom fighter's presence at Dunnottar. He'd never said as much, yet displeasure had been written all over his face on the day Wallace and his men turned up. David De Keith was adept at wearing a mask, but he hadn't fooled Cassian—and Cassian wagered that William Wallace wasn't fooled either.

At De Keith's aggressive behavior, Draco took a step forward, his right hand straying to the dirk that hung at his side. However, he didn't draw it. Cassian's gaze narrowed at his friend's gesture. If things spiraled out of control here, he and Draco might have to fight each other, for he would have to protect his laird.

Reluctantly, Cassian's hand strayed to the hilt of his own blade.

David De Keith ignored them both.

"I'll thank ye for not passing comment on matters on which ye are ignorant," De Keith growled, a nerve flickering under one eye. "The state of my marriage has nothing to do with ye."

Wallace's mouth flattened, although a moment later, he waved the comment away as if it and De Keith's anger held little importance to him. "The fact remains that Irvine and his 'Battle Hammer' shouldn't be yer focus, De Keith. Instead, Edward perches like a carrion crow in Stirling Castle ... and we need to know what his next move will be."

De Keith sneered. "If we wait, we shall see soon enough."

Wallace stared him down. "Edward is a cunning bastard ... we need to be one step ahead of him. And that's why ye need to go to Stirling, under the guise of swearing fealty. Ye need to gain his trust ... and discover how he plans to take the Highlands. If we know what he intends, we can decide how best to defend ourselves ... or even rally the clans for an attack."

A taut silence settled over the solar. It was a large, airy space dominated by a great hearth with a stag's head mounted over it. A heavy claidheamh-mòr—a great Scottish broadsword that had belonged to De Keith's father—hung upon the pitted stone wall opposite the fire place. Beneath the sword was a banner that bore the De Keith clan's crest—a roebuck's head.

"I'm not leaving Dunnottar," De Keith bit out finally.

"Ye are afraid," William Wallace accused, his temper fraying now. "Admit it, man. Irvine is merely an excuse. The truth is that the thought of leaving these sheltering walls makes ye shit yer braies."

De Keith's face reddened. "Careful, Wallace," he ground out, a vein now pulsing upon his temple. "Sometimes I think ye forget ye are a guest here."

"And sometimes I think *ye* forget that I liberated this castle for ye," Wallace shot back, his own voice harsh. "If it wasn't for me, ye'd already be kneeling at Edward's feet."

V

HOPE

CASSIAN STEPPED OUT of the keep into the lower ward and heaved in a deep breath of salt-laced air.

Draco turned to him, a grim smile upon his lips. "Well ... that was entertaining."

Cassian pulled a face. There had been a few moments when he'd thought the argument between De Keith and Wallace would escalate into a fist fight, one that he and Draco would have to break up. However, De Keith had eventually terminated the meeting by storming from the chamber. "Is that disappointment I hear in your voice?"

Draco's smile widened to a grin. "I like a good brawl ... and you and I haven't drawn knives against each other in a long while."

Cassian snorted. It had to be six centuries at least.

"Wallace was deliberately baiting him," Draco continued as the two men made their way down the steps into the lower ward. It was a breezy afternoon, and a zephyr of straw and dust danced across the cobbled expanse in front of them. Around them, the hammering of iron echoed off stone, while the walls above bristled with helmeted figures, their spears outlined against the sky. Dunnottar was readying itself for war. "And De

Keith fell for it. Wallace cares nothing for the laird's supercilious wife."

Cassian raised an eyebrow. It seemed De Keith's wife hadn't impressed Draco; few women appeared to these days.

"You could be right," he admitted, remembering how—upon the laird's exit—Wallace had turned to Draco and flashed him a wolfish smile.

The fact that De Keith hadn't yet agreed to go to Stirling didn't appear to bother him. Wallace wasn't going to let this subject drop.

Massaging a tense muscle in his shoulder, Cassian turned left and headed for the southern gateway, which led out of the fort and down the cliff face to the dungeons. Wordlessly, Draco fell into step next to him. They greeted the guards at the gate before taking the stairs that had been etched into the rock.

What a strange morning it had been. First, he'd stumbled upon Dunnottar's smith aggressing Lady Gavina's maid. And then he'd been summoned to the laird's solar to watch Wallace toy with De Keith. It was a relief to get out of the stifling keep and away from all its tensions for a short while.

Cassian led the way down to the dungeons, moving carefully on the narrow steps. It was a steep drop to where waves crashed against sharp rocks below. The afternoon sun bathed his face, and a brisk sea breeze ruffled his short hair. The sweet scent of summer was in the air, although Cassian frowned at the realization.

"The Broom-star has graced the heavens for well over a moon now." He then cast Draco a look over his shoulder. "The most it has ever remained in the night sky is three months ... time is running out."

Draco scowled. "Just one more line. Can't Mithras grant us that?"

The Bull-slayer has no power over a Pictish curse.

Not voicing his thoughts aloud, Cassian turned his attention back to the perilously steep steps. The fleeting pleasure that the sun and wind on his face brought him faded. His thoughts had become obsessive of late; he could think of little except solving the riddle.

Mortality beckoned like a siren in the distance. They were so close now; he could feel it in the marrow of his bones.

I'll join you soon, Lilla.

An ache rose under his breast bone at the thought of his long-lost love. For many years, every memory of Lilla felt like a dirk to the heart. However, these days the sensation had changed. Now it was a dull ache—a pain that gentled with each passing year.

I'm forgetting her.

Cassian's chest tightened then, and he inhaled sharply. Guilt. It weighed upon him whenever he admitted that three hundred years after Lilla's death, he no longer felt the pain of her loss so keenly.

When he'd confided in Maximus, his friend had told him that the change was inevitable. Such intensity of grief couldn't stay the same with the passing of the years. Cassian had gotten angry at the time, yet secretly he knew Maximus spoke the truth.

He wanted to hold on to Lilla forever. Yet he wasn't able to.

The stairs led down to a stone arch—the entrance to Dunnottar's dungeons. Greeting another set of guards there, Cassian entered the dank tunnel beyond. He and Draco walked past the cells, breathing shallowly as the stench of unwashed bodies and unemptied chamber pots greeted them.

They didn't halt at the cells, but took the passageway at the back of the wide, vaulted tunnel. The pair passed by a small, cave-like alcove that Cassian had turned into a mithraeum. The scent of incense and the warm glow of torchlight greeted Cassian. They continued down the passage and pushed open the door to the second chamber.

A tall, lean man with close-cropped dark hair sat at a table piled high with leather volumes. He was reading by candlelight.

Maximus glanced up when they entered, his peat-dark gaze sweeping over Cassian and Draco's faces. "How did it go?"

Cassian winced. "You missed a fiery argument."

"So, will De Keith make the trip to Stirling?"

"He hasn't agreed yet ... but Wallace thinks he's cracking," Draco replied with a smirk. "William will keep pushing until he gets what he wants."

Maximus nodded, his proud features tensing. He was keen for Cassian to lead the laird's escort to Stirling. They'd almost worked their way through all the histories in De Keith's library—but Stirling Castle would have more. And just maybe, one of them would have the answer they sought.

The answer to who the White Hawk and the Dragon were.

Cassian was in two minds about making such a trip. Although he shared his friend's eagerness to get his hands on more histories, he was reluctant to leave Dunnottar with Irvine's threat of attack looming over the fortress and what it might mean for the riddle. He didn't want the three of them to be separated when the attack happened.

Cassian's attention shifted to the heavy book that lay open before Maximus. "Nothing?"

A crease formed between Maximus's dark brows, and he shook his head. His gaze remained upon Cassian then, his frown deepening. "Heather tells me you had a run in with Blair Galbraith today."

"What's this?" Draco turned to Cassian, his smirk fading. "You didn't say anything earlier."

Cassian shrugged. "I didn't get the chance before the meeting. Galbraith cornered Aila De Keith on a stairwell."

Draco's mouth pursed. Like Cassian and Maximus, he wasn't fond of Dunnottar's smithy.

Remembering the scene on the stairwell, Cassian frowned. Aila De Keith was a sweet-natured, yet innocent, woman. After Galbraith's departure, she'd stared up at him as if he were her brave Lancelot. The intensity in her luminous grey eyes had made Cassian uncomfortable.

"He was trying to take his revenge on me ... and Heather," Maximus spoke up once more. "It seems his cousin's body has been discovered."

This news didn't surprise Cassian; he'd lied to Aila when he'd said the first thing he'd heard was the slap she'd given Galbraith in the stairwell. He'd also heard about the discovery of Cory Galbraith and his men's bodies.

"You knew this would happen sooner or later," Draco pointed out, his tone dry.

Maximus scowled. "Yes, but I don't want the Galbraith laird causing problems for the De Keiths ... or for us ... not when we're so close to solving the riddle."

Cassian moved to the table, lowering himself onto the bench seat opposite Maximus. He suddenly felt bone weary—not so much physically, but in his soul. He saw that Draco wore a frown now. All three of them were desperate.

Freedom was tantalizingly close.

"Any more news from Shaw Irvine?" Maximus broke the heavy silence in the alcove that had become their study over the past month. "Is he readying for an attack?"

Cassian shook his head. As soon as they'd discovered that the Irvine laird wielded the 'Battle Hammer', he'd paid a man he knew well to act as their spy at Drum Castle, the Irvine stronghold. It had been a few weeks, but Cassian's man hadn't sent word that anything was afoot. "Not yet ... but as soon as he does, we'll know."

Maximus leaned forward, resting his elbows on the table while he massaged his temples. "Each discovery we make feels like pure chance. Even after all this time, that witch is still playing with us."

Draco grunted his agreement, while Cassian sighed deeply.

Indeed, that long-dead bandruì wielded the power of life and death over them. She was their mistress, and had been since that fateful day after the Ninth fell.

Cassian felt a dropping sensation in his gut, and a chill washed over him. What if all of this was nonsense? What if they solved the last line and nothing changed?

The witch's riddle suddenly played through Cassian's mind, as it often did, taunting him:

When the Broom-star crosses the sky,
And the Hammer strikes the fort
Upon the Shelving Slope.
When the White Hawk and the Dragon wed,
Only then will the curse be broke.

For years, he'd feared the riddle would get the better of them. For centuries, they'd only managed to decipher the first line. The 'Broom-star' was the fire-tailed comet that appeared in the night sky every seventy-five years. The fort upon the Shelving Slope referred to the old name for Dunnottar.

And they now knew that Shaw Irvine's 'Battle Hammer' was to strike the fort.

Cassian clenched his jaw so hard that pain lanced through his ears. No, he couldn't let himself despair, couldn't let himself believe that the bandruì was simply toying with them.

He had to believe that the curse could be broken.

His attention returned to Maximus. Out of the three of them, he had the most to live for. Ever since meeting Heather, something had changed in the Roman. After centuries as a loner who didn't ally himself with anything or anyone, not only had he recently wed the woman he loved, but like Draco, he'd also willingly joined William Wallace in his cause. These days there was a spark in him that had been missing for so long, and seeing it pleased Cassian.

Warmth replaced the chill in his chest. These two men were his family. The loner and the rebel were the brothers he'd never had in his old life, for he'd been an orphan.

Cassian looked to Draco then and saw that his face was marred by a fierce scowl. Unlike Maximus, who'd joined the Scottish cause because he wanted to be part of something bigger than himself—as he loved a Scottish woman, and her fight was his fight—Cassian suspected Draco had joined for other reasons.

For a long while now, the Moor had sought oblivion, violence, and destruction. The wait at Dunnottar made Draco restless and irritable. Just two days earlier, he'd gotten into a fist fight in the mess hall with one of Cassian's men. Draco was a leashed wolf.

Draco spoke little of the woman he'd once loved. All Cassian knew was that she'd met a violent end, and Draco was part of the war band that wreaked vengeance upon their enemies afterward. The raid was vicious and bloody—and Draco had been a different man ever since. His moods were more mercurial these days, and his behavior more brooding and reckless.

Cassian suspected Draco had done things that haunted him still.

Looking away from his friends, Cassian's gaze fixed on his clasped hands upon the table before him. It almost looked as if he was praying. However, none of them followed the Christian God, but Mithras, the Great Bull-slayer. Cassian prayed morning and night to Mithras in the hope that the Lord of Light might guide his way.

VI

THE BELTAINE BANQUET

"LOOK AT YE, lass." Donnan De Keith greeted his younger daughter with a wide smile. "I've rarely seen such a bonny sight."

"Da, ye are embarrassing me." Aila ducked her head as warmth rose to her cheeks. She wasn't used to being the center of attention, and for a few moments regretted letting Lady Gavina fuss over her all afternoon.

"Stand up straight, Aila," her mother chastised. "Do that lovely kirtle and surcoat proud. Lady Gavina has shown ye a great kindness ... I hope ye thanked her properly?"

"Of course I have, Ma." Aila squared her shoulders, even though her embarrassment morphed into irritation. She hated it when her mother spoke to her as if she were twelve. Smoothing out the skirt of the surcoat she wore over a crimson kirtle, she marveled at the fineness of the silk. She'd never worn anything so lovely.

Frankly, she felt like a fraud for doing so.

She wasn't a lady; surely, folk would look at her askance tonight at the banquet.

They were waiting outside Dunnottar's hall, in a wide gallery, while servants made the finishing touches within. It was growing late in the day; the last rays of the setting sun streamed in through the arched windows behind them, the sunlight sparkling off the North Sea beyond.

The scent of wood smoke wafted in, and despite her nervousness, Aila smiled. De Keith might have forbidden his wife from lighting the Beltaine bonfire on one of the hills west of the castle, but that didn't stop the locals from burning their own fires.

A flash of green caught Aila's eye then, and she spied her sister approaching. Heather's arm was linked through that of a lean, swarthy man. She wore a lovely pine-green kirtle and had woven spring flowers through her thick brown hair. Maximus, as always, was broodingly handsome at her side.

Not for the first time, envy stabbed Aila at the sight of them.

One would have to be blind not to see just how madly in love these two were. Heather had literally glowed ever since their wedding. Upon her return to Dunnottar, Aila's sister had become Lady Gavina's companion, a role she'd continued even after her union with Maximus. She visited Gavina every afternoon, working alongside the lady at her loom.

Aila knew that Heather longed for her and Maximus to have their own household one day, preferably in Stonehaven. She wondered how long it would be until her sister's womb quickened. Strangely, whenever Aila or her mother had brought up the subject of bairns, Heather had gone quiet.

"Mother Mary, what a vision," Heather greeted her sister. "Where did ye get that gown?"

"Lady Gavina loaned it to me," Aila replied stiffly. She hadn't forgotten their argument earlier, or forgiven her sister for her lack of support.

Sensing her distance, the warm smile on Heather's face ebbed a little. Her lips parted as she readied herself to say something else.

But the opening of the doors behind them forestalled her.

The crowd waiting in the gallery flowed into the long hall—a rectangular space flanked by large windows and with a great hearth up one end. The laird's table sat before the fire, while the rest of the tables lined the room lengthwise.

Gazing around, Aila took in the lovely decorations she'd helped put up earlier in the day: garlands of lilac hung from the rafters, the scent wafting through the air, and pots of daisies and roses decorated all the tables and the window sills. Despite the warm evening, a fire crackled in the hearth tonight—for Beltaine was a fire festival, and even if Lady Gavina couldn't have a bonfire this evening, she wouldn't do without fire entirely.

"Come," Aila's mother took her by the elbow and steered her down the hall. "We're seated at the laird's table this eve." The pride in Iona's voice was evident. She loved any occasion where she and her kin got to break bread at the same table as the laird and his wife.

She still had designs on elevating her position at Dunnottar. Donnan was steward here, yet Iona De Keith had wished for a greater standing. She often lamented what a pity it was that Robert and David didn't have any younger brothers—for one would have suited Aila.

Aila's jaw tightened. Of course, she'd hoped that her daughters would wed well. Dashed dreams there—for Heather had wed a foreign soldier, a man without rank or fortune, and Aila had gone into service as a lady's maid.

It looked as if her mother would have to content herself with her current position, for things weren't likely to change.

Taking a seat at the laird's table, between her mother and sister, Aila caught Lady Gavina's eye across from her. The lady flashed Aila a conspirator's grin, and Aila favored her mistress with a nervous smile in return. She knew Lady Gavina was pleased with her handiwork—yet she felt out of place in such finery.

Sooner or later, someone was sure to comment on it, or make fun of her.

But as the hall filled up, and one by one, folk took their places at the long tables, no one did.

Gradually, Aila's nervousness ebbed. However, the brownies in her belly started dancing once more when Captain Gaius appeared at the laird's table. Handsome in a turquoise lèine belted at the waist and dark leather braies, Cassian took a seat to Lady Gavina's left.

Heart pounding, Aila stared down at the pewter goblet of mead that a servant had just poured for her.

Will he look my way?

And to her surprise, when she finally gathered the courage to raise her gaze, she saw that Cassian had.

Meeting her eye, he cast her a questioning look followed by a small smile. He was enquiring after her, making sure she was well after her ordeal earlier in the day.

Swallowing hard, Aila returned the smile, cursing the heat that now crept up her neck. She hated how easily she blushed, especially around the handsome captain.

The laird swept into the hall last. Dressed in a fine velvet lèine, with the clan sash draped across his chest, and chamois braies, he cut a handsome figure. However, the look was marred by the deep scowl that furrowed his face.

Aila watched with interest as David De Keith lowered himself into the carven chair at the end of the laird's table. Surely, he wasn't still fuming about Lady Gavina's behavior?

As soon as the laird had seated himself, more servants appeared bearing trays of food for the banquet.

Aila's lips parted in delight at the array of dishes set down before her. There was a tureen of rich goat stew and roasted haunches of lamb, accompanied by spring greens and an array of breads studded with seeds and nuts. A creamy pudding made with almonds and honey sat alongside the savory dishes, as well as huge bowls of strawberries and pots of thick cream.

It was a feast sumptuous enough for royalty. Glancing sideways at her mother, Aila saw how Iona's gaze gleamed with pleasure. Her mother lived for evenings such as these.

"What an incredible spread, My Lady." Iona caught Lady Gavina's eye and beamed at her. "So much time must have gone into the planning."

"I had help," Gavina replied, glancing at where Lady Elizabeth sat beside her. Robert De Keith's wife was, as always, dressed in dark colors. Yet she'd woven daisies through her golden hair and let it down for once; the flowers softened her austere appearance. Gavina then shot a smile across the table at Heather and Aila. "Elizabeth, yer daughters, and I have spent days making sure everything would be perfect."

David De Keith interrupted them then with a rude snort. He picked up the silver goblet before him and took a deep draft of mead. "Yer brother is readying his 'Battle Hammer', and those English dogs are baying at our door ... and ye women prattle on about a damn banquet."

Lady Gavina's features tightened at the insult. "The folk of Dunnottar need something to bolster their spirits," she replied coolly. "Aye, our land is in chaos once more, but Beltaine has arrived, and we should celebrate it."

The laird sneered before holding his goblet up so that a passing servant could fill it. His gaze raked down the lass serving him, taking in her comely form, dark hair, and pale skin. The look of naked appreciation that followed made Aila's belly tighten. She couldn't believe he disrespected his wife so openly. How often had she seen him leer at serving lasses in the years she'd served Lady Gavina?

Enough times to know that he did it to spite his wife.

Aila took the basket of breads Heather passed her, grateful to shift her attention away from the laird. Still, she found herself fuming on her mistress's behalf.

Lady Gavina deserves so much better.

The banquet began, while a harpist set himself up behind them and began to play. A bright tune filtered through the hall, the music blending with the rise and fall of voices.

Aila passed the basket down the table and watched Captain Gaius help himself to some braised greens. Feeling her gaze upon him, he glanced up. "Would you like some, Aila?"

She nodded, warmth settling in the pit of her belly. Was she imagining things, or had the incident this morning forged a connection between them?

"Aye, thank ye," she replied, reaching out and taking the platter from him. Their fingers brushed accidentally, and Aila stifled a gasp.

It was the first time they'd actually touched.

She would cherish this moment.

Finding it hard not to smile widely at him—for her mother had always said that men preferred demure women—Aila served herself and then handed Cassian the greens back.

The meal would taste even better now.

Cassian nodded to her then before handing the platter to the man seated next to him. His name was Draco, and he'd arrived with the Wallace. He was striking in appearance, with hawkish good looks. The way his hair tightly curled against his scalp fascinated Aila, as did his obsidian eyes.

Cassian and Draco began to talk between themselves then. Disappointment stabbed at Aila's belly. Her brief connection with the captain had been lost.

She wondered if he'd noticed her gown. Lady Gavina had also spent a bit of time on Aila's hair, pinning it high and letting down a few curls to frame her face. Her mistress insisted that she had a lovely neck and should show it off.

Taking a mouthful of stew, Aila marveled at its richness, and at the depth of flavor and spice that had been added to it. However, as she raised the spoon to her mouth once more, she sensed her sister was watching her.

Glancing up, Aila noted that Heather hadn't touched her meal. Instead, her gaze bored into Aila. A line furrowed between her eyebrows. "I'm sorry about earlier," she murmured. "I didn't mean to criticize ye ... I was just being protective."

Aila tensed. "It's forgotten," she lied, keeping her voice light. "Don't fret over it."

Heather didn't reply, although her gaze shadowed. "But I do," she admitted softly. "I don't want ye to get hurt."

VII

THE DANCE

THE WAIL OF the highland pipe echoed through the hall. Its mournful screech blended with the strains of a harp, laughter, and singing. The noise reverberated off the stone walls.

Standing near one of the windows, Aila watched couples move around the floor. It was a rousing folk dance—not a sedate, courtly one.

The banquet had gone on a long while, and then afterward, servants had pushed back the tables and cleared a space in the center of the hall. There was no bonfire to dance around in here, but the fire in the hearth still roared at one end of the space.

Aila was starting to sweat in her lèine, kirtle, and surcoat.

Maximus and Heather swirled past her then, their faces alive with happiness, their cheeks rosy from the warmth of the hall and good food and drink.

Aila's breathing quickened as she watched them.

They look so good together.

Indeed, they did. Heather was all curves and flowing brown hair, her grey-green eyes sparkling, a sultry smile upon her full lips. Maximus's gaze devoured her as he spun her around and then caught her in his arms.

Heather's squeal of delight lifted high into the rafters.

Aila's chest compressed. She wanted a man to look at her like that—and not just any man either.

Tearing her attention away from her sister and brother-by-marriage, Aila's gaze shifted to the opposite side of the hall, where Cassian leaned against the wall. Pewter goblet of wine in hand, he conversed with William Wallace.

The pressure on Aila's breastbone increased. Longing made it difficult to breathe.

Why hasn't he asked me to dance?

Ever since the dancing had begun, she hadn't seen him look her way once.

Not that Aila hadn't caught men's attention this eve. The laird had danced with her earlier—an uncomfortable experience, for his grip on her hand and arm had been too tight, his gaze too intense. After that, one of the Wallace's men, a big warrior with sweaty hands, had drawn her out onto the dance floor.

But Cassian had not.

"Aila." A soft voice intruded upon her brooding. Aila tore her gaze from Cassian to find Lady Gavina at her side. "The man ye wish to win … is it Captain Gaius?"

Aila went rigid. She'd been caught staring. How many other folk in the hall had seen? She dropped her gaze to the floor and considered denying it. Yet the blush that always betrayed her when it came to the handsome captain now burned upon her cheeks, and the kind look on Lady Gavina's face made her swallow the lie.

"Is it that obvious?" she murmured.

"Only because I've been watching ye this eve … wondering who the lucky man is."

Aila huffed a brittle laugh. "Does he consider himself lucky? I don't think he notices me at all."

Lady Gavina's gaze narrowed slightly before she shifted her attention over to Cassian. Draco had joined him and the Wallace now, while a servant refilled their goblets. "Well, I think it's time we changed that."

Lady Gavina picked up the skirts of her dove-colored surcoat and cream kirtle, and walked away.

Aila watched her mistress leave and wondered what she meant by her final comment. But then, when Gavina made her way around the edge of the floor—past where the laird lounged upon his carven chair, his gaze upon the dancing—and headed toward Cassian, her stomach somersaulted.

She suddenly realized what Gavina was planning to do.

Mother Mary have mercy ... no!

Aila cringed back against the wall. Lord, how she wished she could melt into it. Like a hunted hind, she glanced left and right, looking for a place to hide. Yet there was no escape. Horrified, she watched Lady Gavina stop before Captain Gaius and exchange a few words with him.

And then, his gaze shifted across the floor to where Aila stood.

Aila's pulse thundered in her ears, and queasiness rose in her throat. *God's teeth, I can't believe she's done this.*

When Cassian glanced back at Lady De Keith and nodded, Aila's heart began to pound erratically against her ribs.

A moment passed, and then he pushed himself off the wall, handed his goblet to Draco, and headed across the floor—toward Aila.

Mortification pulsed through her. Aye, she wanted this man's attention, but now that she had it, she realized how one-sided her passion had been. Till this moment, she'd longed for him from afar, safe in the knowledge that he didn't feel the same way.

It had been agony, but oddly reassuring.

But now he was walking toward her.

His face was unreadable, his gaze shuttered. That wasn't a good sign.

Nervously, Aila wiped her damp palms upon her surcoat. She couldn't let him see just how on edge she was. A woman worthy of courting should be poised and cool—should behave as if she had men vying to dance with her.

Of course, Cassian knew it wasn't true—or at least he would, if he'd been paying her any attention.

"Aila De Keith," Cassian greeted her with a warm smile. "I hate to see a lass so lovely without a dance partner ... would you join me?"

His words made her already racing heart leap in her chest.

Does he think I'm lovely?

Not trusting herself to speak, lest she trip over her own tongue and make a fool of herself, Aila nodded. He then offered his arm to her, and she took it. A moment later, the pair of them walked out onto the dance floor.

Lady Gavina watched Captain Gaius and Aila join the dancers, and as she did so, a little of the tension within her unraveled.

The music had slowed now as the dancers began the *basse danse*, a slow, dignified dance that contrasted with the lively Scottish circle dance that preceded it.

A smile curved Gavina's lips.

They made a lovely couple: Cassian tall and muscular, Aila willowy and clad in scarlet, her walnut-colored hair piled atop her crown. Gavina was particularly happy with the job she'd done with her maid. Aila was a pretty lass, yet she didn't make the most of herself.

In Gavina's opinion, Aila outshone every other woman in the hall tonight, herself included. The blush upon her cheeks was charming, as was the rapt way she watched Cassian as they danced.

"You shouldn't meddle in the affairs of others, My Lady." A gruff voice intruded then. Gavina tore her attention from the dancing couple, her gaze meeting Draco Vulcan's. The warrior, who'd been talking to William Wallace and the captain when she approached, was scowling at her.

He wore a look of disdain upon his proud features, an expression that immediately made her hackles rise. She received enough such looks from her husband; she wouldn't suffer one of their guests glaring at her in such a manner.

"I'm not meddling," she replied, her tone wintry. "What harm is there in ensuring a woman has a dance partner?"

"You're match-making," he drawled. "Cassian's no fool … we all saw what you did."

Gavina stiffened. He was making it sound as if she'd done something venal.

Next to him, Wallace snorted into his cup of ale. "Leave it be, Draco. What does it matter if the captain enjoys himself? I wouldn't mind a dance with that pretty lass myself."

Gavina cast the Wallace a grateful smile. She appreciated his words. She then cast a cold eye upon Draco once more, taking in his lean, hard-muscled form, haughty face, and penetrating night-dark eyes. The Moor was a good friend of Captain Gaius, but right now she found nothing redeeming about him.

This man was no ally of hers.

"Perhaps ye should enjoy the Beltaine dancing as the captain is," Gavina replied after a long pause. "I'm sure ye can find a woman here who'd take pity on ye."

Aila smiled so widely that her face started to hurt. She'd never enjoyed herself so much. She never wanted this moment to end. Cassian was an excellent dancer. He knew all the steps to the slow dance the harpist was now playing, and the pair of them glided around the floor, moving back and forth like a rising and ebbing tide.

She liked the *basse danse*. It made her feel courtly; for a moment, she was a lady and he her dashing knight.

Back and forth they moved, and when she gently placed her hand over his, a strange giddiness swept over her. His hand was strong and warm, and the light touch of his skin against hers was overwhelming.

The mortification Lady Gavina's bold move caused had vanished. Excitement, a deep, hot pulse in her belly now, replaced it.

All too soon, the dance came to an end. Aila and Cassian drew apart, and he bowed while she dropped into a curtsey.

"That was a pleasure, Aila," Cassian said, his lips curving into a smile, meeting her eye. "It's been a long while since I danced."

"Thank ye, Captain Cassian," she breathed.

He inclined his head. "Captain *Cassian?*"

Heat flared in her cheeks. *What are ye saying? He'll think ye have the brains of a sparrow!* "Captain G ... Gaius ... I meant," she stammered. "Ye are a wonderful dancer."

"You are too kind ... and I must say 'Captain Cassian' has a certain ring to it," he replied, still smiling. Then, to her disappointment, he moved back from her. "Please, excuse me."

Aila kept a smile plastered to her face, even as disappointment arrowed through her. The harpist had begun another slow melody. She'd hoped he'd continue dancing with her—not bow out after just one dance.

Cassian turned and made his way back to Draco and Wallace. Lady Gavina had returned to sit at her husband's side before the hearth. As usual, neither the laird, nor his lady wife, spoke to each other.

The dancing resumed, and Aila realized that she was standing in everyone's way. Hastily, she picked up her skirts and wove a path back to her former place by the window.

However, her heart still raced, and her hand still tingled from his touch.

Taking a goblet of wine from a passing servant, she took a large sip in an attempt to calm her pitching stomach.

Maybe, he's just taking a breather, she assured herself, her gaze flicking over to where Cassian was now talking to Draco, while the Wallace had engaged Maximus and Heather in conversation. *Maybe, he'll ask me to dance again soon.*

But as one song blended into another, he didn't.

VIII

REINVENTION

"YOU DO REALIZE that lass is smitten with you?"

Draco's comment, issued with his usual laconic tone, made Cassian glance his friend's way. "What?"

"You heard me." Draco raised an eyebrow. "Don't tell me you can't see it?"

Cassian frowned. He shifted his attention then, to where a comely figure dressed in plum and scarlet stood alone next to the far window, a goblet of wine clutched in her hand.

Aila De Keith was watching the dancing with a hopeful look upon her pretty face.

"No," he lied. "I hadn't."

Draco snorted. "Unbelievable. I know you can be obtuse sometimes ... but the girl couldn't make her pining for you any clearer."

Cassian stiffened. "Stop talking rot."

Draco gave him a long-suffering look. "She watches you all the time."

"No, she doesn't," Cassian scoffed, irritation surfacing.

Draco shook his head. "She *gazes* at you, man. And tonight, you'd have to be blind not to see it."

Cassian raised his cup to his lips and took a large gulp.

He wasn't blind.

But he certainly didn't need Draco to rub his face in it.

Cassian had caught Aila looking at him a few times over the past weeks, and when he'd come to her rescue that morning, his suspicions had been confirmed. Draco, the smug bastard, was right. The lass was infatuated. Cassian had seen the sparkle in her eyes and the blush upon her cheeks as they'd danced.

"Why do you think the laird's wife asked you to dance with her?" Draco continued, a devilish gleam in his eye now. "She was trying to match-make."

Cassian shrugged.

"So, you aren't going to ask Aila to dance again?"

"No."

Draco cocked an eyebrow. "What ... and break that poor lassie's heart?"

Cassian scowled at him. "This is all a game to you, isn't it?"

Draco smiled back, not even trying to deny the accusation. "I must say, you are providing me with much amusement this eve."

Cassian took another gulp of wine before his gaze shifted back to Aila De Keith. She was lovely indeed in that plum surcoat and crimson kirtle. Her thick brown hair was piled atop her head with ringlets falling softly about her round face.

Years ago, before life took its toll upon him, she'd have been just the sort of woman he'd have pursued. Cassian liked sweet, shy lasses. Lilla had been timid the first time they'd met, but he'd enjoyed seeing her gain confidence as he earned her trust.

Thoughts of Lilla made Cassian clench his jaw. So much time had passed, and yet he still compared every woman to her. These days, however, when he closed his eyes, he had difficulty recalling her face. He remembered that she was blonde and pretty, and that her eyes had been blue—but the cast of her features now escaped him.

Heaviness pressed down upon him as he dwelled upon this fact.

Draco was deliberately goading him, and he knew why. Cassian had grown far too serious of late; his quest to solve the riddle consumed him. They were so close now that he'd become blinkered. He went about his days taking charge as Captain of the Dunnottar Guard, yet his mind was always on that last line of the riddle and the curse that held him and his friends fast.

"For the love of Mithras, don't look so serious about it," Draco spoke up once more. He wore a slightly disgusted expression now. "Not all women want to shackle themselves to you. Some can just be enjoyed."

Cassian cast him a rueful look. "And you think a lass like Aila would take kindly to being *enjoyed*?"

Draco rolled his eyes. "Hades, now you're turning into a monk? Next you're going to start telling me to repent my sins."

Cassian snorted a laugh, the tension between them easing. "I wouldn't waste my breath ... you enjoy them too much."

He glanced over at where Aila was now talking to her sister, Heather.

Draco was probably right. He should relax a little. Comparing every woman to his long-dead wife was pointless. He hadn't taken a lover in a while, and the strain was starting to show. After Lilla's passing, he'd enjoyed a string of women—most of them blonde and blue-eyed like his wife—in an effort to lessen Lilla's loss. Unsurprisingly, it had only made him feel worse.

Cassian frowned, his mood shadowing once more. Maybe it was time to break the drought. Aila De Keith wasn't the right choice though. An infatuated lass would only cause him trouble.

"Are ye enjoying the dancing?" Heather was pink-cheeked and still slightly out of breath. "I swear there isn't a tune those musicians don't know."

"Aye ... it's a fine evening," Aila replied, tightening her grip upon her goblet of wine. Six songs had passed since her dance with Cassian, and still the captain had not returned to her side to ask her for another. "The best Beltaine I remember."

Her voice was brittle, as she couldn't hide her disappointment. This evening certainly was one to remember; never had she swung from such elation to disappointment so wildly. Initially, she'd felt ignored and unwanted, and then when Cassian had danced with her, her spirits had soared. But in the aftermath, she actually felt worse than before. Her chest and belly ached, and she felt a little queasy.

Sensing her mood, Heather stilled. "I am sorry," she said softly. "I know ye wish he'd show ye more attention."

Aila swallowed. "Well, ye did try to warn me," she replied, looking away. Actually, she desperately wanted her sister to leave her alone. Cassian was more likely to approach her again if she was on her own. And the last thing she wanted was her sister's pity.

Heather didn't understand what it was to long for someone like she did for Cassian.

"Maybe this is for the best," Heather continued, her tone still gentle. "Ye need to move past this, Aila. Ye deserve to have men vying for yer hand … let them pursue ye."

Aila's grip upon the stem of the goblet tightened further, and she clenched her jaw. She wished Heather would leave her be.

A short while later, Heather did just that. Their mother called her over to where she was sitting with a group of other wives—women who weren't interested in joining in the dancing.

Mercifully, Aila found herself alone once more.

Her gaze moved across the swirling crowd of dancers to where Cassian had resumed his conversation with Draco.

A knot formed just under her breast bone—and it was slowly squeezing tighter with each passing moment.

She knew she should look elsewhere, yet her attention remained upon Captain Gaius. He leaned against the wall as he spoke to his friend, one hand clasping a goblet. She'd noted what lovely hands he had a long time ago—strong, with long fingers. His touch tonight had felt even better than she'd imagined it would; he'd danced with confidence, and she'd been safe with him. He was a big man, not quite as tall as the Wallace—who was a giant among men—but tall enough to dominate any space he stepped into.

Aila longed to run her hands over the breadth of his shoulders, to lay her cheek against the hard-muscled wall of his chest.

Swallowing hard, she took a large, fortifying gulp of wine.

Heather was only trying to help, only trying to watch out for her, but her concern just made Aila all the more determined.

Other women got the man they desired. Why shouldn't she?

Aila set her jaw, a fluttery sensation rising in her chest.

I won't give up, she vowed. The trouble was that if she wanted to attract the handsome captain, she couldn't remain the way she was: a timid woman who kept to the shadows for fear of being the center of attention.

If she was to be successful, she needed to reinvent herself.

Aila's gaze flicked to where Heather was loudly arguing with their mother over something. Hands on hips, she stood her ground while Iona waggled a finger at her.

Aila's mouth curved at the sight.

If she wanted Cassian, she needed to be more like her sister.

Heather didn't cringe at the sidelines; she might have made a few mistakes along her road to happiness, but she was reaping the benefits now. She'd never have met Maximus if she'd remained under her mother's thumb at Dunnottar, like Aila had.

Aila lifted her goblet to her lips and drained the last of her wine, enjoying the heat that pooled in her belly. It gave her strength.

Glancing over at where Cassian was now laughing at something Draco had just said, the warmth in Aila's belly spread. God's teeth, he was breathtakingly handsome when he laughed or smiled—a rare sight indeed.

I want to be the one to bring joy to his face.

Aila drew in a deep, determined breath. In order to get Cassian to fall under her spell, she was also going to need courage.

IX

LET ME GO

IT GREW LATE, and Cassian stifled a yawn. A surfeit of rich food and drink had made him sleepy. The harpist now played soft, melancholy tunes, and just a handful of couples still danced. Most folk sat at the tables lining the hall, nursing their cups and goblets of mead, ale, and wine.

Cassian rubbed a hand over his face. It was probably time he retired for the night.

He was just about to push himself up off the wall and bid Draco good eve, when raised voices made him glance toward the hearth.

William Wallace had joined the laird and his wife there earlier, and Lady Elizabeth now sat with them.

And to Cassian's surprise, Lady Elizabeth appeared to be arguing with her brother-by-marriage.

"What's this?" he murmured to Draco, digging him in the side with his elbow. His friend grunted, for he'd been on the verge of dozing against the wall. Without awaiting Draco's answer, Cassian moved closer to the group, intrigued.

"If there's a chance Robert can be freed, we must take it, David," Elizabeth said, her voice rising louder still. "Ye cannot sit here and let yer brother rot in an English dungeon. We must get him back. I want my husband returned safely to me."

"Going to Stirling won't achieve that," David De Keith countered. His face was flushed, his brown eyes narrowed. "Best we wait until they decide to free him."

"But that day might never come!" Lady Elizabeth drew herself up. "Ye can't throw Robert's life away."

"Lady Elizabeth is right, of course," William Wallace rumbled. "Longshanks is in Stirling … and he's invited all the northern lairds to visit him, provided they bend the knee. Now is yer chance to go to him and make an appeal for Robert's freedom … ye may never get another opportunity. Surely, yer own brother is worth feigning loyalty for? And while ye are there, ye can find out what action Edward plans to take next."

The laird went still, his gaze swiveling to the Wallace. His lip then curled.

Watching them, Cassian allowed himself a tight smile. William Wallace was a clever man indeed to bring up this subject with Lady Elizabeth present. She was just the ally he needed.

"Wallace speaks true," Lady Gavina spoke up then. Her voice was low and respectful, although Cassian caught the glint in her eye. "We should pay Edward a visit—ye, me, and Lady Elizabeth … we owe Robert that much." She paused there, her gaze flicking to William Wallace. "And take the opportunity to find out what we can."

David scowled at his wife. "As if he's just going to tell us his plans, Gavina. Honestly, ye might have a pretty face, but ye are witless."

Silence followed the laird's insult.

To Lady Gavina's credit, she didn't flinch. However, her gaze shadowed. "Men reveal much when they don't intend to," she replied, her voice subdued. "I don't expect Edward to lay out his plans before us, but he may inadvertently reveal something he hadn't intended."

"Aye, and if ye bring yer lovely wife to Stirling with ye, Edward might be distracted into letting something slip," Wallace added. He was watching Gavina with a keen expression.

Lady Elizabeth wasn't his only ally tonight.

"All of ye are forgetting Shaw Irvine," David De Keith ground out. A nerve flickered under one eye, a sign that he knew this conversation was getting away from him. He was outnumbered, and no one appeared to be taking his side.

The laird was losing the argument, and they all knew it. Cassian tensed at the realization.

He was torn. As much as he wished to remain at Dunnottar, a trip to Stirling would allow him access to its vast library. He could leave Draco and Maximus in charge of things here, and if his spy in Drum Castle got in touch, they'd let him know.

They still had that last line of the riddle to untangle, and their lack of progress was frustrating. It sometimes seemed like the bandruì's riddle only revealed itself when it was ready. Of late, he'd begun to suspect that nothing any of them did made a difference. However, Cassian couldn't give up. Maybe he'd find the answers he sought in Stirling.

De Keith shifted his attention to his wife, staring her down. "Yer brother seeks to take lands that belong to my clan. The moment we leave Dunnottar, he will attack."

"Let him," Wallace rumbled. "Irvine doesn't know that my band and I are here. Ye can go to Stirling, De Keith. I've already assured ye that I will defend this castle in yer absence."

David De Keith's face went slack, and then his mouth flattened into a thin line. For a few moments, Cassian was sure he'd object. De Keith was threatened by the outlaw leader. He had charisma and courage, and inspired loyalty in others in a way that De Keith never had or would. And David knew it.

All gazes shifted to the laird then, and Cassian watched the war waging within the man play out across his face.

"Ye fear I will betray ye, De Keith?" William Wallace broke the weighty silence, voicing the very thing that had been playing across Cassian's mind. The laird frowned, although before he replied, Wallace continued. "I saved Dunnottar once before, David. I rescued ye all from the English ... and if I'd wanted to take this castle for my own, I'd have done so years ago. The distrust I see in yer eyes now offends me." Wallace's tone was gentle, yet there was no missing the steel that lay just beneath.

De Keith's throat bobbed. No one wanted to offend William Wallace. Tales of what he did to those who angered him were now legend throughout Scotland. Cassian had heard that he'd made the dried skin of Hugh de Cressingham—the hated English treasurer he'd killed at the Battle of Stirling Bridge—into a scabbard, hilt, and belt.

Cassian's gaze slid to the wide leather belt the Wallace wore about his waist—was this it?

"I meant no offense, William," De Keith rasped. "But ye can see why I'm hesitant to leave Dunnottar at present." He cast his wife another simmering look. "Irvine will strike the moment my back is turned."

"And as I said, let him," Wallace replied coolly. "I'll shove his 'Battle Hammer' up his arse if he dares bring it here."

"I don't want ye going to Stirling, Aila. It's not safe!"

Aila looked up from where she was laying out kirtles on the bed and trying to decide which ones to pack. Her mother stood in the doorway, twisting the gold band she wore on her left hand—a sure sign she was agitated.

Letting out a long breath, Aila favored her mother with a smile. "Worry not, Ma. The laird has hand-picked twenty of his best warriors to escort us. I'll be fine. Ye wouldn't let Lady Gavina travel without her lady's maid, would ye? Lady Elizabeth is joining us as well ... and bringing Jean, her maid, with her."

Aila had been delighted to discover that Captain Gaius would lead them. They'd journey to Stirling together. Her chest constricted at the thought. If she wanted an opportunity to gain Cassian's attention, this was it. Away from Dunnottar, they could form an attachment much easier. Also, away from her mother, Aila could behave differently. Perhaps this would allow her to break free of her crippling shyness.

"Twenty isn't enough!" Iona De Keith twisted her wedding band once more. "Ye will be going straight into the wolf's den in Stirling."

Aila inhaled deeply. "Please, Ma ... we wouldn't be going if it was that dangerous."

"Ye have never been away from Dunnottar. Ye have no idea how treacherous it is beyond these walls. Look what happened to yer sister!"

Aila straightened up, her smile fading as irritation bubbled within her. "Heather needed to leave Dunnottar," she pointed out, her tone sharpening. "It was the making of her."

Her mother stifled a gasp. "What nonsense is this?"

"It's not nonsense. Heather learned of the world, and I wish to do the same."

Iona's face darkened. "What foolery has yer sister been filling yer head with? I will have words with her."

"Heather hasn't said anything to me," Aila countered. She wished her mother would go away and let her finish packing. They were to leave at first light the following day, and there was still much to organize. "I am more than capable of drawing my own conclusions and making my own choices, Ma."

"Foolish lass," her mother cried, advancing on her. "I'll not have ye travel to Stirling. Edward Longshanks is there. He's likely to have ye all murdered in yer beds!"

"Enough, Ma." Aila grasped her mother's hands and held them fast. She'd rarely seen her this agitated. And now that they stood close, she realized that her mother's grey-green eyes, so similar to Heather's, gleamed with unshed tears.

She's scared for me.

~ 79 ~

"Ma," Aila murmured softly. "I know ye only wish to keep me safe, but ye know ye can't."

Her mother swallowed, her jaw clenching as she sought to keep her agitation in check. Staring into her eyes, Aila screwed up her courage. It was odd, but she'd always let her mother cow her, had always let her decide what was best for her.

Not anymore.

"Ye can't keep shielding me," Aila continued, dogged now that her mind was made up. "I'm no longer that sickly bairn ye used to fret over ... these days I'm no more fragile than Heather is."

Her mother sniffed. "Heather is a lot stronger than ye, Aila ... she always has been. She takes after me."

X

HIGH SPIRITS

AILA TIGHTENED THE palfrey's girth and knocked aside the horse's nose when it took a nip at her.

"That's enough, Dusty," she chastised the dainty dun mare. Even her ill-tempered mount couldn't dim her excitement this morning; she'd awoken long before dawn with a wide smile upon her face that still hadn't faded. "I know ye don't like this, but it's necessary ... or I'll end up hanging under yer belly."

In response, the palfrey flattened her ears back and took another swipe, teeth snapping.

"Careful there." An amused male voice cut in as a hand took hold of the reins and pulled Dusty's snaking head back. "She'll take a bite out of your arm if you don't watch out."

Warmth flowed over Aila, and her breath caught.

Turning, she met Cassian's frank gaze.

"Thank ye, Captain," she murmured, lowering her eyelashes in a way she'd seen other women do. Jean said that men found it attractive. "Dusty's in an ill-temper this morning."

"This mare always is," he replied evenly, not responding to her demure look. "Go on ... finish tightening the girth while I hold her still."

Aila did as bid, cinching the girth up another two notches before turning to the captain once more. "Thank ye," she repeated, offering him a gentle smile.

He returned the smile, handed her the reins, and stepped back. "Ready yerself, Aila," he said with a brisk nod. "We're about to ride out."

Aila watched him walk off, checking the other horses and riders amassed at the western end of the lower ward. Her gaze feasted on him, taking in the breadth of his shoulders, emphasized by the plaid cloak he wore, and the way the wind ruffled his short hair.

Gusts tore across the bailey, snagging at the manes and tails of the horses and making them skittish. Around Aila, the warriors were dressed for travel in quilted tunics, chainmail leggings, and iron helmets. Each man carried a circular wooden shield, and a dirk at his hip. Many bore heavy broadswords. They all wore cloaks and sashes of the De Keith plaid.

A crowd had gathered around the party in the lower ward. Their faces pale and anxious, men and women watched De Keith and his escort ready themselves to ride out. Despite that many warriors—including the Wallace and his men—remained behind, the folk here were still nervous to see their laird depart for Stirling.

Aila didn't share their anxiety. The laird had increased the Guard, and had men tirelessly strengthening the stronghold's defenses, both inside and outside the walls: a deep ditch filled with iron spikes now snaked around the landward side. Every day, more wagons arrived from Stonehaven—the village located just a few miles north of Dunnottar—with stacks of lead and slate, and barrels of pitch to use against any who dared besiege the walls. De Keith had also built up the food stores—just in case Shaw Irvine failed to bring the gates down with his 'Battle Hammer' and tried to starve them out instead.

Shaw Irvine won't attack while we're away, Aila reassured herself. *And if he does, Dunnottar will be well prepared*. Indeed, Lady Gavina wasn't convinced her brother would ever lay siege to Dunnottar. She believed Irvine was merely testing David De Keith.

Comforted by these thoughts, Aila turned back to her mount.

Cassian had been right about Dusty. Her father had gifted her the palfrey, but Aila had never warmed to the mare. She was spirited and willful, and seemed to sense Aila's diffidence. Twice in the past months, she'd tried to throw her. Aila had hoped to ride another horse to Stirling, but it appeared none could be spared.

She would just have to wrestle with her mare.

Aila adjusted the stirrup nearest and turned to face Dusty's rump. She was just about to mount when she spied Heather weaving her way purposefully through the crowd toward her.

Smile fading, Aila waited for her sister. She'd been hoping Heather wouldn't come out to see her off. She just wanted to get away from Dunnottar for a while and forget about her family. After weathering her mother's response the day before, she didn't feel like another scene.

"Were ye going to leave without saying goodbye?" Heather greeted her.

"I knew ye'd find me," Aila replied airily.

Heather frowned. Her expression was guarded this morning. "Take care in Stirling." She stepped forward and enfolded Aila in a hug. "Keep yer eyes and ears open ... and trust no one."

Aila's mouth twitched, and she swallowed the nervous laugh that bubbled up inside her. She was merely accompanying her mistress to Stirling. Most likely, she and Lady Gavina would spend an uneventful week there, while the men discussed important matters, before returning to Dunnottar.

Heather made it sound like she was a spy.

Nonetheless, she didn't bother to contradict her sister, not when she looked so serious.

"I'll be careful," Aila assured her.

Heather's lips parted then, as if she wanted to say something more. But the moment passed, and she stepped back, favoring her sister with a strained smile. The expression was forced, and Aila wondered why her sister's eyes were suddenly so grave.

"Has Ma been talking to ye?" Aila asked, her suspicion rising.

Heather sighed. "She blames me for ye going. Says I have set a poor example."

Aila tensed. Of course, their mother would say that; she didn't seem to think that Aila had a will of her own.

"Ye are all making a storm out of a summer's breeze." Aila leaped nimbly onto Dusty's back and adjusted her skirts. "I'll be back before ye know it."

Cassian led the way out of Dunnottar, next to the warriors carrying the De Keith banner: a long swath of blue, green, and turquoise plaid that snapped and billowed in the strong wind. The North Sea was rough and grey this morning, the surf thundering against the cliffs below the headland. And despite that they had just passed into summer, the air had a sting to it.

The company snaked its way down the winding path and then up the steep slope to the cliff-top opposite the fortress. They then emerged onto the rolling, green hills that stretched away from the castle. As he urged his courser into a trot, Cassian glanced behind him at where the grey curtain wall of Dunnottar reared up against a wild sky.

Before leaving, he'd spoken to Maximus and Draco in the lower ward bailey, and repeated the need for them to remain vigilant—not that either of them needed reminding.

When the hammer strike came, they'd all be ready. Cassian had sent out scouts to keep an eye on the Irvine-De Keith border. Maximus and Draco would send word to Stirling should 'The Battle Hammer' come their way.

Cassian frowned. Despite his precautions, he really didn't want to be away from Dunnottar.

Pushing aside his misgivings, he urged his courser into a brisk canter. Beside him, the banner-men did the same, and suddenly the ground trembled as the party of twenty warriors and their charges joined them.

As always, being on horseback made Cassian feel better; it calmed the urgency within him. The feel of the powerful horse under him—the beast's strength as it lengthened its stride, its black mane rippling in the wind—made him feel connected to the world and everything in it. No matter how many years passed, his love of horses and the joy of galloping across wind-swept hills had never dimmed.

Of late, as much as he enjoyed living at Dunnottar, those great stone walls had started to feel like a cage. It was good to have Maximus and Draco, his blood brothers, nearby once again—but the tense wait while the Broom-star traveled across the sky, the English marched north, and De Keith's war-mongering neighbor readied his 'Battle Hammer' put Cassian on edge.

It felt good to take action of some kind.

The events of last night's Beltaine banquet had also made him uneasy.

The look on Aila De Keith's face when he'd come to her aid with her palfrey this morning had only added to his tension. She was usually so shy, barely able to catch his eye, but she'd actually batted her eyelashes at him.

Poor lass.

Nonetheless, he had to admit she'd looked comely standing there in the midst of his warriors, wrestling with that ill-tempered dun beast of hers. Aila had exchanged the becoming surcoat for a more practical blue kirtle and woolen cloak. She'd braided her long brown hair into a thick plait that hung over one shoulder. The morning light highlighted the strands of gold in it, as well as the milky softness of her skin. Like Heather, she had a round face, although her features were more delicate, and she had her father's smoke-grey eyes.

Her lips had parted as she gazed up at him, and for a moment, Cassian had found himself wondering what she'd be like to kiss.

He'd then caught himself.

He knew Maximus had visited a brothel in the past whenever the urge to bed a woman overwhelmed him. But brothels held little appeal to Cassian these days. There was something about such places that depressed him.

Maybe I should visit a brothel in Stirling anyway, he thought idly.

Cassian's lips flattened, and he let his courser have its head as it thundered onward, kicking up sods of dirt and grass behind it. He needed a woman, but Draco's suggestion that he should satiate himself with Aila was crude and callous.

She was no longer a lass, and had to be in her early twenties at least. But her family had sheltered her, and thus there was a girlishness and innocence to her that made him inwardly cringe.

The wrong man could ruin a woman like that.

"Yer mount is in high spirits today," Lady Gavina commented, casting Aila a concerned look over her shoulder. "Can ye manage her?"

Aila cast her mistress a tight smile. It was an effort to keep Dusty in line behind the ladies and Jean. The other women rode quiet mounts, and Aila envied them. They could just enjoy the journey without fighting their horses all the way. Dusty kept tossing her head, champing at the bit, and even tried to dislodge Aila with a buck or two.

"Aye ... she'll calm down eventually," Aila replied. "I don't know what's wrong with Dusty this morning. Someone must have given her too many oats last night."

"Maybe she just needs to stretch her legs," Elizabeth suggested. "Some horses like to be out front."

Aila nodded, fighting with Dusty once more when the mare tossed her head and side-stepped. She knew her mount liked to lead. The women rode in the midst of the column, while the laird had urged his courser farther up the line. It was a deliberate snub of his wife, although Lady Gavina didn't seem to mind.

In fact, her mistress looked in much lighter spirits than usual this morning. Her pale cheeks had a blush to them for once, and her eyes were bright. Like Aila, she was keen to leave the confines of Dunnottar for a few days.

Catching Aila's eye, Lady Gavina flashed her a smile. "Elizabeth is right. Why don't ye ride up to the head of the column? I'm sure Captain Gaius won't mind. Let Dusty run a little."

Aila glimpsed the knowing look in her mistress's eyes. "Are ye sure ye don't mind?" she asked meekly.

"Of course not." Lady Gavina waved her on.

Not hesitating further, lest her courage fail, Aila steered Dusty out of the column. She slackened the reins just a little, and the mare was off, racing up to the head of the line, kicking her heels behind her.

The horse's exuberance nearly unseated Aila. When she reached the head of the column, where Cassian and the banner-bearers led the way just in front of the laird, her arm muscles were burning from preventing Dusty from careening forward in a flat gallop.

Cassian glanced her way as she drew Dusty up next to his magnificent liver-bay courser. "Aila ... what are you doing up here?"

It wasn't a warm welcome. His tone was clipped, and a frown accompanied the question.

"Apologies, Captain," Aila gasped. "My mount has a mind of her own this morning."

"She really is too much for you," Cassian observed, his frown deepening. "I'll have to speak to your father about getting you a quieter horse upon our return home."

His words stung. Aila wanted to be respected as a competent rider. She wanted Cassian to look upon her with admiration, not with barely concealed frustration.

Suddenly, the plan to force them into closer proximity through riding up the column to join him seemed foolish.

I'm not sure I should have heeded Lady Gavina.

Captain Gaius took his role seriously, as any warrior would. He didn't need a goose-brained woman distracting him.

"I'm sorry," Aila murmured, suddenly feeling a bit foolish. "I'll pull back."

"No need," he replied, his tone abrupt now. Unfastening a lead-rope from behind his saddle, he guided his horse up next to Dusty and fastened the rope to her bit. "This should help keep her in check."

Heat rose to Aila's cheeks. She now heartily wished she'd stayed with the other women farther back in the column. He was going to lead her like a child. And not only that, but he looked irritated about it.

XI

PROGRESS

"DO YE ENJOY living at Dunnottar, Captain?"

As soon as the question left her lips, Aila cringed. All the things she could have asked Cassian, and she'd chosen the blandest question of the lot.

However, Cassian had the manners to at least favor her with a polite smile. "Yes ... I'm fortunate indeed to live in such a beautiful part of Scotland," he replied.

"Ye are from Spain though," she said, drinking in the handsome, if stern, lines of his face. "I have heard that it's a bonny place where the sun shines all year."

Cassian's smile widened at that, and Aila's embarrassment eased.

"I'm from Galicia ... in the north," he replied. "It still gets cold winters."

"What's it like ... yer home?"

Cassian's smile faded, and he shifted his gaze to the road ahead. They'd left the rolling hills surrounding Dunnottar and Stonehaven behind and now rode into the wooded foothills. The bulk of large, forested mountains reared up to the west—marking the beginning of the Highlands. A chill wind buffeted the party, cold for the time of year.

"I don't really remember," he murmured.

Aila frowned. What an odd response. "Have ye been away a long while?"

Cassian nodded. "I became a soldier when I was twenty and left my homeland as soon as I was able." He paused there, glancing back at her. "I had no one left in Spain anyway. I was an orphan ... my parents died of a pestilence when I was barely five winters old."

Aila's breathing hitched, her chest aching at the thought of losing one's parents so young. "What happened to ye after they died?"

"I lived wild ... scavenging and thieving like a rat until I was old enough to enlist."

"And what brought ye to Scotland?"

Aila knew she was interrogating the man, yet it was hard to stem the questions that poured forth. For years now, she'd been awaiting this conversation. And after a frosty start, when she'd appeared at the head of the column, he'd eventually thawed.

Cassian's gaze met hers. "I came here as a mercenary."

"And ye decided to stay?"

His mouth quirked. "It would seem so."

Aila held his gaze, even though shyness suddenly rose up within her and she had to fight the urge to look away. Jean—who seemed so much more worldly than her—had said that eye contact was a clear signal to a man that a lass was interested in him.

The moment drew out, and still they looked at each other.

Eventually, it was Cassian who glanced away first.

Heart racing, Aila allowed herself a small smile of victory. She couldn't believe it; she was actually conquering her fears and talking to the man she longed for. It was a small step forward, but progress nonetheless.

They camped outside the village of Kirriemuir that night. The men erected a tightly-packed circle of tents, just as a vicious squall swept across the hills. It turned the sky the color of slate. The harsh weather made the horses clump together, heads bowed and tails tucked between their hind legs, as rain lashed the company.

Aila untied the saddlebags she and Lady Gavina had packed, her fingers fumbling in haste. Head bent against the icy splinters of rain and ice that howled down from the north, she carried the bags into the large tent that she would be sharing with her mistress, Lady Elizabeth, and Jean.

Her companions were already inside. The ladies were shaking rain off their mantles while Jean bustled about, unrolling furs for everyone to sleep on. One of the men had brought in a brazier and a lump of peat, but it was still unlit. Digging out her flint, steel, and a small bag of tinder, Aila set about lighting a fire. The day hadn't been warm, and the icy rain had made their clothes damp.

Outdoors, the wind and rain hammered the tent, its hide sides billowing and snapping. Aila found it hard not to cringe at the storm's fury. She hoped the men had bashed the tent pegs in well—otherwise they could lose their shelter overnight.

However, the tent seemed to withstand the tempest, and a short while later, the peat started to smoke, sending a choking column of blue-grey fug up through the hole in the roof. Eyes watering, Aila nursed the fire until tender flames took hold. Meanwhile, the ladies had settled themselves on a makeshift seat, made from their saddlebags, as Jean set out a supper.

"It's not much of a meal," Jean sniffed, raising her voice to be heard over the howling wind and drum of the rain above their heads. She was a sweet-faced lass. Aila envied Jean her small, curvy frame and mass of wild red curls that won her much male attention. "Bannock, cheese, and eggs is meagre fare for ladies."

"And it'll do us all fine, Jean," Lady Elizabeth replied. "Frankly, after a day in the saddle, all I want to do is stretch out on my furs and sleep."

Lowering herself into a cross-legged position a few feet back from the crackling brazier, Aila took a bite of bannock and boiled egg. She was ravenous.

Across from her, Gavina buttered a wedge of bannock for herself, her gaze flicking to where Elizabeth sat next to her, peeling an egg.

Watching the two ladies, Aila noted—not for the first time—how different they were. Gavina had an ethereal, delicate quality to her—the effect enhanced by her white-blonde hair. The lady's skin looked almost translucent in the brazier's glow. In contrast, Elizabeth possessed an earthy beauty. Disheveled dark blonde hair framed a strong-featured face, curling over her shoulders in a wild mane.

"I'm glad ye are with us, Liz," Gavina said after a pause. "I intend to make sure David presses Edward about Robert ... but it'll be much easier with ye present."

Elizabeth nodded. "I'm relieved the Wallace managed to convince David to go in the end."

"Aye, although I think William was glad of our assistance," Gavina replied. Her lips thinned then. "David can be bull-headed."

Elizabeth's mouth lifted at the corners. "Aye, but so is the Wallace. He's a clever man ... Robert thought highly of him."

"Thought?" Gavina chided her. "Ye must not talk as if yer husband is dead."

Indeed, the laird had received word just three months earlier that Robert was still alive and residing in an English dungeon. The missive had deliberately avoided telling them exactly where. The English had captured him just over a year earlier during a skirmish near the River Cree on the Scottish-English border.

Elizabeth's dark-blue gaze shadowed. "How much longer will they hold him?"

Gavina clearly had no answer for that, although her face tensed in sympathy. All at Dunnottar knew how close Robert and Elizabeth were. Their son, Robbie, was now three, and Elizabeth clearly worried he would never know his father.

"I miss him so much it hurts to breathe," Elizabeth said finally, breaking the awkward silence. She stopped peeling the egg and lowered it to her lap. "What if I never see him again?"

Gavina reached out then, placing a hand over her friend's. She didn't assure her that he would return—for none of them could make such a promise.

Aila dropped her gaze to her own supper. Elizabeth's pain was palpable, but that was what happened when you gave someone your heart. However, the risk was worth it in her opinion. Elizabeth and Robert's marriage stood out in stark contrast to Gavina and David's.

When I wed, it will be for love, Aila vowed, cutting herself a piece of cheese.

Her stomach fluttered at her resolution. The conversation with Cassian earlier had emboldened her. He was warming to her; she could sense it.

The four women ate in silence, letting the roar of the storm outdoors dominate, before Jean passed around a skin of ale. Meanwhile, the brazier had started to warm the interior of the tent, despite the drafts caused by the buffeting wind. The odor of damp wool and peat smoke caught in Aila's throat and made her cough.

Eventually, Lady Gavina gave a delicate yawn and shifted back from the brazier. She settled down upon the fur Jean had rolled out for her.

"Shall I help ye undress, My Lady?" Aila asked, brushing crumbs off her skirts and rising to her feet.

Gavina shook her head. "I won't bother tonight," she replied. "Not in this weather."

"Neither will I," Lady Elizabeth added. "But can ye comb out my hair, Jean? It feels like a rat's nest tonight."

Aila and Jean went through their usual nightly routine of brushing out their mistresses' long hair. Once that was done, they retired to their own furs on the opposite side of the brazier, near the flap that led outdoors. A chill draft clawed at Aila there, and she was grateful to wrap herself in her still-damp cloak to ward it off.

Lying side-by-side, the two maids huddled under their cloaks.

"Isn't this exciting," Jean murmured, her voice muffled by the screaming wind. "I've never been away from De Keith lands before."

"Neither have I," Aila admitted, glancing up at where water was dripping down from the smoke hole. She edged away from it. "I hope the weather improves though … I was looking forward to the journey, but not in driving rain."

"It's Stirling I can't wait to see," Jean whispered back. "I can't believe the English king is actually there … I wonder if he sports a devil's tail as folk say."

Aila snorted at the ridiculous notion. However, Jean was right about one thing: Edward Longshanks didn't belong in Scotland. She hated the thought of him taking Stirling Castle as his own. Lady Gavina had told her the laird would be expected to swear fealty to Edward— something else that made her tense.

"My sister's been to Stirling," Aila admitted, keen to turn the conversation away from the loathsome Edward. "She says it's a jewel … with the River Forth sparkling in the sun on bright days and the castle rising like a sentinel above it … the brooch that holds Scotland together." Pride tightened in Aila's breast as she said the words.

"And the castle is said to be even bigger than Dunnottar," Jean replied. "I can't wait to explore it."

Aila smiled. She too was looking forward to that. She wondered how long they would remain in Stirling, and whether Lady Elizabeth would be able to soften Edward into releasing her husband. Would Edward reveal his plans now that he'd taken Stirling?

The reminder of the English occupation years earlier made Aila's pride subside, a nervous flutter replacing it.

She rolled away from Jean, terminating the conversation. What a couple of twittering fools they were, treating this journey like a longed-for jaunt. It was a foolish approach to take.

Especially with so much at stake.

XII

JOURNEY'S END

"YOU'RE TOO TENSE, Aila."

Dusty side-stepped and tossed her head, chafing against the third rein that kept her leashed to Cassian's courser. Aila tightened her reins, yet the mare just fought harder. This horse really was too much for her. If anything, the palfrey had become even more hot-headed during the journey south.

She shot Cassian a pained look. In contrast to her rigid posture, he appeared to have been born in the saddle. The stallion he rode, a powerful animal that intimidated Aila somewhat, seemed docile under his firm hand.

"The mare senses your fear," he continued. "Loosen your hold on the reins. The mare isn't going to bolt with me leashing her."

"I'm not afraid," Aila lied, although she relaxed her death-grip on the reins—a relief, for her fingers had stiffened into claws.

Dusty immediately stopped fighting the bit.

"You don't control a horse when you climb upon its back," Cassian added, catching her eye. "You enter into an agreement with it."

Aila frowned. She'd never heard riding described like that. "I don't think Dusty wants a partnership," she muttered as the mare gave a playful buck.

Cassian's lips curved, and Aila's pulse quickened. His smiles really were devastating.

"Try breathing deeply and slowly ... and use your thighs to restrain her," he replied,

Reluctantly, Aila did as bid. It wasn't easy to steady her breathing, especially with his gaze upon her. It thrilled her to be able to exchange a few words with him like this. To her delight, Cassian had sought her out the morning after the storm and suggested that she rode with him again. He'd seen that she was still struggling to control her palfrey, and seemed concerned that Dusty might throw her. Although it was embarrassing—since the other women handled their horses without problems—Aila had also been secretly delighted.

Three more days of travel had passed since that first stormy night—many hours of riding side-by-side.

Aila was self-conscious at having her riding criticized. Nonetheless, his advice worked. As soon as she engaged her thigh muscles, and took a few slow, deep breaths, Dusty quietened a little. The dun snorted and lowered her head.

"See," Cassian said, not without an edge of masculine smugness in his voice. "Trust her."

Aila resisted an indelicate snort. Dusty had already proved herself untrustworthy. "Do horses really sense our moods?" she asked, keen to keep the conversation moving between them.

He nodded. "All animals do. Dogs sense if you fear them or not too." He paused then. "How often have you visited Dusty in her stall over the years?"

Aila glanced away, embarrassed. "Never," she admitted.

She could feel his smile upon her. "Well then ... maybe while we are in Stirling you might want to start doing so. You might find your relationship changes for the better on the journey home."

Aila looked his way once more. Indeed, he was smiling. "How is it ye know so much about horses?"

He shrugged. "I just do ... some folk have an affinity for the beasts." He reached down and slapped his courser's muscular neck. "Rogue doesn't mind me, do you lad?"

Aila smiled, her embarrassment fading. It was strange to finally speak at length to this man. He was different to how she'd imagined. Not as gruff, more philosophical. He had a warmth that drew her in, made her want more.

The real Cassian was even better than her romantic imaginings, although she wished she weren't so easily flustered by his presence.

"We are lucky to have ye at Dunnottar, Captain," she said, forcing herself to conquer shyness and hold his gaze. "Ye are good with both men *and* beasts it seems."

The words were clumsy and came out all wrong. Heat flowered across Aila's chest, and she cursed her gaucheness. However, Cassian didn't seem to mind. Continuing to hold her eye steadily, he smiled once more.

You shouldn't encourage her. Cassian's smile faded as he turned his attention back to the road before them. They were heading down the final incline toward Stirling. The castle reared up to their right, its dove-grey walls outlined against a windy blue sky. *This can't go anywhere.*

Maybe not, but Aila had proved charming company during the journey. He'd been irritated when she'd appeared at his shoulder upon her prancing palfrey that first day, but despite everything, he enjoyed talking to her.

Cassian rarely had long talks with women these days.

He lived in a male-dominated world and took most of his meals in the mess hall. During suppers with the laird, he sometimes exchanged a few words with Lady Elizabeth or Lady Gavina, but the conversation was usually short and formal.

During the journey, Aila had occasionally batted her eyelids or favored him with a longing look, as if she'd studied rules about how to woo a man and kept reminding herself. It was oddly endearing to see her make such an effort, but most of the time, she was just herself—and that was how he liked her. Although she initially appeared timid, she actually had quite a bit to say for herself.

She was full of curiosity about him—*too* curious.

The journey was almost over, and Cassian was relieved about that. However, there was a tiny part of him—a part he dismissed—that was sorry he and Aila would no longer have an opportunity to talk.

Their conversations reminded him of how lonely he sometimes felt. The sensation—a hollow ache in his chest—usually visited him as he lay upon his bed trying to get off to sleep at night.

Cassian tensed his jaw as the feeling surfaced once more. It was just as well the journey was ending. Such thoughts weren't doing him any good.

"The castle is lovely," Aila breathed, her wide grey eyes on the keep perched high upon a rocky crag. The collection of thatch roofs of the town below tumbled down the hillside to where the River Forth sparkled in the noon sun. "Heather told me Stirling was beautiful ... but her descriptions didn't do it justice."

Cassian's gaze followed hers, although his attention focused more on where a blockade of men and horses barred their way into the town. They didn't have to cross the river as they were approaching from the north-east— yet it seemed the English were patrolling all ways in.

"There's no place quite like it," he replied, his attention shifting to the high curtain walls. How many times had he visited Stirling over the years? Too many to count—and yet the sight of that great keep standing guard over the River Forth, a wall of mountains at its back, never failed to make him catch his breath. He remembered the fort that had been here during his early years in Caledonia—the Romans had even occupied it for a time—before the Picts built a stone broch upon the crag.

It was around that time, long before the people of this land worshipped the Christian God, that Cassian, Maximus, and Draco had carved a temple to Mithras out of the rock.

Cassian reached forward and unclipped the lead from Dusty's bridle. "It's best you fall back now, Aila," he said, his manner brisk. Now that they were approaching the wolf's lair, he couldn't afford any distractions. "Rejoin Lady Gavina. The De Keith will need to announce himself."

Aila nodded and drew her palfrey up, waiting to one side while the column rode by. Dusty tossed her head. The mare didn't appreciate being made to wait, but Cassian noted that Aila held the horse in check better than she had earlier that day.

Glancing over his shoulder, Cassian watched the laird urge his courser up the column so he rode directly behind him.

"Ready, De Keith?" Cassian greeted him. "Your welcome party awaits."

The laird wore a strained expression, his gaze narrow as it settled upon the big chainmailed men who barred their path. "How dare they prevent me from entering Stirling," he growled. "This is *our* land."

Cassian tensed at his laird's aggression. As the younger brother, David De Keith had little experience with diplomacy. His brother had known how to treat with his enemies, but it occurred to Cassian then that David's fiery temper could work against him here.

Cassian's mouth thinned. Sending De Keith to Stirling was like throwing a wasp nest into the midst of a banquet. He hoped the Wallace hadn't made an error in insisting De Keith make this visit. Wallace wanted the Balliol family back on the Scottish throne—but his dedication to the cause made him blinkered at times.

"Remember ... you're here to bend the knee," he warned his laird. "Try not to let your disdain for the English show too plainly upon your face."

De Keith muttered a curse under his breath at this, while Cassian urged Rogue forward. Two of the chainmailed English warriors walked out to meet them.

De Keith is in danger here. Cassian schooled his features into an expressionless mask. *As are all of us, if he doesn't do as he promised.*

Clattering up the hill, Aila craned her neck to stare at the towering walls of the castle above her. Excitement fluttered up into her throat, and her pulse quickened.

The rumors were true: Stirling Castle was much grander than Dunnottar. The way in, up a wide road, was definitely more impressive. However, her belly tensed, her excitement dimming, when she caught sight of the two flags flying from one of the keep's towers. The first was white with a red cross—England's Saint George's cross—while the second flag bore three golden rampant lions against a crimson background—the Plantagenet banner of Edward's family.

Aila's mouth pursed, anger dousing the wonder that had consumed her upon riding into Stirling.

The arrogance.

Now that they'd been admitted to Stirling, an escort of English soldiers led the way up the hill. Tension rippled through the company. Lady Elizabeth's pretty face was set in rigid lines, while Lady Gavina had gone quiet and pale. Even Jean, who usually had plenty to say for herself, had lapsed into silence, her gaze wide as she took in her surroundings.

The streets were quieter than Aila had imagined. Heather had spoken of the Riverside market, but there were no stalls along the banks of the Forth today. When her sister had passed through Stirling just over a month earlier, the town had apparently been full of Scotsmen, warriors from the lowland clans who'd rallied to Stirling to help defend it.

But there was no sign of those men now.

Aila swallowed, the fine hair on the back of her arms prickling as she realized most of them were likely dead.

What few folk they spied on the way up the hill peered out from windows and shadowed doorways. Their gazes were fearful, and their faces rigid with distrust.

Finally, the De Keith party thundered through a great stone arch and into a wide outer-bailey. Low buildings—which likely housed the stables, byres, storehouses, and an armory—lined the cobbled space.

More English soldiers awaited them here. The tension within Aila bloomed into panic at the sight of them. Suddenly, Stirling lost its sparkle.

It was impossible to ignore that the English ruled this town and its mighty fortress.

She still remembered what it was like at Dunnottar during the English occupation: how she, her sister, and her mother had feared to wander the keep. She'd also worried for her father's life, for as castle steward, Donnan De Keith posed a threat to English authority. They'd even thrown him in the dungeon for a spell, after first taking the castle, until they could be assured that he wouldn't make trouble.

The English dressed as Aila remembered: many in long hauberks—mail shirts—and chainmail chausses, or stockings. Some of the warriors had pulled up their coifs—hoods made of chainmail. It was a look that she found intimidating.

English and Scot eyed each other warily as De Keith and his followers filled the outer-bailey.

Aila drew up her palfrey and glanced to where Lady Gavina had halted next to her. Meeting Aila's eye, the lady gave her a wary look. "Keep yer wits about ye here, Aila," she warned.

XIII

I'M HERE FOR SCOTLAND

"WELCOME TO STIRLING, De Keith. I'm glad to see at least one of you has the courage to come before me."

Edward of England's deep voice echoed across the Great Hall, breaking the tense hush that had settled when David De Keith entered.

The king spoke French, the tongue favored by the English ruling classes.

Cassian walked at his laird's side, while Gavina and Elizabeth brought up the rear of their small party. A crowd of Edward's retainers drew aside, letting them approach the dais, where Edward sat upon a huge wooden chair.

It had been a long while since Cassian had actually been inside Stirling Castle—the last time was a couple of centuries earlier when the now mighty keep had been little more than a round-tower. This great stone hall with wooden rafters was certainly a magnificent structure.

However, Cassian's attention didn't linger upon his surroundings for long. Instead, it shifted to the man who'd just welcomed them.

He was face-to-face with Edward Plantagenet himself.

Despite his advancing years, the king appeared hale and strong. He looked to be in his early sixties and bore an impressive mane of greying blond hair that flowed over his broad shoulders. A golden, gem-studded crown sat upon his head. He was dressed as a warrior king, in a blood-red surcoat, with a glittering hauberk underneath. A longsword hung at his hip. The man commanded the room.

Even seated, Cassian could see Edward was a tall man. He stretched his long legs out before him and crossed them at the ankle.

Cassian bit back a wry smile. *Longshanks, indeed.*

Watching the English king closely, Cassian understood why Edward of England caused the Scots so much bother. He wore an aura of authority, and as he drew nearer still, Cassian saw the man's ice-blue gaze was flinty when it rested upon David De Keith. A drooping left eyelid marred his even-featured face.

A few feet behind Edward stood another imposing figure: a big man with a hawkish nose. The warrior was clad in chainmail and sported a luxurious red beard.

Cassian needed no formal introduction to know that this was John 'The Red' Comyn, Baron of Badenoch—Steward of Scotland. The man hadn't earned his nickname because of his fiery temper or high coloring, but because of his mane of red hair.

Comyn watched the newcomers halt before the dais without a flicker of emotion on his face. His gaze, when it settled upon De Keith, was guarded. Of course, the Scottish baron had been in control of Stirling before the English attack a month earlier, but wasn't able to hold the castle and township.

It appeared that the baron, who'd become 'Guardian of the Realm' after the forced abdication of his uncle King John Balliol five years earlier, had already bent the knee to Edward.

He wouldn't be standing here if he hadn't.

"You are the first laird of the north to come to me," Edward continued, still in French. Cassian noted that he spoke with a slight lisp, although it didn't diminish the strength of his voice. "I'm pleased to see that the laird of Dunnottar is a *reasonable* man at least."

Cassian cast a glance at where David De Keith had halted next to him. The laird wore a stony expression.

Cassian tensed. They'd already discussed how important it was that the English king thought he'd come in good faith. David had to make a show of subservience. De Keith would need to bend the knee, even if he never intended to honor the gesture. Otherwise, Lady Elizabeth was never going to get her husband back, and Wallace wasn't going to receive the news he so desperately wanted. It would also ensure they could leave Stirling and return home unmolested.

De Keith needed to favor Edward with one of his charming smiles.

Moments passed, and De Keith eventually managed a tight-lipped grimace—however, he didn't kneel as was expected.

The uncomfortable silence drew out, before Edward's greying brows knitted together. Yet he didn't speak. He waited his guest out.

Eventually, David De Keith cleared his throat. A nerve flickered under one eye as he dipped his chin. "Je suis ici pour l'Ecosse," he replied in French, his voice unnaturally rough and his words halting.

I'm here for Scotland. Cassian smiled at this. *Good ... he's finally playing the game.*

"And I hope to do what is in its best interests," De Keith concluded.

Edward's gaze narrowed further before he pushed himself up off his chair, looming over them. He was an imposing sight in his chainmail and crown. He then favored the laird with a cool smile. "That's pleasing to hear, De Keith."

The De Keiths banqueted with the English king that evening in the Great Hall.

As always, Cassian accompanied his laird, keeping one step behind him when they re-entered the hall to find it a very difficult space to earlier that day.

Long tables had been carried in, and flickering torches illuminated the cavernous chamber, bathing the pitted stone walls in warmth. A huge hearth burned at one end of the hall, casting a red-gold glow over the faces of Edward, John Comyn, and the king's retainers as they all took their places at the king's table on the dais.

De Keith was to join them.

"Keep yer eyes open, Captain," David muttered to Cassian. He spoke in Gaelic. "We've truly walked into the adder's nest here." The laird's gaze settled upon the platters of roast meats and steamed greens the servants were placing upon the long table. "I wouldn't be surprised if he tries to poison us."

"Poison isn't kingly," Cassian replied, keeping his voice low. "If Edward wanted you dead, he'd likely just run you through with his sword."

De Keith cast Cassian a frown. He'd been making a statement; he hadn't wanted to be contradicted.

"De Keith!" Edward beckoned to David, motioning to his left side. Comyn 'The Red' sat to his right, his expression as inscrutable as earlier. "Come and sit with me this eve ... so we may speak."

De Keith did as bid, although Cassian noted he now wore a pained look. Those seated upon the dais spread out in a row upon the long table, flanking Edward and facing those seated below. Lady Gavina followed her husband up onto the dais and took a seat to his left. As always, De Keith ignored her.

Cassian sat down between the laird's wife and Lady Elizabeth. Both women looked lovely this eve clad in their best kirtles and surcoats, their hair woven into elaborate twists and braids upon their heads.

Aila will have been busy this afternoon, Cassian thought, imagining the young woman's face creased in concentration as she worked on her mistress's hair.

Cassian tensed. What was he doing thinking about Lady Gavina's maid? He hadn't seen her since they'd ridden into the castle, for she'd been tucked away in the guest apartments. But all of a sudden, a vision of her sweet face, her large grey eyes staring up at him as she favored him with an eager smile, arose before him.

Irritated at how easily a few days in the woman's company had affected him, Cassian shoved the vision of Aila De Keith aside.

A couple of yards away from the king's table, a harpist set himself up near the hearth. He then began to play a melancholy tune. It wasn't one that Cassian recognized, but it was pretty nonetheless: a haunting English melody.

Cassian's attention went to where two burly servants carried a great platter—a huge roast swan, burnished gold with butter—up onto the dais and set it down before the king.

Edward flashed De Keith a wolf's smile. "To celebrate new allies."

Even though he wasn't seated next to him, Cassian felt the laird's tension. He really was useless at keeping his emotions hidden—a poor diplomat indeed. Cassian felt for the pugio at his hip out of habit, tensing when he discovered the dagger wasn't there.

He'd forgotten already that he'd agreed to come to the banquet unarmed.

Cassian didn't like being in here without a weapon to hand, or without any of his men at his back. Now that they were in Stirling, the rest of the De Keith escort were lying low. They wouldn't be needed again until the laird departed.

"Wine?" Edward asked, motioning to a passing servant.

"Aye." De Keith held up his garnet-studded silver goblet to be filled.

Cassian's heart sank. Once De Keith started drinking, he didn't know when to stop.

Edward smiled once more. "I think you'll enjoy this ... it comes from my favorite vineyard in France."

The servants filled up everyone's goblets, Cassian's included. He took a sip of the rich red wine and was immediately transported back to his homeland, to the spicy red wines of Brigantium. He hadn't tasted wine like this in many long years. The lairds and chieftains he'd served over the years occasionally imported wine from the continent, but he rarely got to drink any of it.

"So, De Keith," Edward spoke once more as he watched a servant slice up the swan. He then held out his platter to be filled. "How are things farther north?"

It was a loaded question, and deliberately so. Cassian cut a quick glance to his laird, noticing the way De Keith pinched his lips together.

Lady Gavina cleared her throat. "Things are peaceful in the North, Your Highness," she said in fluent French, "and we wish for them to remain so."

David cut his wife an irritated look, yet she ignored him.

King Edward's gaze shifted for the first time to Lady Gavina. He watched her for a moment—it was a penetrating gaze, yet there wasn't any lechery in it. He merely looked taken aback. Meanwhile, David De Keith's cheeks flushed.

"I don't wish to fight the Highland clans, Lady Gavina," Edward replied, his expression hooding. "If they pledge fealty to me, they shall find I'm a fair and just ruler."

De Keith snorted, causing the king's attention to swivel to him. "De Keith?"

"The clan-chiefs of the North are a stubborn lot, Longshanks," the laird pointed out coolly. "They aren't as *reasonable* as me. Good luck getting any of them to kneel to ye."

The table went silent. Some of the king's retainers seated nearest exchanged scowls.

Cassian sucked in a deep breath. *Great ... we've only just arrived, and the idiot is going to get himself thrown in Stirling dungeon for insulting the English king.*

Next to De Keith, Edward picked up his goblet and took a measured sip. "Longhanks ... now that's a name few men have the balls to say to my face," he replied after a long pause. His voice was low, but it carried across the quiet hall.

De Keith shifted uncomfortably in his seat, his bearded jaw tightening.

"However, I do have another name," Edward continued smoothly. "One that's become very popular over the border." The English king held up his goblet then to De Keith, a smile gracing his lips. "*Malleus Scotorum*: the Hammer of the Scots."

XIV

THE HAMMER OF THE SCOTS

THE HAMMER OF the Scots.

Edward's voice echoed over and over in Cassian's head.

The banquet had finally ended, and the Great Hall emptied out. He was accompanying De Keith, his wife, and sister-by-marriage back to their apartments inside the keep. Outdoors, a slender crescent moon had appeared in the darkening sky. The air against their skin was fresh after the smoky interior of the Great Hall.

But Cassian found it difficult to concentrate on anything except that name.

It's not Irvine's 'Battle Hammer'. Certainty barreled into Cassian. *The Hammer that will strike the fort upon the Shelving Slope is Edward. He's going to attack Dunnottar.*

Cassian's pulse accelerated, sweat beading on his skin.

An aggressive neighbor was one thing, but the King of England with his massive army was another.

How could we get it so wrong? I need to get word to Maximus and Draco.

Cassian would go to the mithraeum and ask one of the guardians to deliver an urgent message to his friends. However, since the Kirk of the Holy Rude would be locked up for the night, he'd need to wait till dawn to do so.

"Loose-lipped woman," De Keith snarled at his wife as she followed him up the stairs into the keep. "Never interrupt when men are speaking."

"I was only trying to help ye, David," Lady Gavina replied. Her voice was soft, with a pleading note to it. "Edward is a dangerous man … can ye not see it?"

"English dog," David spat out the words. "I know how to deal with him."

"By insulting him?"

De Keith turned so quickly that his wife stumbled in an effort not to collide with him. Grabbing hold of her shoulders, he shook her hard. "Folk will have called that bastard worse."

Cassian drew close. He'd never seen the laird manhandle his wife before, but he wouldn't stand by if De Keith got any rougher.

"But, David … ye must play the game," Lady Elizabeth spoke up, her voice low. She halted beside them. The lady's face was pale, her eyes dark with anger as she faced him. "We must convince Edward to release Robert."

"I tire of women telling me what to do," David countered, not bothering to keep his tone low. His fingers dug into his wife's shoulders. Gavina winced and tried to pull away, yet her husband held her fast. "And if the pair of ye don't mind yer tongues, I'll leave ye behind when I meet Longshanks again."

"De Keith." Cassian stepped close then, invading his laird's personal space. "Release your wife … and let us go inside. This is not a conversation you should be having out here."

David De Keith cast him a scowl, hesitating a moment. But Cassian's own stare bored into him. Realizing that he was indeed on the verge of making an ugly scene, the laird reluctantly let go of Lady Gavina and stepped back from her.

Then, with a muttered curse, De Keith swiveled on his heel and stormed into the keep.

"This castle has its secrets, let me tell ye ... I've lived here a few years now, but I still hear tales that surprise me." The young woman leaned close to Aila, her blue eyes widening and an impish smile curving her lips. "Would ye like a tour?"

Aila hesitated. She'd just finished helping Lady Gavina prepare for bed. Her mistress had been subdued tonight, but when Aila asked if anything was amiss, she'd denied it.

She imagined the banquet with Edward had been a tense affair. Aila had gently inquired as to what the English king was like, and Lady Gavina had given her a weary look. "No worse than I expected ... at least he behaved better than my husband this eve."

The comment had intrigued Aila, but since Gavina refused to elaborate on it, she'd emerged from the lady's chamber frustrated. She had a small room next door to her mistress's and was expected to retire to it.

But despite the long day, Aila didn't feel tired. Despite that the sight of all those hauberk-clad English warriors frightened her, she didn't want to lock herself away. Curiosity overcame nervousness. She longed to explore the keep a little. And so, she'd made her way down to the kitchens: a huge cavernous space carved out in the cellar of the keep, where four large hearths glowed and the air was fragrant with the scent of freshly baked bread.

It was there she'd met Fyfa—the wife of Stirling Castle's steward—and the pair of them were just finishing a supper of warm currant buns smeared with rich butter. Rarely had Aila tasted anything so delicious.

Sensing Aila's reluctance to accept her offer, Fyfa rose to her feet, tossed her dark-auburn hair back off her shoulders, and brushed the crumbs from her skirts. "Come on ... Hume lets me go wherever I like in the castle ... and it's bonny at night."

Aila still hesitated. "Is it safe?"

"Of course ... this is still *our* castle. Longshanks is merely an unwelcome guest."

Impressed by Fyfa's fiery response, Aila stood up. She had to stop being so timid. Lady Gavina would be fast asleep now and wouldn't need her till dawn. What would a stroll around the castle hurt? Especially since she'd be with the steward's wife.

They alighted the stairs from the kitchens and left the keep, emerging into the torch-lit inner-bailey beyond. It was a lovely night out; the air was cool yet still, and the sky above was a clear swath of sparkling stars. A sickle moon rode high above them, a silver horseshoe against the inky blanket of night.

Aila breathed in the scent of wood smoke, her edginess ebbing. Woodland surrounded Stirling, so the folk here didn't need to rely on peat to warm their homes. A smile stretched across her face. "It's beautiful out here."

Fyfa shot her a bright smile. "Aye ... the keep and its bailey are grand enough, but they aren't what I love most about this place. Follow me."

And with that, the woman picked up her skirts and led Aila away from the keep. They crossed the inner-bailey, past where guards lurked in long shadows. However, Fyfa didn't appear remotely cowed. Instead, she waved to the English soldiers, called out a cheery 'Bonsoir', and continued on her way.

"Aren't ye nervous?" Aila asked, hurrying after her. "These men aren't Scots ... they can't be trusted."

Fyfa snorted. "No man, Scot or English can be trusted. But fret not ... they know I'm Hume Comyn's wife ... they'll dare not cause us any bother."

The woman, although no older than twenty-five winters, spoke with such authority that Aila found herself believing her. Fyfa led her out of the bailey and through a large walled garden. Burning torches lined the pathways. The scent of lavender and rosemary enveloped them in here, their slippered feet crunching upon the pebbled path. The two women approached a statue at the heart of the garden: the rearing head of a horse. The statue was a fearsome sight, for it was made of a pale sandstone that glowed in the moonlight.

Fyfa paused before it. "It's a kelpie," she murmured, her gaze resting upon the creature's wild face. "Hume's grand-da sculpted it."

"It's magnificent," Aila breathed.

The steward's wife shot her an answering smile. "Come ... this way."

Fyfa continued on, skirting the statue and heading toward the northern edge of the garden, where steps led up to a high wall. Fyfa scaled them, and Aila followed her.

From there, they looked down upon a vast, grassy space, illuminated by the starlight—and at its center was a large, octagonal mound.

"That's the King's Knot," Fyfa explained. "Ye can't see much at night, but there are rose beds planted out there ... the lords of Stirling use the rest of the grounds for hawking and hunting ... and at midsummer, there are jousting tournaments." She paused, casting Aila a conspirator's grin. "Legend has it that King Arthur's round table lies beneath the Knot."

Aila's breathing caught. She loved legends and stories; there were many associated with Dunnottar, but Stirling was all new to her—and it was a place of kings and queens.

"What about the castle's other secrets?" she asked, grinning back at Fyfa. Now that her initial nervousness had disappeared, she was excited to explore the castle further.

Fyfa's gaze glinted in the light of a nearby brazier. "This way then. The best is yet to come."

The woman turned and hurried back down the narrow steps. Aila followed her, although much more gingerly. Even with burning torches and braziers upon the walls, the shadows were deep. One misstep and she'd break her neck.

The steward's wife led her back, through the gardens, across the inner-bailey, and into another large walled space.

"This is the Nether Bailey," Fyfa announced, her voice lowering to a whisper.

Illuminated by burning braziers upon the walls, Aila could see that it was rocky and exposed, and afforded a wide view over the lands below. The fires of the town glowed in the darkness. As her eyes adjusted, Aila caught sight of a row of low-slung buildings with thatched roofs against the northern wall.

"What are those?" she asked.

"Storehouses and workshops mostly," Fyfa replied airily, "but that's not why I've brought ye here. Come … take a look at this."

With that she took a torch from a bracket near the gate and led Aila down to the wall walk.

XV

PROMISE ME

THE TWO WOMEN had finished their tour and were making their way back across the inner-bailey toward the keep, when Aila spotted a tall figure striding across the courtyard toward them.

Her heart leaped against her ribs, and without thinking, she drew closer to her guide.

Fyfa had said it was safe out here, yet maybe she was mistaken.

But as the man drew closer, the tension in Aila's breast unknotted. The breath she'd been holding gusted out of her. "Captain Gaius," she gasped.

Fyfa glanced her way, her gaze sharpening. "Ye know him?"

Aila nodded. "He leads the Dunnottar Guard."

The steward's wife gave Cassian a long, appraising look as he approached. Aila stiffened; it wasn't a look *she'd* dare ever give a man.

Cassian didn't appear to notice Fyfa's sultry gaze. Instead, his attention was riveted on her companion. "Aila," he greeted her brusquely. "What are you doing outdoors at this hour?"

"Fyfa was giving me a tour of the castle," Aila replied with a shy smile. "Stirling is bonny by torchlight. We've just been to the Nether Bailey."

"It's not safe for two women to go wandering about," he replied, casting Fyfa a narrow-eyed look.

"I'm Hume Comyn's wife," Fyfa replied, holding his gaze boldly. "We are perfectly safe, Captain."

A little of the tension upon Cassian's face eased at these words, although his expression remained stern. "All the same ... I think it's time I escorted Aila back to her chamber."

"Of course." Fyfa's mouth twitched as if she was repressing a laugh. "We are done with the tour now."

Not wanting to appear rude, Aila turned to the steward's wife. "Thank ye so much, Fyfa ... I enjoyed that immensely."

The young woman dipped her head. "I shall see ye tomorrow, Aila." She cast another lingering look in Cassian's direction. "Captain."

He nodded, but remained silent, waiting while Fyfa picked up her skirts, turned, and made her way up the steps into the keep.

Once she disappeared inside, Cassian turned to Aila. "Have a care, Aila. We aren't amongst friends here."

The disapproving note in his voice made Aila tense. She'd been happy to see him, but didn't appreciate being treated like an errant bairn. "I'm aware of that," she replied stiffly. "But I wasn't tired, and Fyfa offered to show me the castle."

"Come," he grunted. "Let's get you back to your chamber."

Together, the pair of them made their way inside the keep, past the helmed English soldiers who stood guard at the entrance, and across the hall beyond to the stone stairwell that spiraled up to the floors above.

"Where are ye residing while we're here, Captain?" Aila asked. The silence between them made her uncomfortable, and she missed the easy camaraderie they'd experienced on the journey.

"Just down the hall from you and the others," he replied, his tone gruff.

Aila frowned. His mood seemed dark tonight, and she suspected that her behavior wasn't the reason for it. "Ye seem preoccupied," she ventured. "Is anything amiss?"

He cast her a glance, his gaze shadowed. Side-by-side, they began to climb the stairs. "De Keith has a mouth that could sink ships," he muttered. "During the banquet, he managed to insult Edward."

Aila's mouth thinned. She was torn between admiration that the laird had the courage to do such a bold thing, and concern that he might actually go too far and put them all in danger.

"And Longshanks? Did he bite?"

"Apparently, he's not fond of that name ... so I'd say it softly if I were you."

Aila swallowed a laugh. "Really?"

"Yes, across the border he's fondly known as 'the Hammer of the Scots'."

Aila's step faltered, and she nearly tripped. Cassian caught her by the arm and pulled her up, saving her just in time.

For the barest instant, their bodies collided, and Aila felt the iron strength of his muscular frame against hers. But then he shifted away, and the moment was lost.

"I see the name shocks you too," he observed, his tone wry now.

"How arrogant he must be," Aila breathed, "to call himself that here."

"Oh, he's arrogant," Cassian replied. "And clever too. De Keith needs to watch his step." He paused then before injecting a note of censure into his voice. "As do we all."

They reached a landing and passed by yet another pair of English guards before entering the long hallway leading to the guest chambers. Small, oil-filled cressets lined the grey stone walls, illuminating the hall in a lambent light.

As she walked past Lady Elizabeth's door and then Lady Gavina's, Aila was acutely aware of the tall man who walked at her side.

Reaching her own door, Aila turned to face Cassian.

They were completely alone, for the first time since he'd come to her rescue that day on the stairwell.

Heat rushed through Aila when she tilted her chin to meet his gaze and discovered that he was watching her. The cresset-light played across his tanned skin. It highlighted his high cheekbones and the flecks of gold in his hazel eyes.

The moment drew out, and Aila's chest tightened. The tension was almost unbearable, and so she softly cleared her throat. "Will Edward meet with De Keith again tomorrow?" she asked.

Cassian nodded, his gaze never leaving her face. "They're going hunting in the deer park tomorrow morning ... and will be taking the noon meal together afterward. Lady Elizabeth is keen to broach the subject of her husband's return."

Aila swallowed. "And De Keith?" she asked, lowering her voice to a whisper. "Fyfa says the whole keep is talking about how he's here to bend the knee ... will he actually do it?"

Cassian's features tightened. "He must ... or Edward will become suspicious." He stepped a little closer to her then. "We must *all* be vigilant, Aila. Promise me you'll be more careful in future."

Aila's breathing slowed. He was speaking to her as if he actually cared. The realization thrilled through her veins, causing the heat in her belly to rise up into her ribcage. He was standing so close that if she raised her hand, she wouldn't have to reach far in order to touch him.

As soon as the thought took root in her mind, Aila's pulse fluttered in her throat. And then, without thinking, she lifted her hand and placed it upon his chest. She rested her palm flat upon his leather vest, just below his heart. "I promise," she whispered.

Cassian went still; she actually felt him stop breathing for a moment.

It was bold to touch him like this, but the action had been instinctual. Trying to master the nerves that now writhed in her belly, Aila continued to hold his eye. Spending the evening in Fyfa's company had made her feel braver; the steward's wife was fearless and forthright. She wished she were more like her.

She slid her palm up so that it covered his heart now—and there she felt his strong pulse. It was beating fast.

A thrill went through her at this discovery. She hadn't been wishing in vain after all; he *had* noticed her.

"Aila," he murmured. "Please."

She heard the rough edge to his voice and noted how his gaze shadowed—but didn't heed the warning. She was too caught up in the magic of this moment, in the longing that robbed her of breath.

Aila swayed toward him, going up on tip-toe as she tilted her chin.

Kiss me.

And with a soft sound in the back of his throat, Cassian lowered his head and did just that.

It was the merest brush of their mouths, and yet Aila gasped at the contact. His lips were warm and soft; she couldn't believe that after all these years of wanting, the Captain of the Dunnottar Guard actually looked upon her with desire.

Nervousness assailed her then, for she had no idea how to respond to him. She'd never before been kissed.

However, her gasp seemed to encourage him.

His lips brushed hers again, firmer now, and then Cassian's arms went around her, and he pulled her against him, his mouth claiming hers fully.

Aila couldn't help it—she gasped once more. And when she did, his tongue slid into her mouth.

The sensation was breathtakingly intimate, and excitement pulsed low in Aila's belly, her legs trembling beneath her. His hands slid up her back to her shoulders before they tangled in her hair. Then, cupping the back of her head, he deepened the kiss further.

The intimacy of his tongue exploring her mouth caused an ache to rise in her chest. Shyly, she stroked her tongue against his, responding to him instinctively, even though she hadn't the slightest idea what to do.

Her response may have been untutored, but it appeared to encourage him, for he gave a low groan, his kiss growing urgent and frantic.

Two steps brought the pair of them up against the door to Aila's chamber.

She barely noticed the impact. All she was aware of was the feel of his large, muscular frame pressed up against her smaller, softer body.

He ravaged her mouth with his now, and his hands slid down her back, molding her against him.

Dizziness swept over Aila. The taste of him, his heat, his strength—all overwhelmed her.

It was as if he'd just set her body aflame; she didn't recognize herself or the wild need that clawed its way up from her belly.

And when his hands slid to her bottom, gripping her hard as he pulled her against him, Aila whimpered into his mouth.

Once again, the sounds she made seemed to unleash something within Cassian. One big hand slid down her leg, catching her thigh and hiking it upward. The skirts of her kirtle and lèine slid up, and Aila felt the cool caress of the night air upon her naked skin, but she didn't care.

His wicked mouth pushed all coherent thought from her mind.

Gripping her thigh, Cassian lifted her up and pulled her against his groin. Despite the layers of clothing that separated them, Aila felt him—hard and thick—pressed against her.

Excitement twisted her gut. Aila understood then the smoldering looks that she'd seen Heather and Maximus give each other. She'd had no idea that wanting a man could feel like this; she wasn't herself, but a feverish, aching mess that longed to be possessed. He could take her here, up against the door, and she wouldn't care.

The faint rumble of a man's laughter, coming from within one of the chambers farther down the hall, intruded upon their world.

Cassian stilled, his body going rigid. And then, he tore his mouth from Aila's, lowered her to the floor, and stepped back.

For a few moments, they merely stared at each other. Cassian's chest rose and fell as if he'd been running, and Aila's own breathing came in short, urgent pants.

Her lips parted as she prepared herself to invite him into her chamber. Reaching out, her fingers clasped around the iron handle.

In just a few steps, they would have all the privacy they needed. They could rip away the clothing that separated them, and she could give herself to him entirely.

Her lustiness shocked her, yet she was too far gone to care. She was tired of being timid and prudent. Tonight she wanted to be wild.

But the look upon Cassian's face made the suggestion choke in her throat.

The feral lust had faded, and as she stared up at him, Aila literally saw a shield rise. The need she'd witnessed disappeared, and his handsome features set into a severe expression.

Cassian's hazel eyes veiled, and he took another step back, raking a hand through his short hair. "I'm sorry, Aila," he said roughly. "I don't know what came over me."

"Don't apologize," she gasped out the words, fighting the urge to reach for him. "I wanted it ... I—"

"Goodnight." He turned, cutting her off, and moved away. He was in such haste to leave that he stumbled, yet that didn't stop him.

Aila watched Cassian go, her heart hammering against her ribs. She remained there, frozen to the spot, while he hauled open the door to his chamber and disappeared inside.

XVI

GUIDANCE

CASSIAN LEANED BACK against the closed door and cursed.

Mithras strike his head off, what had possessed him to do that?

Did he have no self-control whatsoever? All it had taken was Aila to place her hand upon his chest, and the iron will he'd prided himself on over the years had literally shattered. If that noise hadn't intruded—that man's laugh—he'd have plowed her, right there in the hallway.

The throb in his groin was almost unbearable. Reaching down, Cassian pressed the knuckle of his thumb hard against it, willing his aching erection to subside. He couldn't believe he'd grabbed her like that and then lifted her up so he could press her against his rod.

His mouth twisted. *The last thing we need around here is another 'hammer'.*

Aila's gasps and moans had turned him into a beast. The soft sweetness of her mouth, the feel of her tongue tangling with his, and the pliant feel of her body against him had turned him witless. He'd been undone.

Groaning another curse, Cassian leaned his head back against the door and tried to calm his ragged breathing.

He wasn't sure what had come over him, yet he didn't like it. Aila De Keith was a virgin, and he'd been on the cusp of ruining her.

This wasn't who he was. He didn't molest women in hallways, especially those who were infatuated with him. The confusion and hurt in Aila's eyes when he'd apologized to her had cut him.

And with a sinking feeling, he realized that, somehow, the woman had gotten under his skin. It wasn't just lust he felt for her, but something stronger—something that disturbed him greatly.

Serves me right, he thought bitterly. When Maximus had confided in him that he was in love with Heather, Cassian had been harsh, derisive. He'd lectured his friend on the folly of falling for a woman when they hadn't yet broken the curse. For all these years after Lilla's death, he'd been so successful at walling off his heart, he hadn't thought himself capable of feeling anything ever again.

But Aila De Keith, with her shy smile and soft gaze, had managed to get past his defenses.

Cassian's jaw clenched. His rod throbbed in time with his heartbeat now. Slowly, he started to unlace his braies. It was no good. He was going to have to relieve himself. And then, afterward, he was going to harden his heart and make sure he and Aila were never alone again.

The Kirk of the Holy Rude was empty when Cassian entered shortly after daybreak. The monks had just filed out after their dawn prayers, and had gone to break their fast. Cassian too had an empty belly, but he had no appetite for bannock, butter, and honey this morning.

Reaching the shrine to Saint John the Baptist, he halted before the bank of candles and withdrew a silver penny from the pouch at his waist. He then slotted it into the iron box before the shrine and lit a candle.

It was his ritual over the years—to light a candle for Lilla whenever he came here.

But he felt like a fraud for doing so this morning. Especially after last night.

Cassian's mouth flattened into a thin line. He was being a fool, feeling guilty when his wife was three centuries dead. Of course, he'd lain with other women over the years. He wasn't made of stone.

But not since Lilla had he responded to one with such passion. He'd lost control. A storm had caught him up, and for a few moments, he'd forgotten who he was and the quest that had driven him for so long.

He'd even forgotten about Lilla.

Watching the candle's tender flame, Cassian sighed.

It had broken him to watch his wife wither and die while he stayed treacherously young. The memory of the agony that had grasped him as he knelt before Lilla's cairn revisited him then.

He'd never weather that pain again. He could not.

Cassian moved to the back of the alcove and pushed aside the slab that hid the passageway beyond. Then he padded inside, lit a torch from the one that burned within, pulled the slab shut, and made his way down to the mithraeum.

The heady scent of incense greeted him, a perfume that always made the years roll back.

As a centurion, he'd worshipped Mithras—the Great Bull-slayer revered by soldiers. After being cursed, he'd thought his faith might fade with the years, especially in a land where no one had ever heard of Mithras.

But in fact, The Bull-slayer had helped keep him strong in the hardest moments and continued to do so now.

Lighting a fresh wand of incense, Cassian knelt before the altar, drew his dirk, and made a shallow cut upon his thumb. He smeared the blood on the stone and bowed his head, letting the smoke waft over him.

"Great God Mithras," he began. "Slayer of the Bull. Lord of the Ages. The wheel turns, and the Broom-star is again in the sky. Draw back the mists and grant three men of the lost legion peace … at last."

It was the same invocation that all three of the centurions used, each time they visited this temple. A plea for Mithras's assistance and guidance.

As he knelt there, Cassian's thoughts turned from Aila to yesterday's discovery.

The Hammer of the Scots.

Never had Cassian visited the mithraeum so hopeful that the curse would be broken. They'd taken a wrong turn in believing that the 'hammer' was Irvine. The truth was both exhilarating and unnerving.

And when the Hammer of the Scots struck Dunnottar, they needed to be ready.

Rising to his feet, Cassian turned to find a hooded figure standing a few yards behind him.

"Good morning, Norris," he greeted the guardian. "I'm relieved to see you up this early."

"Morning, Cassian," the man replied. "I didn't expect to see ye back here so soon."

"Neither did I." Cassian flashed him a tight smile. "Is all well with you?"

"Aye, thanks for asking."

"The English aren't causing you and your family any trouble, I hope?"

Within the recesses of the cowl, Cassian caught the man's answering smile. "Not at present. We're keeping our heads down, like we always do." The man then gestured to the iron box that sat upon the altar, behind the burning incense. "Have ye brought another message for the others? Only Maximus has passed this way recently … there has been no sign of Draco for some while."

"They are both at Dunnottar now, thank you." Cassian stepped toward the guardian, withdrawing a small scroll of parchment from within his leather vest.

"And I do bring another message. I need an urgent favor. Can you take this to Dunnottar ... and deliver it into the hands of Maximus or Draco ... no one else?"

Norris nodded. His features inside the shadowed hood tensed. "Aye, ye want me to leave now?"

"Yes, as soon as you can."

"I will see it done."

"Thank you."

Norris reached out and took the scroll. Then the guardian turned and left the temple without another word.

"That captain of yers is handsome, is he not?"

Aila glanced up from her bannock to see that Fyfa was favoring her with a knowing smile. They sat at the long table in the kitchens, breaking their fast. Fyfa had revealed that ever since Edward's occupation of Stirling, she and her husband were expected to take their meals with the servants.

Indeed, Hume Comyn—a big, muscular man with short dark red hair and a solemn face—was on to his second bowl of porridge at the far end of the table.

Fyfa should have taken her place next to him, but instead, she'd sat next to Aila.

And now Aila knew why.

Her jaw tensed. She wasn't in the mood to discuss Cassian this morning. She was still reeling from the night before, caught between joy and misery. He'd kissed her like she was his world, and then he'd recoiled like she'd just turned into the bean-nighe. She might as well have transformed into the crone who brought an omen of death, for the horror she'd seen in his eyes.

"He's not *my* captain," Aila replied, hoping that the frown accompanying her words would warn Fyfa off. Yet it didn't.

"He's so tall and strong," Fyfa continued, still smiling. "And that accent ... where's he from?"

"Spain."

It was loud in the kitchens, the rumble of voices echoing off the surrounding stone. As such, the other servants were oblivious to the women's conversation. All the same, the subject was making Aila feel nervous.

She was new to this. She didn't understand what she'd done to make him recoil so. He'd acted as if she'd enchanted him, and then he'd come to his senses.

Cassian was a sore subject. She certainly didn't need Fyfa rubbing his attractiveness in her face. She knew just how handsome he was—and now she knew how he tasted too.

"He's got the bonniest eyes I've ever seen," Fyfa continued, seemingly oblivious to Aila's discomfort. "Brown, green, and gold."

Aila tensed. She didn't like the glint in Fyfa's eye. She was a wedded woman, yet that didn't stop her from commenting on Cassian. Aila wondered just how loyal she was to her husband.

Reaching for a pot of heather honey, Aila started to spread it over her wedge of bannock. She wasn't hungry, but she needed something to do.

Feeling Fyfa's gaze upon her, she eventually looked her way. The woman wasn't smiling now; instead, she wore an assessing look, her blue eyes narrowed. "Ye are infatuated with him."

Aila swallowed hard. *Infatuated.* She hated that word. It made her feelings for Cassian sound trivial and childish. "No, I'm not," she snapped. "I'm *in love* with him."

As soon as the words were out, she regretted them. The interest that flared in Fyfa's eyes made her go cold.

Mother Mary, what have I said?

After a moment, Fyfa's expression softened. "Don't look so afraid Aila ... I'm not about to go running through the castle screaming the news." Her tone held a slight note of chagrin, as if Aila's look of panic offended her. "Although I'd like to know what ye intend to do about this?"

Aila put down the spoon she'd been using to spread honey over her bannock. Her stomach now churned. "Last night, after ye left ... he kissed me," she admitted shakily.

A slow smile stretched across Fyfa's face. "And?"

"It was ... passionate ... but then he seemed to regret it. I fear I've chased him off."

Fyfa's smile faded, her expression turning thoughtful. She picked up her cup of warm goat's milk and took a sip. "He's tormented," she said after a pause. "I sensed it the moment he spoke to us."

Aila stiffened. Why hadn't *she* noticed this? It was hardly surprising she hadn't though, given her lack of experience in matters of the heart. Fortunately, Fyfa appeared a worldlier woman. "Tormented?"

"Aye ... but that doesn't mean he doesn't want ye. I wouldn't be surprised if he's had his heart broken in the past and is wary of repeating the mistake. He'll run if ye let him ... but a man like that needs to have his hand forced."

Aila's pulse accelerated—the woman's suggestion both thrilled and terrified her. *But how can I make him to truly want me?*

Sensing her turmoil, Fyfa flashed Aila a wicked smile. "Lucky for ye we met. I can see ye need my help with this ... and fear not, I have a plan."

XVII

A SHOW OF LOYALTY

CASSIAN TOOK A seat upon the dais, his gaze flicking to David De Keith.

A morning out hunting usually put De Keith in a fine mood, but not so today. The laird's face was pinched, his gaze narrowed.

Seated beside him, the English king's expression was also guarded.

Cassian tensed. *He grows suspicious.*

Leaning in, Cassian drew his laird's attention. "De Keith," he said softly, aware that the king was distracted. He was sharing a few words with John Comyn. "Remember what we agreed?" He deliberately spoke in Gaelic, for he didn't want to risk being overheard by the king. However, he still had to keep his voice low—lest Comyn catch his words. 'The Red' kept his counsel close. He'd said very little since their arrival, almost as if he was taking David De Keith's measure.

Like Edward, John Comyn was no fool.

De Keith frowned. "Aye ... and I don't need reminding."

"The king watches you," Cassian warned. "I suggest you stop stalling and bend the knee. Your hesitation is putting all of us at risk."

They were bold words, but Cassian needed to say them. The laird risked putting his wife and sister-by-marriage's lives in danger if he delayed further.

De Keith's mouth pursed. "Stop nagging me, Gaius," he growled. "I'll do it when *I'm* ready." The laird's jaw clenched then, and Cassian once again wondered how the hunt had gone. He hadn't joined them, for Edward, Comyn, and De Keith had ridden out with just a handful of the king's men as escort. Cassian had taken advantage of the time alone to visit Stirling's library.

There was a riddle that had to be solved.

He'd spent a few hours poring over a large volume that chronicled recent political events, but had turned up nothing of value. However, as soon as he was able, Cassian would return to the library and continue his search. Reference to the White Hawk and the Dragon had to be written down somewhere. Perhaps it referred to clan motifs? He needed to do further research.

"Your Highness." A female voice filtered across the table in French. Cassian glanced up from their conversation to see that Lady Elizabeth had now fixed Edward with a steady gaze. "I wish to ask you about my husband, Robert De Keith."

Edward of England smiled coolly back at her. "What do you wish to know, My Lady? I'm afraid I can't reveal his location."

Elizabeth swallowed, her blue eyes shadowing. "Is he well?"

"He is."

"Do you keep him in a dungeon?"

"Yes ... but his cell is a comfortable one. Robert doesn't suffer."

Silence fell then. Cassian was aware that De Keith had gone still. Despite his warning the night before, Lady Elizabeth was still attempting to talk to Edward about her husband. The woman hadn't heeded him at all.

Cassian suspected that David didn't wish to see his brother return to Dunnottar. It would suit him if Robert rotted in an English dungeon for the rest of his life— better yet if Edward decided to hang him, then David's rule at Dunnottar would be assured.

The brothers had never been close, and David had a ruthless streak that Cassian had long been wary of.

We'll never get him to bend the knee at this rate.

"I have a message for my husband," Elizabeth said finally, her voice strained now. "Would you see that he receives it?"

Edward observed her for a long moment before he slowly nodded. He then gestured to the big man standing behind him—a formidable-looking warrior in a glittering hauberk and coif. "Give it to Hugh, and he will personally deliver the letter."

Elizabeth stared back at him. She was usually a woman with healthy coloring, but today her face was pale and strained. Cassian knew the couple were close. She'd worn charcoal and dark-grey kirtles ever since her husband's capture, as if she already mourned Robert.

"When will ye release—?" she asked, her voice barely above a whisper.

"Elizabeth, cease this," De Keith's voice cut through the hush inside the hall. "Don't pester the man."

Lady Elizabeth scowled. Unlike Gavina, she wasn't intimidated by the laird. He wasn't her husband and didn't wield the same authority over her. "It's a fair question, David."

"That it is," Edward drawled. He picked up his goblet and took a sip, his gaze never straying from Elizabeth's pale face. "But one I'm afraid I can't answer." He paused there, deliberately letting his words settle before he continued. The king then glanced over at De Keith. "It all depends on how cooperative your laird is ... I'm still waiting to see a show of loyalty."

"Ye don't want to make Longshanks wait too long," John Comyn's voice rumbled through the solar. "The man's got a mean temper on him."

A few feet away, David De Keith snorted before raising his goblet to his lips and taking a large gulp. "Some of us kneel easier than others, Comyn."

An uncomfortable silence settled in the guests' solar. Cassian drew in a deep breath and bit back the urge to warn the laird to lower his voice.

After the nooning meal, they'd gathered in the large chamber that overlooked the King's Knot and the deer park beyond. Unexpectedly, Comyn had joined them, although he'd taken the precaution of using the servants' stairs up from the kitchen, rather than the main stairwell guarded by English soldiers. It was best that Edward didn't know they were meeting in secret.

Nonetheless, De Keith wasn't being as prudent as the Guardian of Scotland. Standing before the hearth, the laird had virtually shouted his last comment.

"A wise man picks his fights," Comyn spoke up after a pause. "Don't underestimate Edward of England."

"I'm not ... but I'd rather not drop to my knees before him and beg to suck his rod."

Across the chamber, Lady Gavina paled at her husband's crudity, while a few feet away, Elizabeth drew in a shocked gasp.

"David ... please," Lady Gavina murmured, "there's no need for that."

De Keith swiveled, spearing his wife with a withering glance. Gavina sat near the window, a spindle in one hand and a basket of bright red wool upon her lap.

"Mind yer manners, De Keith," Comyn growled, his bearded face creasing into a scowl. "There are ladies present."

The laird sneered, before he lifted his goblet once more, draining it.

"We have to think of Robert," Lady Elizabeth said, her tone wintry. "If we cooperate, Edward might release him."

"I'm far more concerned with finding out what Longshanks is planning," De Keith shot back. "And then getting safely back to Dunnottar."

Elizabeth gasped. "But Robert's *yer* brother!"

The laird ignored his sister-by-marriage and crossed to the side-board. He went to pour himself a cup of wine. "This jug's empty," he snapped, turning to his wife. "Where's that maid of yers?"

"She'll be next door, folding and pressing our washing," Gavina replied stiffly.

"Well, get her in here!"

His wife cleared her throat. "Aila," she called.

A long moment passed, and then the door to the next room opened and a comely brown-haired lass entered.

Despite his previous determination to wall himself off to Aila De Keith, Cassian went still at the sight of her.

As always, she wore her long walnut-colored hair unbound, although today she'd pulled the front of it back so that it didn't annoy her while she worked. Her cheeks bore a becoming blush, and her moss-green kirtle clung to her supple curves.

Before he could stop himself, Cassian's gaze roamed over her, remembering just how soft and warm her body had been pressed up against his. Her hair had smelled of lavender. And when his attention rested on her full mouth, his groin tightened at the memory of how she'd tasted: sweet, fresh, and all woman.

Hades, I have to stop this.

Cassian tore his attention from the lovely maid, his pulse racing now.

Did he have no self-control at all? Hadn't he vowed the night before that he would distance himself from Aila from now on? And yet all it had taken was for her to step into the room and his resolve splintered.

He didn't understand. For long years, he'd found it easy to keep himself walled off from women. None of the lovers he'd taken since Lilla had come close to capturing his heart; he'd made sure of that.

Aila was shy, unsure of herself, and achingly young compared to his old, weathered soul, and yet when he'd kissed her, he hadn't been the one in control.

"Fill this jug with wine," De Keith ordered, shattering Cassian's reverie. He picked up the offending item and shoved it at her.

"Aye, De Keith," she murmured. Her gaze shifted around the solar, taking in the tense faces. She would realize that she'd just walked into a heated discussion. She looked at Cassian last, and treacherously, his gaze sought hers.

And for an instant, they merely stared at each other.

Cassian's breathing quickened. This wasn't what he wanted. Why couldn't he stop from gawking at her?

And then Aila dipped her chin, severing the connection. A moment later, she left the solar, clutching the jug to her side.

Cassian watched her leave, and when he turned his attention back to his companions, he saw that Lady Gavina was observing him, her gaze curious.

Swallowing hard, Cassian frowned. Had he been that obvious?

"If ye are keen to learn of Edward's plans ... I can be of some assistance." John Comyn spoke up once more. He lounged in a high-backed chair by the hearth. However, the man's gaze was cool when it rested upon De Keith. "There are benefits to *kneeling* to the English king."

Cassian pressed his lips together, fighting the urge to smile. He liked Comyn; the man wasn't easy to offend, and he was also sharp.

His lack of wine momentarily forgotten, De Keith turned to him. "What have ye learned?"

Comyn raised a ruddy eyebrow. "A few nights ago, I shared a few horns of mead with the king ... and discovered some things." The big man paused here, aware that all gazes in the chamber were now riveted upon him. He smiled, enjoying the moment. "The first is that we should be wary of his son ... Edward, the newly appointed Prince of Wales."

De Keith frowned. "Go on."

"Prince Edward commands part of Longshanks' army," Comyn continued. "He has a force of around three hundred soldiers, and has taken control of the Solway coast. The prince is green and under his father's control ... but Longshanks boasted to me of his military prowess. He shares his father's ambition to rule Scotland."

De Keith's frown deepened into a scowl. "One Edward of England is bad enough," he muttered. "We don't need to deal with another." He paused then, his features tightening. "And what else?"

Comyn's mouth quirked. "This may be of real interest to ye ... Longshanks believes the time isn't right for a campaign into the Highlands. He'll not strike north for a year or two yet."

Cassian tensed. Comyn was surely mistaken. If the 'Hammer' that the riddle spoke of was Edward—and he felt certain it was—an attack had to come soon. Or else it would be too late for this coming of the Broom-star. *This news makes little sense.*

Oblivious to his captain's turmoil, David De Keith's face visibly relaxed at Comyn's revelation. "He fears the northern clan-chiefs?"

Comyn snorted. "Longshanks fears few men, De Keith." His gaze glinted then. "However, this brings me to the last thing I discovered while Edward and I were drinking together. There are two Scots who concern him ... William Wallace ... and Robert Bruce. He currently has spies out searching for Wallace."

"I hear he's in France," Lady Elizabeth replied. The cool calm of her voice impressed Cassian, as did the fact she'd spoken up before De Keith dropped them all in it. Cassian didn't dare glance the laird's way, in case Comyn was watching their reactions to his news.

"Aye ... that's what most folk say," Comyn replied. "But there are rumors he's returned. Longshanks is certain he was spotted in Inverness." The baron paused there, his mouth pursing. "He hates Wallace ... swears he won't rest till the man is swinging from a gibbet."

"And Robert Bruce?" De Keith asked, deftly turning Comyn away from the subject of the freedom fighter.

'The Red' flashed him a humorless smile. "Like me, Bruce has been appointed 'Guardian of the Realm' ... yet many believe he has much greater ambitions." The baron paused there, his gaze narrowing. "Longshanks went on crusade with Robert's father. The two of them are firm friends, but Edward doesn't trust his son ... he believes Robert Bruce wants the Scottish throne for himself."

XVIII

THIS IS FOLLY

"I'M NOT SURE this is wise."

Fyfa Comyn favored Aila with a sly smile in response. "Love isn't wise, Aila. But if ye wish to win this man, ye will have to be brave." The steward's wife then dipped her finger into a vial of rose perfume and began dabbing it on the sensitive spots just below Aila's ears. She then applied some at the hollow of her throat and upon the underside of her wrists. "Men love a woman's perfume," she assured her. "This will drive him wild."

Aila looked down at the thin shift she was wearing. "I think I'll keep this on under my robe," she said softly. "I can't go before him naked."

Fyfa gave a frustrated snort. "Bravery ... it's the only way ye will prevail." She stood back then, her gaze meeting Aila's. "Remember, fortune favors the bold. That's my clan motto. Before I wed a Comyn, I was a MacKinnon."

Aila's heart started to race at these words. "Aye, but have ye ever done something like this?"

Fyfa smiled. "How do ye think I won my husband?"

Aila's gaze widened. "Ye went to his chamber wearing nothing but a robe?"

Fyfa nodded. "We'd been dancing around each other for a while, but I knew that if I didn't take the initiative, Hume might never make his move. Some men need a little ... encouragement."

"And was he pleased that ye came to him?" Aila licked her suddenly dry lips. When Fyfa had initially suggested they work on a plan to win Cassian, she'd been pleased. But now, as they stood alone in Aila's tiny bed-chamber, while the moon rose in the sky and the rest of the keep slumbered, she suddenly wished she hadn't taken the woman up on her offer.

He'll think me too forward.

And yet she hadn't missed the look on Cassian's face earlier that day. The hunger she witnessed in his eyes when she walked into the solar had made her step falter. She'd seen his struggle.

Maybe Fyfa was right. It was up to her to bridge the gulf between them.

Fyfa favored Aila with another knowing smile. "Now, remember what I said earlier." The steward's wife packed away the perfume into the basket she'd brought with her. She'd oiled and brushed out Aila's hair till it fell in glistening waves over her shoulders, and all the while had given her instructions on how to approach Captain Gaius. "Keep yer voice low and soft ... and maintain eye-contact. If he looks hesitant, move in close and touch him. Don't let him send ye away."

A chill feathered down Aila's spine at these words. What if he did?

She couldn't stand the humiliation; she'd never be able to look at him again.

"I'm not sure I'm brave enough for this," she admitted shakily, watching as Fyfa made for the door.

Turning, the steward's wife flashed her a warm smile. "Aye, ye are ... ye just mustn't listen to the voice in yer head that keeps ye from reaching for yer desires. Ye look beautiful, Aila. And remember what I said ... fortune favors the bold."

And with that, Fyfa exited the chamber.

Alone, Aila smoothed her sweaty palms upon the shift. It was made of thin linen and reached mid-thigh.

There was no way she was taking it off, no matter what Fyfa said. She wasn't that bold. Reaching for her robe, Aila wrapped herself in its soft folds. Her legs were shaking now, and she felt a little sick.

Perching on the edge of her narrow bed, she gathered her courage.

It had been a strange day. She'd interrupted that tense discussion in the solar after the nooning meal, and when she returned with wine for the laird, De Keith had scowled at her so darkly that she nearly wilted under the force of his glare. He'd then snarled at her for being so slow.

However, she hadn't really cared, for just being in Cassian's presence had made her pulse race, her blood heat. Dressed in a mail shirt and leather leggings, he'd been dangerously handsome. His gaze had tracked her across the room.

Aila smoothed out the folds of her robe. *He wants me*, she reminded herself. *I have to keep telling myself of that.*

She did, but that didn't mean Aila didn't tremble with nerves when she finally padded out of her chamber.

She left her move as late as she dared.

Occasionally, Lady Gavina needed her assistance after bedtime, but tonight, her mistress was silent. She had no excuse to tarry, no reason not to go to Cassian, and yet she delayed.

Letting herself out into the hallway, she started to sweat. The air was cool, the glow from the cressets staining the stone walls. As she'd expected, there wasn't anyone about—although she knew that English guards would be posted on the landing beyond, surveying everyone who came up and down the stairwell.

Barefoot, Aila moved down the hallway toward Cassian's door.

Dizziness swept over her. She was really starting to struggle with this.

Grow a spine, she chastised herself as she stopped before the door. *What would Heather do in a situation like this?* The thought made her rally; her elder sister had always seemed fearless. In fact, she'd admitted to Aila that after their arrival in Dunnottar, she'd eventually sought Maximus out—a meeting that had resulted in a steamy encounter in one of the guard rooms.

And now Heather was happily wed to Maximus. Maybe if she hadn't been courageous that day, things might not have ended so happily?

Coward. What are ye waiting for? Indeed, she'd been standing in front of the door for a minute or so now.

This wasn't going to get things done.

Dragging in a deep breath, Aila raised her hand and gently knocked upon the door.

And then she waited.

At first nothing happened.

Moments passed, stretching out. Aila's already racing heart started to thud painfully against her ribs.

Had he even heard her? She hadn't knocked that loudly, for fear of waking up the others who lay slumbering in the nearby chambers.

I should return to my own bed. She took a step back, feeling sick. *This is folly.*

And then the door opened.

Cassian stood there, dressed only in a pair of braies.

For a few instants, the pair of them merely stared at each other, and then Cassian's gaze narrowed. "Is something wrong, Aila?" he murmured. His short hair was mussed with sleep, and the burnished light of the cressets played across the muscular lines of his bare torso. Aila's gaze settled upon the strange mark he bore upon the right side of his chest: an eagle with its wings spread.

Her mouth went dry at the sight of him, her heart now pounding wildly.

"No," she whispered. "Can I come in? I wish to speak to ye."

Cassian's gaze slid over her, taking in the robe she wore and her bare feet. "You want to enter my bed-chamber?"

Aila nodded.

His throat bobbed. "This isn't a good idea. Please go back to bed."

Aila's chest constricted. She'd feared this might happen, even though Fyfa had assured her that a little reticence on his part was to be expected.

"I can't," she whispered, cursing the way her voice now wobbled. "I must speak to ye first."

He stared at her, his hazel eyes hooding in a way that made her lower belly catch alight. "You do realize what you're doing?"

Aila nodded once more, not trusting herself to speak. She did realize—although it was taking every last bit of courage to continue.

Fortune may have favored the bold, but she felt about as brave as a mouse.

Another long pause drew out, and then Cassian stepped back, opening the door so that she could enter.

Remembering to keep breathing, Aila walked into his bed-chamber.

The room was similar in size to her own, with a small hearth burning in one corner that illuminated a simply furnished space and a narrow bed against one wall. But unlike her chamber, this one had a tiny shuttered window.

The door shut behind Aila with a soft thud.

And then she found herself alone with Cassian in his chamber.

Turning to him, she wished her belly wasn't churning so violently. She clearly didn't have the nerve for this; the fear of rejection was overwhelming.

"What is it you want?" he asked. There was a hardness to his tone that cowed her. However, it contradicted the heat in his stare and the sharp rise and fall of his chest. She wondered why he seemed to blow so hot and cold with her. Surely, if he wanted her like she did him, he didn't need to fight it?

"I'm not a bairn, Cassian," she replied softly. "Ye don't need to treat me like one. If I come to ye, I do so willingly."

His expression shadowed. "Are you a virgin, Aila?"

His question made her draw in a sharp breath. It was an intimate thing to ask, and yet considering that she'd invited herself into his chamber, it was a fair one.

"Aye," she murmured, shrugging off her thick woolen robe, letting it pool to the floor. Despite that she wore the thin shift underneath, she felt exposed. Yet she kept her shoulders back and continued to hold his eye. She couldn't let him see just how nervous she was. "But I wish to give my maidenhead to ye."

His features grew taut, even as his gaze raked over her. Glancing down, she saw that her nipples were hard and clearly visible through the gauzy material of her shift. She hadn't had the nerve to come before him naked, but she may as well have been.

"Why?" he grated out the word. "Don't ye wish to wait for a husband?"

Aila's gaze snapped back up, and she raised her chin as she met his eye once more. "I want ye ... I've wanted ye for a long time ... and I believe ye feel the same way."

"You want me to *bed* you ... nothing more?" His tone turned incredulous.

Aila's heart shrank at the question. No, she wanted everything. She wanted Cassian Gaius body and soul, but she couldn't bring herself to admit it.

Fyfa had counseled her to remain emotionally reserved, no matter how physically heated their encounter became. "A man should feel he's the one to make the next move," she'd advised with a cheeky smile. "Give him the illusion of control, even if ye are the one in charge."

The urge to laugh rose up within Aila. Her nerves were getting the better of her. She wasn't in charge of this situation in the slightest.

However, reminding herself of Fyfa's advice, Aila let the moment draw out, and when she finally answered him, her voice was low but firm. "Aye."

XIX

WANT

CASSIAN STARED BACK at Aila, noting the tension upon her face, the gleam in her smoke-grey eyes.

She was lying. Aila's infatuation was clear. She wasn't going to admit it to him, but she believed herself in love.

He should send her away. He certainly shouldn't have let her into his bed-chamber.

But now she stood before him clad only in a flimsy shift that showed every curve, her full lips parted with want. The scent of rose enveloped him, blending with the sweet smell of her clean skin.

His groin started to ache, and hunger tightened his chest, making it hard to breathe.

He needed to rip open the door and order her out, and yet he didn't move.

As if sensing his indecision, Aila stepped close to him. And like she had the evening before, she raised her hand to his chest, splaying it over his heart.

But this time no clothing separated them, and the feel of her palm against his skin seared him like a brand.

Cassian sucked in a shocked breath.

It still surprised him that so shy a lass could arouse such a response in him. Aila was painfully inexperienced.

Yet there was a sensuality to her that triggered a primal response within him. It made Cassian lower his shields. It made him cast aside everything he'd worked hard to keep at arm's length for so long.

Aila made him want.

She'd be able to feel his thundering heart under her palm. She'd bewitched him. He literally couldn't move, couldn't speak.

With her other hand, she gently traced the lines of his chest, her fingertips sliding across the Eagle mark above his right nipple.

Her touch left a trail of fire in its wake.

He had to send her away.

"I'm yers, Cassian," she whispered. Only the faint tremor in her voice gave her nervousness away. But the lack of polish to her seduction, her vulnerability, made aching need spiral up inside him.

He groaned a curse and placed his hands over hers, and then, with the blood roaring in his ears, he bent his head and kissed her.

She tasted incredible.

A heartbeat later, he let go of her hands and pulled Aila hard against him, his hands cupping her face as his mouth ravaged hers. She kissed him back with equal ferocity. The night prior, there had been a slight reserve in her; he'd sensed that she'd never been kissed before.

But now she was ready for him. Her tongue danced with his, exploring, caressing, tasting—and when she gently bit his lower lip and dug her fingernails into his upper arms, the last of Cassian's own resolve snapped.

He reached down and ripped the shift off her. The sound of rending fabric filled the bed-chamber, but neither of them noticed or cared.

Now Cassian had moved, he couldn't stop touching her.

Hades burn him to cinders, she smelt good. The scent of rose wreathed around them, and the taste of her skin, as his mouth trailed down her neck, turned his hunger into a rampaging beast.

Picking Aila up, he carried her over to the narrow bed and lay her down upon it.

Seeing her laid out there—her pale, shapely limbs glowing in the firelight; her pert breasts straining toward him, their hard, pink nipples begging to be sucked—Cassian caught his breath.

Aila stared up at him, her full lips swollen from his wild kisses, her walnut hair spread out in waves across the pillow.

He had to have this woman.

Cassian unlaced his braies and then pushed them down over his hips, letting them fall to the floor.

He watched her gaze widen, fastening upon his erection. Glancing down, Cassian saw that his rod was swollen and hard. Such a sight would frighten many virgins, but Aila stared at it as if she'd never seen anything so wondrous.

The hunger on her face made lust barrel into him. The wanting was so fierce now that he felt maddened by it.

Cassian went to her, crawling over Aila and kissing her once more. The kiss was wet and desperate now—their tongues, lips, and teeth clashing as hunger took them both. And all the while, his hands were everywhere. He ached to touch this woman.

Ripping his mouth from hers, he then cupped her breasts in his hands and pushed them up to greet him, before he greedily suckled her nipples. Her sighs and groans filled the chamber. She writhed under him. Cassian sucked harder still, and then gently nipped a nipple with his teeth.

Aila gave a soft cry, her fingernails raking down his back as she bucked her hips against him. She may have been a maid, but her body knew what it wanted.

Cassian parted her legs and stroked the wetness between them. She was soaking, her thighs slick with need for him. The musky scent of her arousal made his stomach muscles tighten, his rod quivering and throbbing now.

But he would make himself wait a little longer.

Spreading her thighs wider still, he lowered his head between them, his lips trailing along the softness of her inner thigh.

Aila gasped, her body going rigid against the bed.
He was touching her *there*.
She threw her head back, her eyes fluttering shut as she gave herself up to sensation. She wasn't a complete innocent. She'd heard about the things that men and women did together, although when Fyfa had tried to mention this act earlier in the evening, Aila's cheeks had burned like two hot coals.
They weren't any longer.
His lips and tongue were relentless, and before she knew it, Aila was arching up against him, her soft pleas filling the chamber. And then when her thighs started to tremble uncontrollably, she bit down on her lip.
The urge to scream her pleasure clawed its way up within her. Yet even lost in this storm of passion, she knew that to do so was unwise.

Rising up between Aila's thighs, Cassian gazed down at her.
She lay there panting, her body trembling in the aftermath of the peak he'd just brought her to.
An ache rose in his chest, warring with the throb in his groin. He had to be inside her.
Now.
Cassian moved across Aila, his mouth capturing hers once more in a hungry kiss, and then he slowly eased himself into her.
Despite her readiness for him, she was tight, and so he gradually worked his way in, halting when he met resistance.
Breaking off the kiss, he stared down into her wide grey eyes. They were glazed with desire, yet they would soon be clouded with pain. "This will hurt," he warned her softly, "but not for long."
She nodded, and the look of trust upon her face caused his chest to constrict.

He thrust into her then, and her gasp filled the room, her body going rigid under his. Murmuring soothing words, he trailed kisses up over her jaw before covering her soft mouth with his once more. And when she sighed against his lips, he knew the pain had passed.

Cassian moved gently inside Aila at first, letting her adjust to the size and feel of him. Her warmth, wetness, and tightness made it difficult to restrain himself. Sweat beaded upon his skin with the effort he was making to go slowly. But as Aila began to moan and writhe against him, her hips angling toward him with each thrust, his self-control started to slip.

The urge to let go, to seek oblivion in this woman overwhelmed him.

The weight of the years had become such a burden, as had his long quest to break the curse. But right now, none of that mattered. All he wanted was to lose himself inside Aila.

With a strangled groan, he let himself go, plunging into her now, gripping her hips as he drove deeper.

And Aila rose to meet him. Her legs wrapped around his hips, and she pulled him hard against her with each wild thrust.

Cassian was lost. The last of his restraint splintered, and he took her in a frenzy, as if his very life depended on it.

And when he shattered, the world went dark for an instant.

David De Keith slapped the young woman across her bare backside. "Go on, Jean ... ye had best get back to yer own bed now."

With a groan, the fire-haired lass rolled naked off the bed and reached for the lèine he'd stripped off her earlier. The faint glow of the hearth on the other side of the chamber gilded the neat, lush lines of her body, and David drank her in.

The only good thing about Elizabeth insisting on accompanying them on this trip was that she'd brought her comely maid with her.

David had managed to entice Jean into his bed around two months earlier, and many lusty nights had followed. Usually, after the first few encounters, David tired of plowing the same woman—but not Jean.

Such a lovely field to plow.

Padding to the door, she cast a sultry look over her shoulder.

De Keith's rod hardened in response, and the urge to order her back to bed rose within him. However, the night had stretched out and dawn wasn't far off now. She needed to return to her room before Elizabeth called for her.

Lying back upon the bed, amongst the rumpled sheets that smelled of their coupling, David listened to the door thud shut behind Jean, leaving him alone inside his bed-chamber.

And as soon as she departed, his thoughts shifted from his lover, to what she'd just revealed.

There's a secret exit here.

It seemed that Gavina's maid had been exploring Stirling Castle, and had learned of a hidden door in the Nether Bailey—one that Edward apparently didn't know about. Excited about her find, the maid had shared the news with Jean earlier in the day.

Staring up at the rafters, David contemplated his situation—and as he did so, his pulse quickened.

This news gave him an idea.

XX

SECRETS

AILA ROSE FROM the bed and padded barefoot across to the shuttered window. Opening it just a crack, she saw that outdoors the eastern sky was starting to lighten.

She needed to get back to her room.

Turning, Aila's gaze settled upon the man still asleep upon the bed.

Cassian lay on his back, one arm covering his face. His chest gently rose and fell; he was in a deep sleep, and she didn't want to disturb him.

Even so, Aila lingered there a moment, her gaze devouring the sculpted splendor of his naked body.

Last night was better than any of her fevered fantasies.

She'd had no idea that coupling could be like that— even though Heather had hinted a few times that with the right man the experience could be unforgettable. At the time, she'd thought her sister was showing off, that her passion for Maximus had turned her a bit goose-witted.

But now she realized what Heather had meant.

Cassian had consumed her.

After the first time he took her, they'd lain together gasping. But she'd barely recovered when he rolled her over, pulled her up onto all fours, and took her again. The new position had been as exciting as the first one, and he'd ridden her just as hard.

Aila's legs still felt weak, and the sting between her thighs reminded her they'd coupled a number of times throughout the night. The last time, she'd sat astride him.

Aila's breathing caught at the memory of how powerful she'd felt, riding him, his fingers digging into the soft flesh of her hips as he urged her on.

Bending down, Aila retrieved her woolen robe and wrapped it around her. She also picked up her torn shift; she'd have to see if she could sew it back together. Her fingers tightened around the soft material, as she remembered how he'd ripped it off her and the savage lust in his eyes when he'd picked her up and carried her over to the bed.

Her knees wobbled. She wanted to relive it all again.

But instead, instinct drove her toward the door. Lady Gavina was an early riser and would call for her shortly.

Casting one last, longing look at Cassian, Aila fought the urge to move over to the bed and kiss him. However, he was sleeping so deeply, it would be a shame to wake him.

Letting herself out of Cassian's bed-chamber, Aila gently pulled the door shut behind her. She was about to veer right and head back to her own chamber, when she realized someone else had just stepped through another doorway farther to her right.

Jean stood there, clad only in a sheer, ankle-length lèine, her red hair tumbling messily around her shoulders.

Aila's breathing caught when she realized the maid was standing before the laird's door.

She's De Keith's lover.

The laugh that had interrupted Aila and Cassian's kiss the other evening. It had been David De Keith.

Aila stared at Jean, watching as the lass's face paled and understanding dawned in her eyes.

She knew where Aila had spent the night too.

The moment drew out, both women frozen like deer in a hunter's sight. In other circumstances, Aila might have found such a tableau ridiculous. But not this morning.

She couldn't believe that Jean was so foolish as to be led into the laird's bed, or that she'd been so careless herself, not to check the hallway was empty before stepping out into it.

Jean's throat bobbed, even as her mouth thinned. Aila recognized the expression as a warning. The two maids shared each other's secret now. If Aila didn't want everyone to know about her and Cassian, she wouldn't say a word about what she'd just seen.

Cassian stirred and stretched, wakefulness stealing upon him slowly.

Well-being filtered over him. His body felt free of tension, his muscles loose and relaxed. The aftermath of the night's passion still ebbed over him like gently lapping waves.

Cassian's eyes flickered open.

Aila.

He was alone on the bed. His lover had gone.

His brief sense of peace—a sensation that had eluded him for so long he'd forgotten what it actually felt like—dissipated, and Cassian sat up.

The fire in the hearth had gone out, although it wasn't cold in the chamber. Nonetheless, his skin prickled as the memory of everything he'd done the night before crashed into him.

Muttering a curse, Cassian ran a hand over his face.

What's wrong with you, man? Did he have no self-control at all?

No, when it came to Aila De Keith, he did not. He'd sneered at Maximus's inability to stay away from Heather, and yet he wasn't any better. Aila only had to fix him with that limpid look, and his resolve not to touch her melted.

And now you've gone and bedded her. He'd stolen her maidenhead, something she should have reserved for her future husband.

But at least he hadn't planted his seed in her belly.

Swearing once more, Cassian rose to his feet and crossed to a small table where a jug of water and a wash bowl sat. Splashing himself with cold water, he tried to shove the images of last night to the back of his mind.

Aila was fire.

Had it been like that with Lilla?

With a jolt, he realized that, all these years later, he couldn't actually remember. His memories of his beloved wife were of other things: the way she laughed when he teased her, how she sang to him in the evenings, and her habit of warming her freezing hands and feet on him in the winter.

He knew he'd loved bedding Lilla—but these days he couldn't remember the details.

This morning, all he could think about was Aila.

She'd been a virgin, and yet as soon as the pain of that moment had passed, she'd met him with a hunger equal to his own.

Cassian's jaw clenched. He'd let depravity get the best of him last night, for he'd taken her again and again— each time more wildly than the last. And each sigh she'd given, each low moan, had fueled a madness that had possessed him body and soul.

He'd rutted her like a randy old goat, driven by a hunger he didn't even understand.

Had she left without waking him out of mortification? It wouldn't have surprised him.

Cassian dried himself off with a scratchy length of cloth before hauling on his clothing. His mood was now dark, his brow furrowed.

Denial wasn't good for a man.

Over the years, both Maximus and Draco had warned him that he couldn't go on clinging to his wife's shade. It wasn't as if he hadn't lain with women over the years, but he kept the act brief and emotionally distanced. He'd avoided intimate relationships.

"Lilla wouldn't want you to live like this," Maximus had said once, many years earlier when they'd run into each other in Perth. "You aren't a cold bastard like me ... find yerself another woman to spend some years with."

Cassian had snarled back that Maximus wouldn't know what Lilla had wanted, and that if he didn't want a busted nose, he'd shut his mouth. With a rueful grin and shake of his head, Maximus had done as bid.

But he'd been right. Cassian had missed the connection he'd shared with Lilla. He'd been holding back for too long—and it had turned him into a lust-filled beast.

Aila hadn't complained, yet she'd done a foolish thing appearing at his door like that, ready to seduce him without a thought about what it might cost her.

He'd need to make things clear next time he got a private moment with her. Aila had given him everything last night. She hadn't wept or told him she loved him, but he'd seen her feelings writ clear upon her sweet face and in her soulful grey eyes.

But Cassian couldn't return her feelings, and the sooner she understood that, the better.

Pulling on his boots, Cassian tore down his cloak from a hook on the wall and strode out of his bed-chamber.

He had to talk to her, but if he waited till later, the resolve might leave him.

I have to do it now.

It was later than he'd realized—Cassian had slept in well past dawn. He found Lady Gavina and Lady Elizabeth breaking their fast together in the guests' solar, but there was no sign of Aila.

"She's downstairs in the kitchen, Captain," Lady Gavina told him, a groove appearing between her eyebrows when he enquired as to Aila's whereabouts.

Thanking the lady with a brusque nod, Cassian moved to retreat from the solar. However, Lady Gavina spoke up, preventing him.

"What do ye want with her?"

"The steward's wife is looking for her," he replied, tensing. The curiosity in the woman's eyes made him uncomfortable. "It seems they've struck up a friendship."

Hastily quitting the chamber before Gavina could question his feeble excuse, Cassian made his way downstairs.

The kitchens were hot and smoky, the air heavy with the scent of freshly baked bannock.

Cassian usually looked forward to breaking his fast in the morning, and when he'd awoken earlier, his belly had grumbled.

But this had to be done now.

He found Aila seated at the far end of a long table, chatting to that sly-eyed woman she'd befriended since her arrival here—the steward's wife.

Both women glanced up as he approached. Fyfa favored him with a slow, flirtatious smile, while Aila's cheeks blushed prettily. He should've known that woman, Fyfa, was involved somehow.

Misgiving rose up within Cassian then. Coming down here wasn't clever. If he'd thought his plan over, he'd have waited till Aila made her way back upstairs. It wasn't wise to draw attention to both of them like this. Nonetheless, it was too late to turn back now.

"Captain," Aila greeted him, lowering the wedge of bannock she was eating. "What are—"

"Can I speak to you a moment, Aila?" he cut in.

Her gaze widened. "Now?"

"Yes ... if you don't mind?"

Not taking her attention from him, Aila rose to her feet. She ignored the grin the steward's wife shot her and edged out from behind the table.

XXI

LAST NIGHT WAS MADNESS

HE'S COME LOOKING for me.

Aila followed Cassian up the stairs. Her heart raced. The bannock she'd just eaten churned in her belly as excitement caught her up in its thrall.

Cassian had just walked into the kitchen and asked to speak to her alone—in front of everyone.

Jean was there too, seated farther down the table. She'd have seen him. Maybe they wouldn't need to keep things secret for much longer after all.

The only thing that concerned Aila about his abrupt appearance was the sternness upon his face.

However, she wasn't surprised either; he was hardly going to seek her out with a love-struck expression, was he?

Halfway up the stairwell, Cassian turned and drew her into a shadowed alcove. This was a storage area. Bulky cloth sacks surrounded them, and Aila inhaled the musty scent of oats and barley.

They were alone here. Did he intend to sweep her up in a passionate embrace, to kiss her senseless as he'd done the night before?

Aila waited, breathless, yet Cassian did neither of those things.

Instead, he stood there, his hazel eyes narrowing as they fixed upon her. It was dimly lit in the alcove, with just a faint glow from the cressets on the stairwell. However, there was enough light for her to see that he was in a very different mood to last night.

"Cassian?" She reached for him, but he moved back, out of reach. Aila lowered her hand, a chill washing over her. "What is it?" she whispered. "Has something happened?"

He shook his head. "Last night was a mistake," he said. His voice was so different, so hard and cold. Where was the lover who'd held her in his arms and whispered endearments in her ear while she trembled and gasped?

Aila stared at him, momentarily lost for words. His declaration was a slap across the face.

When she didn't respond, Cassian continued. "I can't give you what you seek, Aila. I can't love you ... or wed you."

An ache twisted deep in her chest. "But we lay together," she whispered. "I thought—"

"It's not possible," he cut her off, his tone sharpening. "I did warn you."

"But why?" She hated the sound of her voice, the pleading note to it, yet she couldn't help but ask the question. She had to know.

His shadowed gaze guttered. "My reasons don't matter. I'm sorry, Aila. I shouldn't have bedded you. I shouldn't have taken your maidenhead."

Her eyes stung as tears threatened. Her throat was suddenly so tight that it was difficult to speak, and yet she forced herself. "I gave it to ye willingly, Cassian. And I'd do it again, a hundred times over."

He shook his head, his jaw clenching. "I've taken something you should have kept for a husband," he rasped. "But since I cannot father children, you will be spared an unwanted bairn at least."

Aila flinched at his bluntness. She hated the cold way he was addressing her. This wasn't Captain Gaius—the honorable warrior who'd spoken to her so gently, who loved her last night like she was the only woman alive.

What reason could he possibly have for treating her so callously?

"I d—don't understand," she stammered. "This doesn't make any sense. Last night ye—"

"Last night was madness." Once again, he wouldn't let her finish her sentence, and somewhere deep inside her, deeper than the shock and hurt, the heat of anger kindled.

"No, it wasn't," she shot back, her fists curling at her sides. That was better—rage felt stronger than tears. He'd stood there, as cold as a carven marble effigy, and ruthlessly ripped her heart to pieces—but she wouldn't let him get away with it. "Ye are lying. I know ye care ... I saw it."

Cassian shook his head. "You're comely and sweet, Aila De Keith ... few men could resist you. We had an enjoyable night together, but it ends here between us. You aren't to visit me again. If you do, I shall turn you away ... and I'd like to spare both of us such a scene."

Comely and sweet?

Aila's churning belly clenched. She stared at him, fury rendering her immobile. She was so angry that it literally stripped her of the ability to speak. She didn't have her mother or Heather's quick, fiery temper. Instead, she was more like her father. Her anger was difficult to rouse, but when it did stir, it was a dark beast ripping at her insides, snarling to get free.

Aila's fisted hands clenched. If there had been a suitable object within arm's reach, she'd have grabbed it and hurled it at his face.

How dare he tell me last night meant nothing?

"Liar," she finally gasped. But he merely stood there, his gaze upon her, his face stony. She was looking up into the face of a stranger.

"No," he murmured. "I was *lying* before ... this is the real me."

Aila fled then. She had to, before she flung herself at him and raked her nails down his face.

~ 165 ~

To think she'd believed him a kind and decent man. To think she'd imagined he *cared* for her.

She'd been living a fantasy—one he'd just rudely woken her from.

She flew up the stairs, away from the kitchens, and sprinted across the wide entrance hall, nearly colliding with a group of English guards who were exiting the keep.

One of them laughed and made a grab for her, calling out something in French.

Aila ducked, avoiding being caught, before she snarled an insult in Gaelic and lunged for the stairs.

Male laughter followed her, although the guards didn't.

Aila took the steps two at a time, her pulse vibrating in her chest. Reaching the landing to the guest apartments, she sprinted past the bemused guards standing watch there and fled along the hallway.

Inside her tiny chamber, she flung herself face down upon the bed and let the full weight of her humiliation and grief hit her. Raw sobs ripped at her chest, tearing at her throat.

The agony of it made her want to die.

Cassian lingered in the alcove after Aila fled.

He let her go, listening as her hurried footsteps disappeared above, before he emerged. He didn't go down to the kitchen to get himself some bannock, and he didn't go up to the solar where De Keith would be breaking his own fast this morning. The laird was expecting him, for they were supposed to go over the plans for the day.

Instead, Cassian went outdoors. He needed to walk, to be alone for a while.

He left the keep and strode across the inner-bailey to the walled garden beyond. Despite the warm breeze that stirred Cassian's hair, ominous-looking clouds hung overhead. Bad weather was likely on its way.

Cassian walked into the garden, his feet crunching on the pebbles that covered the network of paths. At the center of it all was a carven statue of a kelpie head—a horse-like, shape-shifting water spirit that inhabited the lochs and pools of this wild land.

Cassian paused before the statue. The creature's head was thrown back, its wild mane flowing behind it. Kelpies were just one of the many spirits and mythical beasts of Scotland's folklore. After all he'd seen and done over the long years of his life, Cassian knew better than to dismiss them all out of hand as fantasy.

Suffering the bandruì's curse had opened his eyes to the fact that there were many things that couldn't be explained.

Cassian swallowed, in an effort to loosen his aching throat. He shifted his attention from the kelpie and looked up at the cloudy sky. Was that druidess looking down on him and smirking at his misery?

For he *was* miserable.

His chest burned with every inhale.

Saying those things to Aila had cost him, but they were necessary. He'd let himself get too close to her; drastic measures had to be taken before he fell for the winsome Aila De Keith.

Fool, you left it too late, a cruel voice whispered. *The damage has already been done.*

Aila wouldn't forgive him for this—and he didn't blame her.

Pain darted through Cassian's left ear, and he realized he was clenching his jaw so tightly that the muscles were starting to cramp. Raking a hand through his hair, he turned on his heel and stalked out of the garden.

Enough. He couldn't let this mess with Aila distract him from his purpose. De Keith needed guidance at present, and there was still a library full of books that he needed to return to.

Comyn's revelations sat uneasily with Cassian—he suspected Edward had lied to him about his plans. His gut warned him that the Hammer would strike the Fort upon the Shelving Slope. And soon.

Breaking the curse was the only thing that mattered. He couldn't let himself love another woman, not while he remained immortal.

He'd never put himself or anyone else through that agony ever again.

XXII

NEVER MY INTENTION

LADY GAVINA GLANCED up from the small leather-bound book she was reading by the window. Her gaze grew wide when it settled upon her maid.

"Heavens, Aila. What's the matter?"

The lass's face was blotchy, her eyes swollen and red. She'd just carried a stack of clean linen into Gavina's bed-chamber and placed it on the end of the bed.

"Nothing," she whispered, before she turned and attempted to hurry from the room, gaze averted.

"Aila!" Gavina put down the book and rose to her feet. "Stop ... what's happened?"

Her maid halted, and still facing away from her, covered her face with her hands.

Gavina watched her shoulders start to shake.

Rushing to her, she enfolded Aila in a hug. It was the first time she'd ever embraced her maid—for Gavina wasn't used to physical contact with others—but she couldn't let Aila weep like this.

The muffled sounds of her sobs cut Gavina to the quick.

"It's nothing, My Lady," Aila gasped. "I'm just foolish. Please ignore me."

Gavina's mouth thinned. As if she'd ever do such a thing. Taking Aila by the hand, she led her over to the window seat and gently pushed her down onto it. Then, lowering herself before the young woman, she met her watery gaze.

"I can't ignore such suffering," she said softly, "especially from someone who has been so good to me. Please tell me what ails ye."

Aila stared back at her, anguish twisting her pretty face. Her mouth trembled, and she clutched at Gavina's outstretched hands.

"I made a mistake, My Lady," she gasped. "I let myself believe in fairy tales ... and now I see they don't exist. They *never* existed."

Gavina's breathing constricted. Aila had always been so light-hearted, so full of hope. Her sunny disposition was a balm to Gavina's soul, a reminder that there were some folk who believed happiness was possible. But someone had stripped that from her sweet-tempered maid. Someone had just crushed her spirit.

Gavina stiffened, her temper quickening. She intended to find out who.

Cassian didn't realize he had company in the library at first. Deep in concentration, he was bent over a large book, his finger tracing the page as he read. It was only when the soft scuff of footfalls shattered the silence that he glanced up.

Lady Gavina glided toward him.

"My lady," Cassian greeted her, rising to his feet. He resisted the urge to slam the book shut or try to cover up what he was doing. It was patently obvious that he was reading, and he didn't want to arouse suspicions.

"Captain," Gavina acknowledged him. Her attention flicked to the open volume upon the table. A bank of candles nearby illuminated the bookshelves lining this windowless space and the huge oaken table in the center of the chamber. "What are ye reading?"

"A history, My Lady."

Gavina glanced back at him, her gaze questioning. She appeared surprised he could read, yet was too polite to say such a thing outright. Indeed, there were few men in his position who could read. Soldiers didn't usually need such a skill.

"Of what?"

"The Histories of the Clans."

She inclined her head. "And such things interest ye?"

Cassian smiled. "History is a passion of mine," he replied.

Curiosity gleamed in her blue eyes before her expression tensed and her brow furrowed. For the first time since he'd come to live at Dunnottar, Lady Gavina De Keith looked at Cassian as if she disliked him.

"I apologize, My Lady," he said quietly, motioning to the volume upon the table. "If this offends you, I shall put the book away."

Her lips compressed. "No, *that* doesn't offend me."

Cassian stiffened at her tone. Pretending he hadn't noticed her frosty attitude, his gaze flicked to the small leather-bound book she carried. "I see that you too like to read?"

"Aye," she admitted, her gaze still guarded. "Although my preference lies more in folk tales and legends. I've just finished this book of short tales, among them is 'The Doomed Rider'. Do ye know it?"

Cassian nodded. He'd heard the tale about a Kelpie's dark prophecy. "It's one of my favorites."

Gavina's frown deepened. "Ye are a true enigma, Cassian Gaius," she murmured. "A Spaniard who has made Scotland his home ... risen swiftly to the rank of captain in Dunnottar... and with an interest in our history and folk tales."

"I've lived here awhile, My Lady."

"Aye, but ye keep yer own counsel." She paused then, her chin lifting. "When ye aren't breaking hearts."

Cassian stilled.

Aila has told her. He couldn't believe she'd been so indiscreet. Did she want to utterly ruin herself?

A nerve ticked in Lady Gavina's cheek, almost as if she'd read his thoughts. "No, my maid didn't come complaining to me ... but when a woman is so deeply hurt, it's impossible for her to hide her grief."

Cassian drew in a slow, deep breath. "It was never my intention to hurt Aila," he said stiffly. His voice now held a note of warning; this wasn't a discussion he intended to have with the laird's wife.

Lady Gavina arched a slender eyebrow. "Really? Ye didn't think that by swiving and then spurning her, ye'd not wound her?"

Coldness swept over Cassian. "It's more complicated than that, My Lady ... and, if you don't mind, I'd rather not—"

"Oh, but I do mind." She took a step toward him, angling her chin higher in order to continue to hold his eye. "It's bad enough that ye bed my maid under my very nose ... but now ye dishonor her. What if her womb quickens?"

Tension coiled within Cassian, his skin prickling. He had to get out of this library and away from this woman's outrage. "That won't happen."

Her mouth pursed. She didn't want to be indelicate, yet he could see she didn't believe him.

"Ye are fortunate, Captain, that I am merely the laird's wife, and not the De Keith himself," she ground out, her heart-shaped face taut and pale. "For I wouldn't tolerate a man such as ye to lead *my* guard."

XXIII

SAVIOR OF THE REALM

THE LIGHT WAS fading and a chill wind buffeted David De Keith when he walked into the walled garden. Pulse racing, he feigned a relaxed posture, circling the beds of herbs and sweetly scented flowers, before making his way to the center of the space, where the kelpie statue sat at the garden's heart.

Spots of rain hit his forehead, and the dark clouds hovering to the north warned that the short spell of fine weather they'd been enjoying was about to end.

David continued his circuit around the garden, and all the while, he could feel cold steel pressing against his calf.

He'd hidden a dirk in the back of one of his long hunting boots.

Longshanks had agreed to meet him here.

De Keith slowed his step, passing under a trellis of gillyflowers. He'd been nervous that the king would refuse to meet him alone, for David had insisted that neither of them have an escort of guards.

Not even Comyn was invited to this meeting.

The De Keith laird's mouth thinned. 'The Red' was a traitor in his eyes. He'd knelt too easily to the English. De Keith wasn't going to do the same.

Instead, he was going to make himself a hero.

David glanced back at the towering walls of the keep.

He hated being here in Stirling. Each meeting with Edward was a kick to the bollocks. His father would turn in his cairn at the thought that one of his sons was about to kneel before an English king.

David clenched his jaw. *Robert would never suffer this.*

It was true. His proud brother was festering in an English dungeon, but he hadn't submitted to their rule. David would never live it down.

He'd initially agreed to play the Wallace's game—but he wouldn't any longer. Hot pride surged within him. *I won't bend the knee to an English king.*

He wouldn't let history remember him as the craven laird who'd knelt before the 'Hammer of the Scots', while the other northern chiefs refused.

Before he left Stirling, he'd ensure that history recorded him as a hero.

As the man who'd rid Scotland of Edward Longshanks.

The laird emerged from under the trellis and stopped before the kelpie statue. The fading light highlighted the beast's profile, and patriotic pride surged through De Keith, causing his chest to swell.

John Comyn was currently a Guardian of the Realm, but *he* would be named its savior.

He would kill Edward of England and let his blood soak into Scottish soil.

He'd have little time left after that—for the castle was full of English soldiers—but De Keith had a plan. After Jean had whispered to him about a hidden way out of the keep, David had known what he must do. The existence of the exit made escape possible.

And once Edward was dead, he'd make straight for it.

He'd have to leave the others behind, but no doubt Comyn and Captain Gaius would ensure the women came to no harm. And even if Gavina and Elizabeth ended up suffering as a result, he didn't care. He'd had enough of those meddlesome women, especially his Irvine wife—a woman he'd never wanted to wed.

He'd be sorry to abandon Jean though—she'd been a real delight—but he certainly wasn't going to put himself at risk to save a servant.

The crunch of booted feet on gravel made David turn.

Edward had entered the garden and was walking toward him.

De Keith watched the King of England approach. The man reminded him a little of his elder brother, Robert. Long and lanky, he had a stalking gait—a warrior's walk. As always, he wore a chainmail hauberk with a scarlet surcoat atop it. He wasn't a young man, yet the years did not appear to have bent or weakened him.

The laird suppressed a frown at the sight of the chainmail; that would make Edward harder to kill. The king's coif was lowered at least, leaving his neck exposed.

Determination coiled in David De Keith's belly. *I will strike him in the throat.*

"Another ale." Cassian called out, waving to the inn-keeper of *The Golden Lion*. The man wore a harried expression as he served two English knights—big men in hauberks, their broadswords hanging conspicuously at their sides.

The inn-keeper nodded, while the English soldiers glanced Cassian's way. Their gazes narrowed.

Cassian stared belligerently back at them. The mood he was in, he welcomed an outlet for his simmering temper.

Go on, insult me ... start a fight.

But, perhaps sensing his aggression, and maybe not in the mood to draw swords this evening, the two knights turned back to their tankards.

Cassian's lip curled. *Typical.* How many times over the years had he entered a tavern, just looking for some peace and a cool tankard of local ale, only to have an idiot provoke him. But when he was in a confrontational mood himself, everyone else just wished for a quiet evening.

"Yer ale." The inn-keeper carried across a fresh tankard and set it down before him. Cassian sat at a booth in the corner, a shadowy spot that afforded him a clear view of the whole common room. He always chose his seat in these places carefully. Even in his present mood, he still liked to keep an eye on his environs.

Cassian handed him a coin, and the man went on his way.

Taking a deep draft, Cassian wished he'd ordered something stronger. This ale wasn't having the slightest effect on him. He needed his senses to dull, for the ache under his breastbone to ease, and for the bunched muscles in his neck and shoulders to relax for a short while at least.

But there was to be no respite.

Reclining against the back of the booth, Cassian ran a hand over his face.

He had no one to blame but himself for this mess.

He'd known that spending time with Aila De Keith was foolish—he'd known, and he'd ignored his instincts. It was hard to think straight when she was near, and on the two occasions she'd reached out and placed a hand upon his chest, he'd lost his wits.

He imagined Maximus and Draco sitting opposite him then. The former would be favoring him with an exasperated look, while the latter would likely be wearing his best 'I told you so' smirk.

His own arrogance had gotten him into this. He'd thought he could go through life without connection, without letting himself go with a woman.

But Aila had taught him that, underneath his defenses, he was achingly lonely—and his hubris had been his undoing.

Cassian took another gulp of ale, wincing at the memory of Lady Gavina's cutting words.

Of course, the laird's wife didn't understand. And he wasn't about to explain the situation to her.

Hades take them all. This was why Maximus had chosen to live a solitary life for so many years.

People could be incredibly wearing.

Once more, he lifted the tankard to his lips and took a deep pull. *The Golden Lion*, one of his favorite establishments in Stirling, had an odd atmosphere this eve. Apart from one or two stalwart locals, English soldiers filled the tables and booths. There was a watchful, tense atmosphere within the common room.

Cassian had come here looking for some escape, but *The Golden Lion* wouldn't provide it.

If anything, the ale just darkened his mood further.

All he could think about now was the hurt in Aila's smoke-grey eyes. The look on her face still tormented him. She'd actually flinched. He hadn't wanted to be hurtful, or to wound her, but he'd been desperate.

Whenever he trod gently, he just got himself deeper into trouble.

In order to drive the reality of the situation home, he'd had to be brutal—but he still regretted hurting her.

"I take it you're not about to bandy words again, De Keith?"

Edward's greeting made anger coil in David's belly. The English king's arrogance had goaded him from the moment he'd walked into the Great Hall three days earlier. Since then, the two of them had played a game— one that Longshanks was slowly winning.

But David De Keith was about to turn the tables on him.

"No, Your Highness," he replied in French, meeting the king's eye. "That's why I wanted to see you alone. It isn't easy for a proud Scot to humble himself before an Englishman. I'd rather not have an audience when I do this."

Edward's gaze glinted.

He thinks he's beaten me.

De Keith's jaw clenched at the victory he saw in the king's piercing blue eyes.

David had begun to realize his limitations of late. For years, he'd chafed at the fact that he'd been born the younger brother—that Robert was laird and *he* wasn't. When Robert had been taken by the English, David had seized the opportunity presented to him. Finally, he led the De Keith clan. Yet that responsibility came at a price.

As laird, he had to manage the likes of Wallace, a man he didn't trust in the slightest. And then there was Shaw Irvine, who broke truces and intended to lay siege to Dunnottar. But the worst of it was having to deal with Edward Longshanks.

The hate that boiled within him whenever the English king drew near made it hard to hide his true feelings.

Robert always said I'd make a poor diplomat. David fought the urge to scowl at the thought. *Aye, but I'll be the man to end Longshanks' life.*

No, he wasn't a diplomat. He'd been born to do greater deeds. He'd show them all.

Edward shifted his gaze from David's momentarily as he glanced up at the darkening sky. "Hurry up then," he murmured. "Let's get this over with. Kneel before me, man, and pledge your troth."

De Keith bowed his head, feigning submission.

Heart pounding now, he stepped forward and lowered himself on one knee. But as he did so, his right hand strayed to the back of his boot and the dirk he'd hidden there.

XXIV

STORM UNLEASHED

CASSIAN CLIMBED THE slope toward the walls of Stirling Castle. The biting wind gusted into him, bringing with it droplets of cold rain. Bowing his head, he grimaced. It was easy to forget that it was summer when the weather changed like this.

Keen to get indoors, Cassian increased his pace. The Bull-Slayer take him, he'd consumed enough ale tonight to bring most men to their knees, yet his gait was still steady. The curse was working against him, keeping his mind clear and his senses sharp even when he sought oblivion.

Before him loomed the great stone archway that led into the outer-bailey. Shadowed figures, hunched in their cloaks, their faces obscured by helms, watched him approach.

The English guards didn't greet him, and he ignored them. However, no one blocked his path either, for they'd seen him depart earlier. They all knew he was a member of the De Keith party.

The outer-bailey was deserted. The worsening weather had driven folk indoors.

Cassian crossed the courtyard, passed the stables and storage buildings, and entered the inner-bailey through another archway. The keep rose before him, its solid walls leached of color against a leaden sky.

A storm was about to unleash itself upon them.

Even so, Cassian didn't feel like re-entering the keep just now. He might accidentally see Aila; it was best if he kept a low profile for the next few days.

Coward. He grimaced at the thought. He was—but if he'd listened to the voice of reason that had counselled him wisely ever since his departure from Dunnottar, he wouldn't be in this situation.

Despite the buffeting wind, he'd hopefully find refuge in the walled garden to the north-west of the keep. He wasn't ready to see anyone at present, and the garden had given him some solace earlier that day.

Cassian altered his direction, steering himself toward the rose entwined archway that separated the inner-bailey and the garden beyond.

He'd just stepped through it when a sight in the heart of the space, below where the Kelpie's head reared skyward, made him halt.

Two men were fighting.

And not two soldiers or servants—but Edward of England and Laird David De Keith.

For an instant, Cassian merely stared, hardly able to believe what he was seeing.

De Keith had just drawn a dirk. He slashed it wildly at Edward's throat, the thin blade flashing in the gloaming.

Edward ducked back, just barely avoiding being cut across the windpipe. He moved fast, despite that he was much older than his opponent, his red surcoat billowing in the wind.

Cassian remained frozen, his gaze riveted on the two men.

He'd witnessed a lot of fights over the centuries, and he knew that there was nothing he could do. By the time he reached them, it would be over.

De Keith wielded the blade savagely, but without precision. His wild slashing would be his undoing. Both men wore chainmail, so there were few vulnerable spots to attack—but to have any chance of success, accuracy was required.

As he watched, Edward retaliated.

The English king ducked again, caught De Keith by the wrist, and twisted hard. The laird cursed and released the dirk.

Edward moved with breathtaking swiftness then, revealing himself for the warrior he was. He scooped up the dagger, grabbed De Keith by the hair, and yanked his head back—and then he drove the blade into his throat.

One heartbeat passed, and then another.

Edward withdrew the dirk blade and stabbed De Keith once more. A choking sound drifted across the garden, blending with the whistling wind. The laird fell to his knees, mouth gaping, eyes bulging.

A chill swept over Cassian.

Idiot ... what has De Keith done?

The thought brought Cassian out of his reverie. Swiveling on his heel, he turned and sprinted back across the inner-bailey toward the keep.

Aila was having difficulty focusing.

She sat in the guests' solar, along with Lady Gavina, Lady Elizabeth, and Jean, while the wind battered at the closed shutters. A draft managed to claw its way into the chamber. It feathered across Aila's face and made the fire in the hearth gutter.

Across the solar, she could hear the soft cadence of the ladies' voices. However, she paid no attention to their conversation.

Instead she stared down at the hem she was mending. It felt as if she were moving through porridge this evening.

Once the storm of hurt and anger had spent itself, once the tears had burned themselves dry, Aila felt like a husk. She'd gone blindly about her duties for the rest of the day. Supper was approaching, yet she had no desire to go down to the kitchen and join the other servants. She hadn't eaten anything since dawn; her belly was a hard knot of misery. The thought of forcing food down made her feel sick.

She longed for Lady Gavina to dismiss her for the rest of the evening, to see to her own needs for once. Instead, Aila wished to return to her tiny chamber, curl up on her bed, and pretend the world didn't exist.

The ache in her chest was almost unbearable, and every time she relived those moments in the alcove, bile crept up her throat.

She felt such an utter pudding-head.

I should never have taken Fyfa's advice. Aila swallowed hard at how eagerly she'd listened to the steward's wife. She'd been furious at Fyfa earlier, yet now that anger turned upon herself.

Aye, Fyfa had advised her, but it was Aila who'd presented herself at Cassian's door, who'd blindly followed the words of someone she hardly knew.

Such had been her desperation.

Aila's throat constricted as shame washed over her.

Ma and Da can never find out.

Iona De Keith had strong views on how women should behave. Heather had once roused her fury when she'd run off with Iain Galbraith, but Iona also kept a judgmental eye on other women residing within the stronghold.

There had been a tragic incident involving a maid at Dunnottar around four years earlier. The lass had fallen in love with one of the Guard—a callous man who'd used her and then refused to wed her. She'd been so distraught afterward that she'd thrown herself off the walls and died upon the jagged rocks below the fortress.

After the lass's shocking death, Iona had made a comment that Aila had never forgotten. "No man is worth killing yerself over," she'd sniffed. "A woman who believes in her own worth would never let herself be treated that way in the first place."

Harsh words, yet years later they mocked Aila.

She too was a foolish woman. She'd woven a fantasy about Dunnottar's handsome captain, built him up into someone he wasn't. She'd taken every kind word, every smile as evidence that he felt the same way as her, ignoring the facts that were plain to everyone else.

No wonder Heather tried to warn me.

Aila swallowed hard, remembering the concern that clouded her sister's eyes on the day they'd departed Dunnottar.

She didn't want to go back there. She just wanted to hide away from the rest of the world. Forever.

The door to the solar crashed open then, jerking Aila into the present.

Cassian strode inside.

Her heart lurched. For a brief instant, she cringed in her seat, wishing the floor would open up and swallow her.

But then she saw his face. He was out of breath, although his expression was steely.

"Captain?" Lady Gavina greeted him coolly. "Why are ye—"

"Your husband has just tried to kill Edward," Cassian cut her off. "I saw them in the walled garden. The king wrested the dirk off him and stabbed him in the throat with it."

A strangled cry filled the solar. But it was not Lady Gavina who had made the horrified sound, but Jean.

Aila's gaze jerked to her. The maid's face had turned the color of milk. Eyes glittering, she reached up and clutched her throat. "No!"

In an instant, everyone in the room knew Jean's secret.

Across the solar, Lady Gavina's face paled. "David," she breathed. "The Lord have mercy on us all ... what have ye done?"

"We're trapped in here." Lady Elizabeth lurched to her feet, the wool she'd been winding onto a spindle tumbling to the ground. Her voice rose as panic seized her. "Edward will have us all hanged for treason."

The shock of Cassian's news settled over Aila, puncturing the fog of misery that had cloaked her all day.

At that moment, her unhappiness ceased to matter.

Lady Elizabeth was right. De Keith had just tried to assassinate the English king, and Edward would be out for blood.

Aila jumped to her feet, her pulse thundering in her ears. "We have to run ... before he sends his guards to fetch us."

Cassian swiveled to her, scowling. "We'd never get through the gate."

Aila shook her head. "There's another way ... a secret way ... out of the castle. Fyfa showed it to me the other evening. It's a door in the wall in the Nether Bailey. Edward doesn't know about it."

Aila had been nervous as she followed Fyfa down the wall walk that first evening in Stirling. At first, she hadn't been able to see anything but the long-shadowed expanse of wall. But halfway down, Fyfa showed her a wild growth of gorse that grew up against it. The sweet scent of its flowers had drifted over the women. Edging around its prickly branches, Fyfa had gingerly pushed them aside to reveal a small wooden door. "It's a secret way out," she'd whispered. "Some of the Scots who reside here know of it ... but Longshanks doesn't."

"Why didn't ye use it when Stirling came under attack?" Aila had asked. Fascinated, she'd resisted the urge to open the door and see where it led.

Fyfa had snorted. "My husband is a Comyn ... they don't run from the English."

"But he's ruled by them now."

"Aye ... but since the English have taken Stirling before and then lost it, all we have to do is wait," Fyfa had replied with a confidence that awed Aila. "Longshanks will never keep hold of this place ... just as he will never break the Scottish spirit."

The discovery had been so exciting that Aila hadn't been able to keep it to herself. Jean's eyes had gone as wide as moons when she'd heard the tale the following morning. Yet now, at the mention of the secret door, the maid wore an odd, almost guilty look.

Aila was just about to question her about it when Cassian cut in. "Are you sure?"

"Yes, I've seen it. The door is hidden behind a gorse bush part way along the wall."

Cassian stared at her. His expression was difficult to fathom, although his eyes gleamed. He was already planning ahead.

Breaking eye contact with Aila, Cassian turned back to the other occupants in the solar. "Follow me. Quickly!"

"Wait ... but shouldn't we fetch our cloaks and belongings?" Lady Gavina asked, her voice shaky.

"Take a cloak and nothing else," he replied curtly. "If we're going to make it out of Stirling Castle, we have to go now."

XXV

THE WAY OUT

THE FOUR WOMEN followed Cassian down the hallway. He didn't lead them back to the main stairwell, past the guards, but instead in the opposite direction—to a service stairwell used by servants that led down to the kitchens.

The same one that Comyn had taken when he'd met with them.

Now that Cassian knew of the secret way out of the castle, he moved with purpose down the dimly lit steps. They were perilously narrow, yet he didn't slow his pace.

Edward would be summoning his guards. There was a real risk they wouldn't even make it to the Nether Bailey before they were caught.

Cassian was focused now. Nothing else mattered but getting these women safely away from Stirling. They would have to leave the other men of their escort, and their horses, behind. But there was no time to warn the warriors, and horses would only hamper their escape.

The kitchens were busy, a cacophony of shouting cooks making final preparations for supper. Servants hurried to and fro, carrying tureens of stew and baskets of bread.

A couple of them noticed the party that appeared from the service stairwell.

One of the cooks nearest the stairs—a big man with a florid face and a harassed expression—scowled. "What are ye lot doing down here?"

"Just passing through," Cassian replied, ushering the women ahead of him across the floor to an archway. "And if you have any love for your fellow Scots, you'll forget you ever saw us."

The cook's expression tightened, his mouth thinning. A moment later, he gave a reluctant nod and turned away, before bellowing across the kitchen. "Fergus! Stop yer idling!"

"Where does this passage go?" Lady Gavina whispered to Cassian when he joined them.

He flashed her a grim smile. "To the eastern side of the inner-bailey, a short walk to our destination."

"We'll never make it!" Jean's voice echoed shrilly against the surrounding stone.

"Lower yer voice, Jean!" Lady Elizabeth snapped. She then turned to Cassian. "She has a point though, Captain ... we'll not reach the door without being spotted."

"We won't," Cassian agreed, drawing his sword. The dull scrape of steel filled the cramped tunnel. The light of the nearby cressets gleamed against the pointed, double-edged blade and its bronze handle. The women's gazes settled upon the blade, and then Lady Elizabeth's brow furrowed.

Cassian's mouth lifted at the corners as he suppressed a smile. They'd expected him to carry a claidheamh-mòr—a great Scottish broadsword, not this shorter, thinner blade. He wielded a *gladius hispaniensis*—a Spanish sword made of folded Toledo steel. The weapon had been with him for many long centuries.

Noting the doubt upon the women's faces, Cassian flashed them all a tight smile. "Fear not ... a blade like this is ideal for fighting your way out of a castle."

And it was. His gladius had been forged for use on the battlefield at close quarters, to cut and thrust with while holding a shield in the opposite hand. He never went into a swordfight without it.

Cassian led the way toward the heavy wooden door that would take them into the inner-bailey. "Keep a few yards behind me till we reach the door," he instructed. "I'll likely need to clear a path for us."

He glanced over his shoulder then, his gaze finding Aila's.

Her round face was pale in the dimly lit tunnel, her grey eyes huge and dark. And yet she wore a resolute, determined expression that he welcomed.

Aila De Keith was brave. He just hoped the other women had the same mettle, for tonight, they would be hunted prey. He wasn't afraid for himself, but these women's lives were his responsibility.

"Where exactly is the door?" Cassian asked after a pause.

"On the southern side of the Nether Bailey." Her voice was low and steady, giving him further reassurance that she wasn't going to panic the moment they stepped outside. In contrast, Jean was ashen-faced and trembling beside her. "Look for the gorse bush."

Cassian nodded before turning away. He moved to the door and threw it open, leading them out into the night.

Aila pulled up the hood of her cloak and bent her head against the icy onslaught of rain and wind. It was dark outdoors now, and the few pitch torches that still burned on the walls hissed and smoked.

The foul weather was their ally though.

Gripping Jean by the arm, for the lass kept stumbling as they fled across the pebbled expanse of the inner-bailey, Aila kept her gaze fixed upon the dark figure leading the way.

Cassian was little more than a broad-shouldered outline against the shadowy night beyond. Occasionally, she caught a glint from his drawn sword blade. His confidence and cool head awed her. The man was truly a soldier.

From the moment he'd burst into the solar, he'd taken charge.

They were still in the midst of danger, and yet she trusted him.

As Cassian had anticipated, they didn't reach their destination without running into trouble.

Two English guards barred the way into the Nether Bailey, but Cassian was on them so fast the pair barely saw him coming.

Pained grunts reached Aila.

She pulled up short, causing Lady Gavina to run into her back. "Wait!" she whispered to her mistress. "It's not safe yet."

Beside her, Jean whimpered. Aila tightened her grip on the lass's arm. "Courage," she murmured. "Hold fast, Jean."

Ahead, Cassian turned—two figures lying prostrate upon the ground before him—and motioned for the women to follow. He then slipped through the archway behind the fallen guards into the Nether Bailey.

Darkness shrouded this corner of the fortress, making it difficult to find their way to the unruly clump of gorse that signaled the way out.

A lone brazier smoked and hissed upon the walls. On the verge of going out, it threw out a little light over the exposed grassy area beneath it.

The four women followed Cassian along the wall walk, using their hands to guide them.

Aila halted when she heard Cassian mutter a soft curse up ahead.

"I've found the gorse bush," he announced, his tone rueful. "Thorny bastard."

In other circumstances, Aila might have smiled. However, she felt sick with nerves. The howl of the wind cloaked any noise they made, and she couldn't yet hear any shouting from the keep behind them. But the guards would come soon enough.

They had to get out of the castle grounds now.

A squall hit the Nether Bailey—freezing rain slashing against their faces as they edged up to where Cassian had spoken. It was difficult not to blunder straight into the spikey growth of gorse. Aila managed to pick her way around it, following Cassian's lead, and squeezed in behind him through the gap between the gorse and the secret doorway.

The creak of iron filled the night when the door opened on rusted hinges, and once again, Aila was grateful for the howling storm.

"Are you all with me?" Cassian asked. She couldn't see his face, although from the clarity of his voice, he must have twisted toward her.

"Aye," Aila replied. "We're ready."

"We don't know what lies beyond this door," he admitted, his tone growing grim. "But the cliff face is on the other side of the wall, and without torches to light our way, we risk toppling to our deaths."

Jean whimpered again. Aila silently clutched the maid to her. Although she didn't voice her own fear, it welled up inside her nonetheless.

"Follow me out slowly, and only advance forward a few steps when I let you know the way is clear," Cassian concluded.

With that, he pulled the wooden door toward him and moved through the narrow archway.

Muffled shouting some way off reached them then, piercing the howl of the wind.

Lady Elizabeth breathed a curse. "They're after us."

It was time to go.

Aila followed Cassian outside, stifling a gasp as the full force of the wind hit her in the face. She'd thought the storm had been violent inside the walls, but beyond their sturdy protection, the wind clawed at her—making their escape even riskier.

The four women clung together, inching their way through the door and onto the pebbly slope below.

Aila's belly pitched. They were so exposed up here. One misstep and it would be over. Back in Dunnottar, she avoided walking too close to the ramparts. But out here in the dark, with the wind pummeling her, she was standing on the edge of a precipice.

Outside the wall, the women halted as instructed and waited for Cassian's signal.

It took a while.

Aila peered into the stormy darkness, her eyes straining. She tried to catch sight of him. Her eyes were gradually adjusting to the gloom, but the storm had closed them in, obliterating the night sky and the fires of Stirling burning below.

"There are stairs," he called back finally. "This way."

Doing as bid, Aila inched her way down the slope a few feet.

"Slide down the stairs on your backsides," Cassian instructed. "We're going to have to feel our way down. It'll be slow, but it's safer."

None of his companions argued with him. Right now, no one was worried about dirtying their clothing.

Her pulse beating in her ears, Aila obeyed. She let go of Jean, who now trembled against her, and lowered herself to the ground. "Come on, Jean," she whispered. "Just do as he says, and we might get through this."

Then, feeling her way with her feet, Aila shuffled onward. She found the first step and slid down onto it, and then the next.

It seemed to take an age to descend the steep, torturous stairway leading down from the Nether Bailey.

Impatience thrummed through Cassian. He too shuffled down the steps on his backside. The buffeting storm made everything more dangerous. His cloak was sodden, and the wind had plastered it against his body. He'd long since pushed back the cowl as no one could see him out here anyway.

Behind him, he could hear the scraping sounds of the women following. He hadn't cautioned them again, for it was unnecessary. All of them understood just how dangerous this was.

Eventually, Cassian reached the rocky bottom of the volcanic outcrop on which Stirling Castle perched. He rose to his feet and waited for the women to join him.

They were on the edge of the town now; the gabled roof of the Kirk of the Holy Rude rose up to his left, a dark outline against the faint glow of lanterns.

Cassian's jaw clenched as he considered his next move. There were a few options open to him. He could try and hide the women in Stirling itself—if the kirk had been open, he'd have taken them down to the mithraeum. But the kirk was barred at this hour, and such a move would only trap them all in Stirling. By the time they tried to leave, the hills would be crawling with English soldiers.

Tonight was their best chance of escape.

It was either the river or the hills.

The river was the riskier of the two options, for he'd have to steal a birlinn from Riverside before they could sail downriver with it. Cassian frowned then. The tide was out at this hour. The decision was made for him: he would have to take the women cross-country.

His frown deepened to a scowl.

Without horses and hampered by long skirts, the women wouldn't be able to travel fast.

Turning, his gaze settled upon a cloaked shape that drew close. "Cassian ... we've made it?" Aila's breathless voice reached him.

"For now ... are you all still with me?"

"I think so."

Cassian raised his chin, eyes narrowing. High above, he spotted the glow of torches. The chatter of raised, angry voices drifted down the cliff toward them.

The English had discovered the secret door, and were now following them down the cliff face.

Cassian dropped his gaze to the four women who'd halted before him, their faces pale smudges in the darkness. Their lives were in his hands now; he couldn't fail them. "Come," he said gruffly. "It's time to run."

XXVI

THE WOODLAND GLADE

AILA LAY UPON her back and drew in deep gulps of air. Her lungs burned, her back ached, and her legs no longer had any strength in them. If Cassian hadn't let them halt in the woodland glade, she would have collapsed.

A few yards away, she heard a soft retching sound. Exhaustion had dug its claws into them all. She wasn't sure which of her companions was being sick in the bushes, but Aila wasn't surprised. She too fought the waves of nausea that washed over her.

Too exhausted to even lift her head, Aila stared up through the embracing tree limbs overhead at the lightening sky.

Had they really run all night?

She wasn't even sure how they'd managed it—only that fear of capture had driven them on.

Cassian had led them over the rock-studded hills away from Stirling, careful to keep the women off the road. And all the while, the storm had screamed across the hillsides like an enraged fury.

Without Cassian, they would never have made it this far. Without his impressive sense of direction, they'd have wandered lost and likely fallen into a ravine.

He was their savior.

Dragging in another deep breath, Aila inclined her head to spy Cassian seated a few feet away. Unlike her, he didn't lie sprawled on his back. Instead, he leaned against the trunk of a birch.

Now that dawn filtered across the world and the storm had spent itself, she could see him properly for the first time since their escape.

Cassian's chest rose and fell sharply. Sweat slicked his handsome face and plastered his short brown hair to his scalp.

Feeling her gaze upon him, he shifted his attention to her, but Aila hurriedly looked away.

She was torn. She was grateful to him—his bravery and quick thinking had saved them—but his courage didn't cancel out what happened between them. It didn't erase his cold, callous words.

But ironically, the journey here had given her time to think. And as Aila slowly mulled events over in her mind, she'd come to realize that she was largely to blame for this mess.

She'd thrown herself at him.

Mortification, hot and prickly, swamped her then as she recalled how he'd warned her off. Yet she hadn't listened. Her own willful blindness had gotten her into this situation.

Cassian was an enigma, a man who clearly hid something. She burned to know why he was so guarded with his heart—yet the searing humiliation she'd suffered at his hands prevented her from pressing the issue.

Coward.

Keeping her gaze averted, Aila rolled over onto her side, away from him. She could still feel him watching her, but she focused instead on her ragged breathing and pounding heart—only now it wasn't just caused by exhaustion.

Nausea hit her, and Aila swallowed down bile. She drew in a deep breath, fighting the urge to be sick. Fear and urgency had driven her during the night, and had given her a respite from her misery. But as sun filtered over the glade—illuminating a mossy space with a burn trickling through its center, fringed by spindly birches—the ache in her belly returned.

She wouldn't meet Cassian's eye—she was too embarrassed to do so. The less contact the pair of them had, the better.

Once they returned to Dunnottar, they could go back to their old lives.

Only, I shall never forget him. The thought rose, unbidden, but Aila shoved it back. *No, I must.*

Aila sat by the fire and turned two large grouse over the glowing embers. The gamey aroma of the roasting bird filled the glade. Her belly rumbled in response. She'd eaten virtually nothing over the past few days and was starting to feel dizzy.

The three other women sat around the fire with her, their faces drawn and pale. Cassian wasn't present. He'd gone to scout the area, to make sure the English weren't nearby. But before going off on patrol, he'd hunted them some grouse.

In Cassian's absence, the women had hung up their sodden cloaks to dry upon the boughs of the birches while they cooked the grouse. Aila longed to be able to change her lèine and kirtle, for her skirts were now filthy and the still damp fabric itched her skin.

"Robert is doomed now." Lady Elizabeth's broken whisper interrupted the gentle crackling of the fire. Sorrow etched her face.

"Don't say that, Liz." Lady Gavina reached out and placed a hand on her sister-by-marriage's arm. "Ye don't know for sure."

Elizabeth's throat bobbed. "David's behavior won't go unpunished. Edward will take his vengeance out on the De Keiths."

"Robert isn't David," Gavina replied firmly. "Even Longshanks will realize that."

The look Elizabeth gave her told them she doubted the English king would show her husband any mercy.

Aila glanced down at the grouse. The skin was starting to blister; the birds were almost cooked. Turning the roasting grouse over the fire gave her something to do—stopped her thinking about everything that had happened.

Around her, a sunny afternoon turned golden and the shadows lengthened. The violent storm had swept away the clouds and allowed the sun to bathe the world once more.

Summer had returned.

However, Aila felt as if winter had taken up residence within her. There was a chill in her chest that wouldn't thaw.

"Longshanks has enough to contend with at present." Gavina continued after a pause. "His hold on Scotland is tenuous at best ... Robert won't be his focus."

Shifting her attention from their supper, Aila noted that Elizabeth's gaze glittered. "I want to hope," she admitted softly. "But I'm not sure my heart can take it."

"Worrying about Robert is all well and good, My Lady," Jean spoke up, her voice brittle. "But it's yer own neck ye should be concerned about." She glanced around the darkening glade. "Where's the Captain? We should be moving on."

"We won't be leaving here until dusk settles," Aila replied. "It's not safe to travel in daylight. The storm has passed ... it should be a fair night and the moon is waxing, so traveling won't be difficult."

Jean's mouth pursed. "Captain Gaius should be here ... protecting us."

"He'll be back soon enough." Elizabeth cast Jean an irritated look. "Ye should be pleased that he's gone to scout. Edward will have soldiers out looking for us."

Jean dropped her gaze. "Aye, My Lady," she murmured, chastised. "I am indeed grateful."

"We have much to thank the captain for," Gavina added softly, before sighing. "We'd have never gotten this far without him."

Aila swallowed to ease the sudden tightness in her throat. Her mistress was right, of course. Nonetheless, she didn't want to think about Cassian, let along talk about him.

At that moment, the man himself appeared at the edge of the glade. Cassian's face was inscrutable as he strode across to the fire and lowered himself down before it.

"Any sign of the English, Captain?" Gavina greeted him.

Cassian shook his head. "We got a good head-start on them it seems ... although they will pick up our trail soon enough."

Lady Elizabeth exchanged a worried look with her maid at this, while Lady Gavina's attention remained upon Cassian. "Back in Stirling ... did ye see it happen, Captain? Did ye see David die?"

Cassian raked a hand through his hair. The gesture caused a visceral reminder in Aila, of how she'd threaded her fingers through those soft strands when they'd lain together. Longing pulsed through her before Aila clenched her jaw. *Stop it.*

Oblivious to the war Aila was waging, Cassian nodded. "They were in the garden ... David went for Edward with his dirk." he paused then, scowling. "But he was no match for him. Edward disarmed him in a couple of moves before stabbing him twice in the throat."

Gavina swallowed hard. "What was David thinking?" she murmured. "This wasn't what we'd planned. All he had to do was feign submission to the king and gather details that could help us." She broke off there, shaking her head in despair. "But no, he had to go after glory. Selfish, vain man!"

A sharply indrawn breath filled the glade. All gazes shifted to where Jean sat. Scorn twisted the maid's face. Gone was the mask of gentle subservience she usually wore when in the presence of the ladies. She was now glaring openly at Lady Gavina.

"Ye are a cold, hard bitch," she choked out the words. "Yer husband has just had his throat cut, and ye sit there dry-eyed, condemning him. No wonder he couldn't stand ye."

XXVII

HOLDING BACK

THE WORDS FELL heavily in the warm afternoon air. Suddenly, it went quiet in the glade, save for the crackling of the fire and the gentle gurgle of the burn.

When Lady Gavina spoke, her tone was as wintry as her expression. "And ye wouldn't condemn him for putting all our lives at risk?"

The maid didn't answer. She merely stared at Gavina, her eyes burning with fury. But Aila could sense the lass's grief. It pulsed just beneath the surface.

"How long have ye been stealing into his bed?" Gavina demanded. Her small frame had gone rigid, and her blue eyes were narrowed.

"Two moons," Jean replied, raising her chin in defiance.

"And do ye think ye are the first servant to spread her legs for him?" Jean flinched, but Gavina continued, leaning toward the maid now. "Do ye actually think he *cared* for ye?"

"He did." Jean bit out the words. "What we had was special."

Aila's heart twisted as she watched the pain on Jean's face. Poor, foolish wench. Was that how *she* appeared to Cassian?

Gavina's mouth twisted. "Ye weren't special to him. David De Keith loved no one but himself."

Aila's breathing caught. Gavina had played the role of long-suffering wife for years now, despite the laird's callous behavior. He'd never bothered to hide his disdain for her, or hidden his outrageous flirting with other women in her presence. And all the while, Gavina had put up a stoic front.

But the Lady of Dunnottar was done pretending none of that had hurt her.

Jean glared back at Lady Gavina for a long moment. But then her face crumpled. It was an awful thing to see, to watch a woman's heart break. For a few instants, Aila forgot to breathe. Suddenly, her own unhappiness, her own disappointment, paled to insignificance.

Jean's grief enveloped them all.

"I loved him." The words ripped out from Jean in a high, keening wail, and then she buried her head in her hands and began to weep in deep, rending sobs that echoed through the clearing.

Instinctively, Aila moved across to Jean and put a gentle arm around her shoulders. But the lass didn't notice. She was too lost in misery.

Aila glanced then back at Lady Gavina. She'd expected to see her mistress still angry, her eyes full of self-righteous rage, but the look upon her face made Aila still.

Her heart-shaped face had drained of color, and her mouth trembled. She watched Jean weep, her eyes glittering—not from rage this time, but from sadness.

Supper was a tense, somber meal.

The party ate in silence. Jean refused to touch the pieces of roast grouse that Cassian handed her, so he laid them on a piece of moss next to her. The girl would likely want some later.

The grouse was tough and very gamey, but nobody complained.

Across the fire, Aila ate hungrily. Cassian did his best to keep his gaze off her, yet when she licked the grease off her fingers, he couldn't help but stare.

His belly clenched.

What was it? Lust? Loneliness? Regret? Perhaps a blend of all three.

Wariness settled over Cassian then. Aila De Keith, with her sweet face and guileless eyes, had done something to him, had woven an enchantment around him.

He'd once dismissed her as a bashful lass. But that had all changed once they left Dunnottar. And their escape from Stirling had shown that she was courageous. Her soft speech and gentle manners hid a core of iron.

He'd underestimated her.

Aila's attention cut to him then, and she caught him watching her.

Face rigid, she stared back. And as the moment drew out, he saw anger shadow those smoke-grey eyes, turning them hard and flinty.

She hated him now—and rightly so.

Cassian broke eye contact. Leaning forward, he fed some sticks onto the fire.

It's better this way, better she thinks I'm a heartless rogue, he reminded himself. *Anger is easier to deal with than sorrow.*

Cassian's mouth compressed. Who was he trying to fool?

He'd seen her reaction that morning in the alcove, had watched her happiness splinter into a thousand pieces by his hand.

Her rage was a shield, as was his indifference.

The party finished their supper of grouse in silence and waited while the shadows lengthened further and dusk settled over the woodland.

Finally, Cassian rose to his feet, kicked dirt over the embers of the fire, and swept his gaze over the faces of his companions.

All four women were tense, their expressions guarded. This would be a subdued journey.

"We'll set off now," he informed them, his voice splintering the silence. "Sound travels at night so keep your voices low—if you need to say anything at all." Looking at their pale faces, Cassian knew he didn't have to worry about that last warning. None of them looked in the mood to chatter amongst themselves.

They left the birch-lined glade and headed through the press of trees. Cassian had deliberately taken them cross-country, away from open land, any villages, and the roads that wound their way through the wooded hills and valleys that spread north of Stirling.

The good weather continued, and as the last of the daylight faded and the stars came out to play, Cassian was able to use them to check their position.

While he'd been out scouting, he'd discovered they were a little farther west than he'd thought, and so he angled a path north-east through the trees. The Highlands rose up to the west, and he didn't want to take them in that direction. Dunnottar lay on the eastern coast.

The Broom-star was clearly visible in the night sky, and the sight of it brought Cassian solace.

It may not be long now.

Despite everything, they were still the closest they'd ever been to breaking the curse.

The events of the last day had pushed all thoughts of the riddle from his mind—something that rarely occurred. But seeing the bright star with its fiery tail brought everything back.

Ironically, he should be grateful to De Keith. He'd been concerned, after speaking with John Comyn, that the Hammer of the Scots wouldn't attack soon. But after the attempted assassination, an assault was likely not far off. Fate had swung events back in their favor.

The 'Hammer' would indeed strike the fort upon the Shelving Slope—and the attack wasn't likely far off.

But for now, Cassian had to set the curse and its enigmatic riddle to one side. His sole focus was to get these women home.

Aila picked up her skirts and traversed the burn. Cold water seeped through her boots and chilled her feet, but it couldn't be helped. Even with the moon lighting their way, it was impossible to pick her way across the stream without getting wet.

Ahead, Cassian made his way up a slope, moving like a shadow between the dark outlines of pines.

Gritting her teeth as her leg muscles ached, Aila scrambled after him.

Behind her, she heard Jean mutter something under her breath. However, Gavina and Elizabeth had been impressively stoic. Aila expected both ladies to complain of aching feet and tiredness, yet they pressed on without a word.

They'd just stopped for a brief respite, and had drunk from a cool spring. Generally, it wasn't wise to drink from springs and streams in the wilderness, for many folk sickened after doing so, but thirst made the choice for them. They'd never make it back to Dunnottar otherwise. Fortunately, Cassian seemed confident he knew the watering holes that were safe, and those that were to be avoided.

Aila did her best to avoid making eye contact with Cassian during the times she was forced to interact with him. His presence was a constant reminder of her foolishness. Yet she was aware just how dependent they all were on him.

Even so, when she'd caught him staring at her just before dark, frustration had welled up within her. His expression had been shuttered, yet she'd seen the heat in his eyes.

And curse him, he'd kindled the same response within her.

Knave! He has no right to look at me like that, she railed to herself as she marched up the slope, the scent of pine enveloping her. *Not after he cast me aside.*

The thought made her so furious—both at him and herself—that her belly started to hurt.

She really needed to have it out with him; she wanted some honesty. She was tired of avoiding eye contact, of acting as if nothing had happened between them. When they reached Dunnottar they would resume their old roles, but tonight she longed to speak her mind.

Aila tripped over a stump and stumbled forward, catching herself on a pine branch. Up ahead, Cassian plowed on, oblivious to the storm growing within her.

Clenching her jaw, Aila staggered up the hill after him. *Things can't go on this way,* she thought grimly. *I'm going to have to face him.*

The night stretched on, seemingly endless. And all the while, the moon traveled across the sky before setting behind a wall of towering pines.

Cassian led them away from the steep valleys carpeted in conifers, to a woodland of oak and ash. Aila was starting to stumble from exhaustion, her breathing labored, when he finally halted.

They stood in a shallow valley, where a creek trickled over mossy rocks. A line of ancient oaks, their boughs stretching toward the earth like supplicating arms, surrounded them.

Cassian swiveled on his heel and cast a gaze over his exhausted companions. "Dawn isn't too far away." They were his first words in hours. "We'll rest here awhile."

Too tired to even respond, Gavina flopped down on the ground near the creek. She then pulled off her boots, so that she could inspect her feet. Likewise, the others sat down, their breathing loud in the predawn stillness. Above, the sky had changed from black to indigo.

Cassian moved away from the women, taking a seat under one of the spreading oaks.

Aila watched him go.

Her belly tightened. This was how it would be for the rest of the journey: him leading the way and them hurrying after him like frightened ducklings.

Her desire for confrontation still smoldered, and although her body cried out for rest, the need to clear the air with Cassian grew stronger.

Drawing in a deep breath, Aila picked up her skirts and followed him to the mighty oak.

Cassian spied her approach, although his expression was difficult to read in the dim light. "What is it, Aila?" he asked, his tone guarded. "You should really rest ... while you can."

Aila frowned. His cool manner just strengthened her resolve. It unfettered the last of her reserve. It was time for some plain speech; she needed to say this before her courage deserted her.

"I'll rest in a moment," she said, facing him, hands on hips. "But there are things that must be said." She broke off, aware of his steady gaze upon her. Aila sucked in a deep breath. "Firstly, I want to apologize."

He visibly stiffened. "Look, Aila ... I don't think—"

"I threw myself at ye, and I'm sorry for it."

"This isn't your fault," he replied, his voice strained.

"All the same, I should have heeded ye." Her jaw firmed. "I admit my part in this mess, Cassian. Despite yer warnings, I said I was comfortable just spending the night with ye—but it was a lie ... I'd hoped for more. Now all I ask in return is the same honesty from ye." She swallowed as tension crackled between them. "Tell me the real reason why ye spurned me."

XXVIII

THE SUN RISES

CASSIAN WASN'T SURE how to respond. His first instinct was to make some excuse, as he had back in Stirling, but as the moment stretched out, the words wouldn't come. He was weary, both in body and soul—and the angry woman standing before him deserved the truth. "It seems I underestimated you, Aila," he said softly. "You aren't an easy woman to fool."

Aila folded her arms over her chest and stared down her nose at him. "Why would ye want to fool me?"

Cassian heaved a sigh. "Sit down ... I'd prefer not to explain this with you looming over me."

Aila didn't move.

"Please. You'll want to be sitting down when I tell you this."

Silently, she did as he asked, sinking into a cross-legged position a few feet back from him. "Go on," she said stiffly. "I'm listening."

Cassian watched her shadowed face. It was too dark for him to make out the details of her features, yet he could sense just how on edge she was.

You don't need to tell her everything.

Was it too late to make up a plausible story? Aila wouldn't know any different. He could tell her an altered version of his tale, yet keep the immortality out of it. He could make her pity him, weep for him even.

Cassian's throat constricted. No. He wouldn't do that. It would be disrespectful to both Lilla and Aila. She demanded honesty, and his conscience wouldn't let him have a moment's peace until he spoke the truth.

Of course, it would be the death-stroke between them. She'd recoil once she knew what he really was. But that would be for the best.

Clearing his throat, Cassian inhaled slowly before speaking. "I'm not who you believe me to be. I'm not like other men." His gaze fused with hers. "I can't ... die."

"Excuse me?" Aila's voice hardened; she clearly thought he was toying with her.

"Over a thousand years ago, I marched into Caledonia with the Ninth legion of the Roman imperial army," Cassian pushed on. He'd set himself on this course now. He wouldn't stop until she knew the whole story. "We'd been sent to put down the Picts, but in the end, they bested us ... and after the final stand in the far north of this land, I was taken captive."

Aila had gone dangerously still, but she said nothing.

Cassian continued. "A Pictish druidess cursed me to an immortal life. I cannot leave the boundaries of Scotland, I cannot father children ... and I cannot die."

Aila made a soft, choked sound. "May the devil blind ye," she finally managed. "I can't believe ye would make up something like this ... just to rid yerself of me."

Cassian shook his head. "I know it sounds far-fetched ... but it's true. Every word."

"*Far-fetched?* That's a pretty word for a filthy lie!" Aila's voice rose as she scrambled to her feet.

"Wait, Aila." Reaching up, Cassian undid the leather vest that covered his chest and opened it to reveal the faded design of the eagle above his right nipple. Even in the murky light, the inked mark was clear. "I am a centurion of the Ninth ... this is the mark of my legion. I had it carved into my flesh on my twenty-first birthday."

He swallowed hard. "As I told you on the journey from Dunnottar, I grew up an orphan, running wild on the streets of Brigantium in Hispania. When they let me join the legion, it was the proudest moment of my life. I lived to serve Rome ... but that empire fell long ago, and here I remain. Cursed. Immortal."

Aila stared down at him for a long moment before her lip curled. "I can't believe I have wasted all this time longing for a deceiver such as ye." Her voice shook as rage seized her.

Cassian held her eye, something deep within his chest twisting. She didn't believe him—which called for drastic measures.

He drew the pugio from his belt.

The large, leaf-shaped blade of his dagger gleamed in the dull light. To the east, the first glimmers of dawn were teasing their way through the trees. The timing was perfect. He didn't want to do this—not least of all because it would hurt—but she wouldn't believe him otherwise.

They weren't alone in the clearing. If he revealed who he was to Aila, the other women would discover his secret too. But it couldn't be helped. Cassian's breathing quickened. He was desperate for her to believe him now. To think he'd condemned Maximus for telling a mortal woman their secret—and he'd done the same thing. But now he'd revealed who he was, he'd take this to the bitter end. He had to *show* her who he really was.

"This dagger has been with me since the beginning," he said, running his finger along its whetted blade. The pad of his finger stung as it drew blood.

Aila continued to stare at him, disgust written across her features. She clearly thought him raving now.

Cassian's fingers flexed around the handle of the pugio, and then he drew in a deep breath, bracing himself for the agony that would follow. "I'm sorry you have to see this ... but it's the only way you are going to believe me."

And then he turned the blade upon himself, gripped both hands around the hilt, and drove it straight into his heart.

Aila screamed, the terrified sound echoing through the trees.

The man had lost his wits.

Unease had stolen over her when he'd drawn the odd-shaped dagger, and her belly had tightened when he'd run his finger along the exposed blade. But she'd never anticipated his next move.

And now the dagger was buried to the hilt in the left side of his chest.

In his heart.

Bile surged up Aila's throat as she staggered back from him.

Cassian's face contorted, his eyelids fluttering in agony. "Mithras," he croaked, his jaw bunching as he arched back against the tree trunk. He then yanked the blade from his chest.

Horrified, Aila watched dark blood ooze from the wound.

"What have ye done?" Her words came out in a wail. "Cassian ... why?"

Panic surged through her, followed by a wave of nausea. Forgetting her horror, as fear for his well-being swamped her, she rushed back to him, her hands fumbling for his. Cassian had just dealt himself a mortal wound. He was about to die.

Cassian's gaze snared hers, and for a moment, the rest of the world fell away.

"It's the only way you'd believe me," he gasped, his fingers tightening around hers. "I'm sorry, Aila."

"Aila! What is it?" Lady Gavina appeared at her shoulder. Aila twisted around to see the others had rushed up behind her.

All three women stared at Cassian, horror etched upon their faces.

Still clutching Aila's hands, Cassian lay back against the oak, panting. Pain glazed his eyes.

"Ye stabbed him?" Jean demanded, horrified.

"I didn't!" Aila choked out, her gaze returning to the wound on his bare chest. "He did this to himself. I don't—"

"Watch me," Cassian cut in, his voice a dull rasp. "I should be dead by now ... but still I breathe. And with the rising of the sun, I shall be made whole once more."

Lady Elizabeth gasped. "What is the man raving about?"

"He says he's immortal," Aila replied, her voice wobbling. "And he just stabbed himself to prove it."

"Cassian." Lady Gavina moved forward, her gaze riveted upon the bleeding wound. "What possessed ye to do something so foolish?"

Cassian favored Lady De Keith with a smile that was more of a grimace. "To prove a point, My Lady. Watch now ... the sun rises."

Aila disentangled her fingers from his, swallowing down the urge to be sick. She was trembling now, for horror had chilled her blood.

But as she looked on, her heart thudding dully against her ribs, the sun crested the tops of the woodland to the east and bathed the valley in golden light. It crept over Cassian's prostrate form, and his eyes fluttered shut.

To Aila, he looked on the verge of death.

Why? The question was a silent scream within her. A boulder sat on her chest now, making it difficult to draw breath. Aye, she'd been angry and hurt that he'd spurned her, but she didn't wish him dead.

The moments drew out, and then before their eyes, the wound upon Cassian's chest started to mend.

Beside Aila, Jean gasped, while Elizabeth muttered a very unladylike oath.

Indeed, the stab-wound was knitting.

"I don't believe it," Gavina breathed. "He's actually healing."

Cassian's eyes flickered open, a grim smile stretching his lips as the wound disappeared entirely, leaving only bare, unblemished skin. Even the blood he'd lost was gone. It was as if he'd never stabbed himself.

"Lord have mercy on us all." Gavina shifted closer still and then reached out, touching the spot with her fingertips, as if to make sure her eyes weren't deceiving her. "What is the meaning of this?"

"I'm immortal, My Lady," Cassian murmured. However, his gaze was now upon Aila. "I was cursed over a thousand years ago. Aila wanted to know why I pushed her away, why I can't give her my heart ... and this is the reason." His attention never wavered. "I had a wife once. We lived together for fifty years before old age took her from me. I thought I knew what binding myself to her meant ... but I didn't understand what it is to remain young and healthy while the woman you love withers before you. And when she died, I wasn't prepared for the agony. It broke me ... and I swore I'd never love like that again."

Silence followed this explanation, interrupted only by the twittering of the early dawn chorus. Aila stared at Cassian. She understood his words, yet she could barely take them in. She was still reeling from the fact that he'd stabbed himself and then healed with the rising of the sun.

Heart galloping, she slowly reached out and, like Lady Gavina, touched the place where he'd stabbed himself. The skin was warm, healthy.

She couldn't take it in.

"Ye are the devil," Jean whispered, a tremble in her voice. "Only Satan could rise from the dead like that."

Cassian huffed a humorless laugh before pushing himself up and relacing his vest. "I wish that were true, Jean," he murmured. "It would certainly make for a happier existence than my current one."

"Lucifer!" Jean's tone turned shrill now.

Aila tore her attention from Cassian to see that Jean was backing away, pointing an accusing finger at him. "The Angel of Darkness is among us."

"I'm not the devil," Cassian replied, impatience creeping into his tone. "I've already explained what I am."

Jean's pointed finger started to shake. Her face was a mask of revulsion. Aila tensed. Jean had been through a lot in the past two days. She'd lost her lover, been forced to flee through the wilderness, and had now watched a man rise from the dead. It was too much for her.

"Jean," Aila moved toward the maid, reaching for her. "Please, calm yerself."

Jean shook her off. "Ye spread yer legs for him ... that makes ye Satan's consort."

Elizabeth drew in a shocked breath at this revelation; clearly, Lady Gavina hadn't told her about Aila and Cassian.

Aila's cheeks flamed, and she recoiled as if burned. She hadn't expected Jean to turn on her.

"Enough, lass." Elizabeth turned to her maid, her tone sharp. "We don't need yer hysteria on top of everything else. Get ahold of yerself."

"I'll not stay in his presence." Jean continued to back away from Cassian, her gaze flicking from face to face. "And if ye do, he'll steal yer souls away."

And with that, the young woman turned on her heel and fled.

"Jean!" Elizabeth started after her. "Wait!"

XXIX

A LONELY THING

AILA AND GAVINA remained under the oak with Cassian. Both women were seated now. The shock of this discovery had made Aila's legs go weak. She wasn't sure she could actually get up and walk away.

"We should go after them," Aila said after a long pause. "Jean will come to grief on her own."

"You won't catch her," Cassian replied, a wry edge to his voice. "And she'd rather starve out in the wild than suffer Lucifer's company. We can't force her to remain with us."

Aila rounded on him. "How can you make light of this?"

He merely cocked an eyebrow in response.

Gavina cleared her throat. "So, this is real, Cassian? Ye haven't just worked some elaborate trick for our benefit?"

He shook his head. "I'm not a warlock, My Lady. The only power I wield is to heal from my injuries ... age and sickness don't touch me, but I can't enchant anyone." His attention shifted back to Aila. He was watching her warily, as if he expected her to turn on him again. "Are you afraid of me, Aila?" he asked softly.

She held his gaze, not sure how to respond. Truthfully, she didn't know. Unlike Jean, she wasn't convinced he was Satan or a demon of any kind—but at the same time, she didn't understand any of this.

Wordlessly she shook her head, and his features relaxed. He leaned back against the tree trunk, closing his eyes. Suddenly, he seemed tired, despite his youthful appearance. It was a weariness that had nothing to do with physical exhaustion.

He was fatigued by life.

"How old were ye, when ye were ... cursed?" Gavina asked, breaking the heavy silence.

"Twenty-eight," Cassian replied. His eyes remained closed. It was clear he didn't want to continue speaking about himself.

Sensing this, Lady Gavina rose to her feet, cast Aila a penetrating look, and then moved out from under the oak's canopy. "Let's all get some rest," Gavina advised. "We've still got a lot of ground to cover."

Aila nodded before she shifted a little farther away from Cassian. She then stretched out on her side. The shock of everything crashed into her. Weariness descended like a heavy cloak, pressing her down into the ground.

She still had questions for Cassian, yet she didn't have the energy to interrogate him at present.

I'll just close my eyes for a few moments, she promised herself. *And then I'll face him again.*

Aila rose slowly from a deep sleep. Her eyes were gritty, and her head felt as if it were stuffed full of wool. With a groan, she rolled over onto her back and rubbed a hand over her face. She'd only meant to doze, but the fogginess behind her eyes told her that she'd been asleep for a while.

"I was wondering when you'd wake up," a male voice greeted her. "I've never seen anyone sleep so soundly."

Tensing, Aila removed her hand from her face and inclined her head, focusing upon Cassian. He still sat, leaning up against the oak, watching her.

Around them, the sun blazed over the shallow valley where they'd taken refuge. However, under the oak's protective canopy, it was cool and shaded.

"What time is it?" she asked groggily, propping herself up on her elbows.

"Mid-afternoon," he replied. "I've just been out scouting again. I climbed up onto a ridge and caught sight of riders far to the west ... moving in our direction. We will have to move on soon, if we want to have any chance of escaping them."

Aila sat up, her gaze shifting to the creek that meandered through the vale, where Elizabeth and Gavina sat. The ladies appeared deep in conversation, their heads bowed together.

"Where's Jean?" she asked.

"Lady Elizabeth lost her in the trees."

Aila glanced back at Cassian. He wore a shuttered expression, viewing her under hooded lids. He was watching how she'd react to him now.

Aila breathed a curse and scrubbed her face with the back of her hand. "She shouldn't be out there on her own."

Cassian gave a soft snort.

Aila's brow furrowed. "What if the English catch her?"

"That's a possibility."

Her frown deepened. "Ye are acting like ye don't care."

"She made her choice, Aila. You can't shield her from that."

"But she was afraid."

"And so are you ... but you didn't behave as she did ... and neither did Elizabeth or Gavina."

Aila went still. Of course, he thought she was frightened of him. In truth, after his revelation, her skin had crawled at the idea that she'd actually lain with him.

The man was over a thousand years old after all.

It was unnatural. It was wrong. And yet, his gaze this afternoon was warm upon her skin. She could almost believe that she'd dreamed that awful scene. He hadn't really stabbed himself in the heart, had he?

Cassian's belly rumbled then, making him wince.

"What's wrong?" Aila asked.

"I'm starving," he muttered. "It always happens after I recover from a mortal wound ... I get the appetite of a famished hound."

"But we don't have any food."

"No." His belly growled once more, as if in protest this time.

Their gazes held for a few moments, and then Cassian reached out and ran his hand down the scarred bark of the great oak that sheltered them. "This tree is old," he murmured. "Around the same age as me, I'd say." He paused then, his fingers flexing against the bark. "It's dying."

Aila stiffened and glanced around her. "How can ye tell?"

"Some of the branches are withered. They say that oaks take five hundred years to grow and five hundred to die. This ancient beauty has stood here for a thousand years, but its time is coming to an end."

Aila inclined her head, studying his face. "Ye sound wistful."

"I am ... it's a lonely thing, Aila ... living forever."

She bit her bottom lip, fighting the sympathy that welled up within her now.

Ye are too soft-hearted, lass, she chided herself. And it was true. When Cassian had told the sad tale of the woman he'd loved and lost, her anger toward him had dissolved.

The enigma had been solved. Cassian was so full of contradictions; she'd known he was holding something back, but she would never have guessed the real reason.

And somehow, the truth—as outlandish as it was—set her free.

He'd been trying to protect her.

Careful, she cautioned herself. *This changes nothing.*

With this reminder firmly in place, she rose to her feet and brushed the leaves off her skirts. "So, the curse can never be broken?"

He glanced up, spearing her with a frank hazel-eyed gaze that still robbed her of breath. "Well that's the thing, Aila," he murmured. "It can."

She ran until her lungs felt as if they were on fire, until her legs trembled under her and she was forced to halt. Bent double, Jean sucked in deep breaths of air.

She'd done it.

Lady Elizabeth had tried to catch up with her, but Jean was younger and faster. She'd sped off through the trees, twisting and turning like a hunted doe. Eventually, her mistress's cries for her to stop faded.

After a while, all she could hear was the whisper of the breeze through the trees.

Lady Elizabeth had abandoned the chase.

Holding her side, for a stitch stabbed her through the ribs, Jean straightened up, grimacing.

She couldn't believe those foolish women had remained with that demon. They'd been as shocked as her when he'd healed from a mortal wound to his heart with the coming of the dawn. Yet they'd all just stood there like lackwits.

Jean's mouth twisted. She wouldn't be surprised if he'd robbed them all of their souls by now.

Whispering a prayer under her breath, Jean crossed herself. Her mother had always warned her that the devil appeared in many guises and one must be constantly on one's guard.

How right she was.

The thud of hoof-beats shattered the woodland's hush then, followed by the snapping of twigs.

Jean froze. She was trying to decide what to do, when a group of men on horseback burst through the trees. Their glittering hauberks and white cloaks immediately gave them away, and Jean's breathing hitched.

The English.

A big knight atop a charcoal destrier reined up in front of her. The beast pawed the ground, and Jean shrank back. Staring up at the knight's helmed face, she felt her knees wobble under her. He had cold, grey eyes.

"Qui êtes vous?" The knight barked.

Jean shook her head and backed away from him. She knew a little French, but fear robbed her of the power of speech.

One of the men called out something, and the knight's wintry gaze narrowed as he observed her.

He'd obviously just learned who she was.

He swung down from the saddle and advanced on her, a gauntleted hand reaching out to grasp her by the arm. He then growled something else, and Jean's blood ran cold.

A scream rose in her throat, and she stumbled backward. For the first time since fleeing her companions, she regretted her behavior.

"Please, help me," she gasped. "If ye want the Scots, I can take ye to them ... but please spare my life."

However, as she gazed up at the huge knight and his terrifying, iron-clad face, despair twisted in her chest. Foolishly, she'd run from the arms of one devil to another.

XXX

UPON THE HILLTOP

AILA FOLLOWED HER companions out of the woodland and across gently undulating hills. A cool breeze tugged at her hair out in the open; they had been sheltered from the wind in the trees, but now that they were traveling through more exposed country, she was glad of the woolen cloak about her shoulders. The dusk was setting, making the air grow colder still.

They'd set off before nightfall this time, a somber party of four instead of five.

None of them mentioned Jean, although Elizabeth wore a pinched, haunted expression.

Both Gavina and Elizabeth had kept their distance from Cassian since the incident earlier that day. However, like Aila, they continued to travel with him. They all knew they'd never reach Dunnottar without his assistance.

And as before, Cassian strode ahead, his gaze scanning their surroundings. He'd doubled back earlier, his face grim when he returned to the women. "They're gaining on us," he'd reported.

Aila glanced around nervously as she walked. *I hope Jean is safe wherever she is.* It felt exposed out here on the hills, especially after traveling through woodland for the past two days. However, she imagined this new terrain was a good sign.

Surely, they were approaching De Keith territory?

Glancing up, she saw the moon had risen, clouds racing before its silvery face. Although once their eyes adjusted to the darkness, they could see well enough.

Cassian certainly seemed confident that they were heading in the right direction.

Of course he does. The man's spent the last millennium in this land.

The thought made a shiver ripple down her spine. She couldn't imagine what it was like to live that long. What things must he have witnessed over the years? He would have seen the land of the Pict kingdoms turn into Alba and then into Scotland. And all the while, he was trapped here.

But there was a way out.

The bandrui who'd cursed him had provided him with a riddle to solve, and just one line remained.

It had made little sense to Aila, even when Cassian told her the meaning of all but the last line.

Her gaze shifted then from the waxing moon, to the fire-tailed star that stood out brightly against the black curtain of night.

The Broom-star, Cassian had called it.

Folk at Dunnottar had been talking about the star since late spring. Many said that its appearance heralded change, although David De Keith had been obsessed that it was an ill-portent. But the fiery star was of no concern to him now.

The laird had sealed his own fate the moment he'd drawn a knife on the English king.

Aila's mouth thinned. An idiotic act they were all going to pay for.

She broke away from the ladies now, walking but a few yards behind Cassian. As if sensing her nearness, he slowed his pace and allowed her to catch him up.

"How far are we from Dunnottar?" she asked.

"It lies in that direction." He pointed to the north-eastern horizon. "And if we keep walking at our current pace, we'll reach it around dawn."

Relief suffused Aila, and she let out a sigh.

Cassian cut her another look then, this one veiled. "You are a resilient lass, Aila."

She arched an eyebrow in response. "Well, Lady Gavina and Lady Elizabeth have both weathered the shock ... I wasn't going to let them show me up."

He nodded. "Over the years, I've noticed that women are often stronger than men ... especially in the darkest of times." He paused there. "When I arrived in this land, and we faced the Picts ... many women fought among them."

Aila's gaze widened. "Women warriors?"

He favored her with a weary smile. "Terrifying they were too."

Aila took this in, her skin prickling in delight. How different things were these days. Ladies like Gavina and Elizabeth lived cloistered existences, while most other women spent their lives toiling and bearing bairns. She'd never heard of a woman picking up arms and fighting alongside her menfolk. She'd always thought women lacked the physical strength and the killer instinct that made men so dangerous.

"This news surprises you?" Cassian asked, his smile warming.

"Aye ... I'm just trying to imagine such a thing," she murmured. "And I admit, I have difficulty."

"Times were different back then ... Scotland has changed much with the centuries." He paused, slowing his pace a little and moving closer to her. "I owe you a number of apologies, Aila."

She huffed, but didn't contradict him.

"I hurt you."

Aila tensed. "Ye did, but I'd prefer to look forward now," she replied, injecting a crisp tone she didn't really feel into her voice.

"I know you do, but I'm sorry nonetheless. I also ask your forgiveness for what I did in that valley ... it would have been a gruesome thing to witness."

Aila sucked in a breath. "It was."

"I was desperate, but I should have warned you."

Aila shot him a rueful look. "It wouldn't have made any difference ... seeing a man stab himself in the heart would never have been pleasant, even if you'd announced your intention first."

Cassian snorted and opened his mouth to say something else. However, instead he came to an abrupt halt.

"What is it?" Aila stared up at his face, all hollows and angles in the moonlight.

Cassian knelt and placed a hand flat upon the ground. "Horses," he said, his tone hardening. "They've caught up with us."

At that moment, the rumble of thundering hoof-beats cut through the night air.

"Gavina, Elizabeth!" Cassian called out. "To me ... now!"

The ladies rushed forward, their faces taut and pale.

"Get behind me," he instructed. "All of you."

The three women did as bid. Cassian then drew the dagger from his belt and handed it to Aila.

"You may have to use this." Cassian's gaze gleamed as he stared down at her. "Wait till your attacker is close and then go for the throat or eyes ... their torsos will be protected by chainmail, so don't try to stab them there."

Aila's heart started to pound a tattoo against her ribs. She wasn't sure she could stab anyone. *If only I were a fearless Pict warrior woman.* But pushing down her fear, Aila nodded.

There was no more time for talk then, for dark shapes emerged from the night and barreled toward them.

"Lord have mercy on us," Elizabeth whispered from behind her. "They're going to run us down."

Even Cassian couldn't protect them from being trampled by warhorses.

Aila gripped the dagger's handle tightly and braced herself for impact.

Cassian watched the horses approach, chainmail and steel glinting. He'd drawn his sword and was ready for them, even if the knowledge that this was going to hurt turned his belly sour.

It would be worse for the women he was trying to protect.

I've failed. Pain lanced across his chest.

But at the last moment, the riders pulled up, their huge destriers snorting and squealing. They then drew out in a circle around the man and three women who stood upon the hilltop.

"Did you really think you'd outrun us?" A deep voice boomed through the night. A massive knight drew up his warhorse a few yards back from Cassian. He spoke French. When Cassian didn't reply, the man gave a low, humorless chuckle. "We found your friend. The woman was witless ... kept screaming that she'd fled Lucifer." A heavy gaze settled upon Cassian. "Was she speaking about you?"

"It seems so," Cassian replied, his voice cool and even.

"What have you done to Jean?" Elizabeth shouted.

"She's dead," the knight said flatly, swinging down from his horse. "The king has ordered that you all die."

Elizabeth choked back a sob, while Lady Gavina whispered a prayer.

Cassian's lips thinned. Prayers weren't going to save any of them now. He kept his attention riveted upon the knight. The man drew the heavy broadsword from his side, and the sound of steel scraping against leather rent the night.

Drawing in a deep, steadying breath, Cassian readied himself for combat. He would fight to the bitter end, but that wouldn't help these three women.

Aila's going to die.

Cassian's belly clenched into a hard ball. Being immortal didn't give him the power of ten men. He could still feel pain, could still be brought to his knees by injuries. They could cut him to pieces, and he'd still heal with the rising of the sun—but Aila, Gavina, and Elizabeth wouldn't.

And when he rose from the dead, he'd find the mutilated bodies of the women he'd failed to keep safe.

The big knight came at him then. He wielded the broadsword double-handed, the heavy blade slicing through the air.

One of the women screamed. It was a heart-rending, chilling sound that carried far across these lonely hills.

Gritting his teeth, Cassian swung his gladius high and lunged forward.

XXXI

MERCY

THE MOMENT THE huge knight swung for Cassian, Aila's heart leaped into her throat.

We're doomed.

At least half a dozen more men had dismounted and now encircled them. Closing in like wolves, they drew their swords, but didn't attack—not yet. Once their leader brought down the women's protector, it would be over.

But Cassian wasn't so easily beaten. Aila shifted close to the ladies. However, her gaze remained riveted upon him.

Gilded by moonlight, he feinted, parried, and attacked with a fluidity that was breathtaking to watch. His blade became little more than a silver blur. He fought like a man who'd had years to practice—an ancient warrior.

Cassian was a big man, but his opponent was huge, and he wielded a lethal broadsword. Yet, Cassian brought him to his knees with a vicious stab to the leg.

The knight roared, swinging his blade around to intercept Cassian's next strike just in time. He then bellowed, "Attaque!"

The surrounding men moved. An English soldier leaped toward Aila before Cassian intercepted him and drove his short, sharp blade into the man's throat.

But the first knight wasn't done for yet. He lunged to his feet with a roar and swung at Cassian's neck.

He'd have decapitated him, but Cassian ducked, and the blade whistled overhead.

Suddenly, Cassian was surrounded on all sides. He hissed as one of the English blades found its mark, cutting through his chainmail.

Aila's knees threatened to buckle, a cry rising in her throat.

She knew he couldn't die, but she didn't want to see him cut to pieces in front of her either. Not only that, but he was the only thing standing between them and the English soldiers.

Heedless, Cassian fought on, savage now.

But it was hopeless. They all knew it.

Gavina screamed, and Aila twisted around to see that one of the soldiers had grabbed her. He had hold of Gavina's hair and was dragging her away while she kicked and clawed at him.

Terror jolted through Aila.

He's going to rape her! I have to do something.

The knife didn't sit easily in Aila's hand, yet she tightened her fingers around the hilt and gathered her courage. Gavina fought the soldier like a hell-cat, clawing, biting, and kicking. Her fury was slowing him, but if Aila didn't act now, it would be too late.

Jaw clenched, she flew at the soldier—and slashed him across the throat.

The feel of steel slicing through flesh made Aila's stomach heave, but she went through with it, reeling back as darkness bloomed across his pale throat.

Eyes startling white in the hoary light of the moon, the soldier stared at her an instant, his mouth working in a soundless curse. And then he crumpled.

Gavina's breathing came in rasping sobs as she scrambled away from her attacker. Wild-eyed, she clutched at Aila and Elizabeth, and the three women clung together. But men closed in on them on all sides now, cutting them off from Cassian.

Aila gripped the dagger tighter still, although she was shaking so violently that she wasn't sure she'd be able to wield it. All the advancing soldiers were wary of her now.

The man nearest grimaced, his teeth flashing white in the darkness before he muttered something in a tone that needed no translation.

Aila broke into a cold sweat, a sob rising within her. She wanted to be brave, but these men terrified her.

And then the twang of a bow-string cut through the night.

The soldier who was just moments from making a grab for Aila stiffened. His face then contorted in agony, and his knees gave way beneath him. When he toppled forward, Aila spied a fletched arrow embedded between his shoulder blades. It had pierced the chainmail.

Out of the darkness, the silhouettes of men appeared. Prowling close, they drew a net around the cluster of figures standing upon the brow of the hill.

Aila choked back a whimper. Her heart was beating so wildly now she couldn't hear anything else. She moved forward, shielding Elizabeth and Gavina. However, the dagger she held out before her shook.

Were these men friend or foe? She wouldn't let her guard down, for they could easily be outlaws looking for unsuspecting travelers on the hills.

But as she looked on, steel flashed, and the dark-clad men engaged the English soldiers.

Aila spied Cassian then. He'd just managed to kill the huge knight who led the patrol. Sweat glistened upon Cassian's face when he straightened up, gasping for breath. His gaze swung left and right, taking in the scene around him.

The choking sounds of dying men echoed over the hillside as the newcomers finished off the remaining English.

One of the English soldiers threw down his sword and sank to his knees.

"Pitié!" The man gasped. "Je me rends!"

Aila's French was very poor, but even she understood the soldier. He was pleading for mercy, surrendering himself to them.

A dark shape emerged from the night, and a man clad in a rippling cloak strode toward the kneeling soldier.

In the moonlight, Aila saw that the soldier had removed his helm. He was young—barely older than seventeen winters at most.

Barely more than a lad, and yet a man all the same.

And as the newcomer neared, he pushed back the cowl that hid his identity.

Aila sucked in a breath. She recognized him.

It was Draco. The Wallace's right-hand. A patrol from Dunnottar had found them.

Approaching the English soldier, Draco's hawkish gaze fastened upon the man's face.

"S'il vous plait," the young man gasped, his voice breaking. "Aies pitié!"

But Draco didn't answer. Instead, he drew the dagger at his waist and struck.

The English soldier gave a soft, choking gasp and then crumpled to the ground, his throat cut.

Suddenly, there was no sound but the wind whistling across the hilltop. Draco wiped his knife off on his cloak and then resheathed his blade, his gaze surveying the three women clinging together.

Cassian staggered across to where Aila still stood before the ladies. He moved awkwardly, favoring his right side. His gaze traveled down the length of her body, checking for injuries, before it rested upon the bloodied dagger she still gripped.

Cassian met Aila's eye then, and he managed a tight smile. "I knew I could rely on you, Aila."

"Drag the corpses into a pile and burn them."

The men of Wallace's patrol got to work. Sitting on the brow of the hill, hunched over the deep wound in his left flank, Cassian listened to Draco's voice carrying through the predawn stillness. The patrol dragged the bodies of the fallen English soldiers into the gully below and lay them upon a pyre of dry reeds before setting it alight.

Cassian sat, unmoving, watching the smoke snake up into the cobalt sky. The Broom-star was fading from sight. The sunrise wasn't far off.

Once he'd overseen his men, Draco joined Cassian on the hilltop. "Norris reached us at Dunnottar," he murmured, shifting to Latin so the women seated nearby couldn't catch his words. "The Hammer isn't what we thought it was?"

Cassian shook his head, grimacing. The throbbing in his side made him feel sick; dawn couldn't come soon enough. "It's not the 'Battle Hammer' that will strike Dunnottar," he agreed between gritted teeth. "But Edward, the 'Hammer of the Scots'. And if Longshanks didn't have a good reason to attack Dunnottar before, he does now … De Keith tried to kill him and got his throat cut for his trouble."

Draco's gaze widened as he took in this news. He then flashed Cassian a grin, his teeth white in the dim light. "It looks like the Wallace is about to meet his old foe again."

Cassian grunted. "If he's wise, he'll leave Dunnottar. Longshanks wants his guts."

Draco chuckled, although the sound had no humor in it. "No chance of that … you know how much that man loves a good scrap."

Blood stained the peaty earth, the offal stench of it making Aila's already delicate stomach churn all the more. With the rising of the sun, the slaughter around them upon the hill became evident.

Cassian sat a few feet away with Draco, his face pale, his features pinched. He'd suffered a deep cut to his flank. But as the first glimmers of sun touched him, his expression relaxed, and he no longer hunched over.

Just like the morning before, he was healed and whole once more.

Aila watched the two men converse quietly. She wondered if Draco would question Cassian about his injuries. Would he be surprised to see his friend healed so quickly?

Dark smoke wreathed up in the gully below from the pyre, staining the lightening sky. Elizabeth watched it, her face grim. However, Aila noted that Gavina's attention was upon Draco, a deep crease etched between her finely arched eyebrows.

"Why didn't ye show him mercy?" She eventually spoke up, her cool voice cutting through the dawn hush.

Draco glanced toward the lady, his own brow furrowing. "Excuse me?"

"That lad asked for clemency," she continued, holding his gaze. "Why didn't ye give it to him?"

Draco shrugged. "That *lad* would have raped you if given the chance, *My Lady*."

Gavina stiffened. Her cornflower-blue eyes shadowed.

When she didn't reply, Draco frowned. "Is that the thanks I get for coming to your rescue?"

"Of course I'm grateful for yer assistance," Gavina replied stiffly." Her face had gone taut. "But when a man goes down on his knees and surrenders ... it is honorable to spare his life."

Draco's mouth twisted. "Honorable?"

"That's enough, Draco," Cassian cut in, a warning edge to his voice.

Draco snorted, yet heeded his friend.

Another silence settled upon the hill-top—this one fragile. Gavina turned her attention away from Cassian and Draco, her gaze traveling toward the north-eastern horizon. The Lady of Dunnottar's expression was now shuttered. Aila sensed she wished she were already home—far away from all this brutality and bloodshed.

The hush drew out, and then Cassian and Draco resumed speaking once more. Aila had overheard them exchange a few words earlier, and once again she realized they conversed in another tongue.

She watched them for a few moments before stillness crept over her. Her breathing slowed, suspicion flowering.

Cassian. Draco. Maximus. Latin names. Friends who'd come together at Dunnottar. Foreign men who'd made Scotland their home.

Aila's breathing quickened. Her thoughts started to whirl. "Cassian," she gasped. "Ye aren't the only one who's immortal ... are ye?"

Cassian's attention cut to her, his face suddenly strained. Next to him, alarm flared in Draco's dark eyes. He flinched, as if Aila had just struck him, before he turned to his friend, his voice rough. "You told them?"

Cassian nodded. "My hand was forced."

Aila stared at the two men. "Maximus too?" she demanded.

The merest nod of Cassian's chin confirmed her fear. Her pulse started to gallop.

Does Heather know about this?

She remembered her sister's shadowed gaze when Aila had revealed her feelings for Cassian, and how she'd tried to steer Aila away from him.

Suddenly, everything fell into place.

Of course, Heather knew.

Heat ignited in Aila's belly. *She knew, and she didn't say anything.*

Draco muttered a curse, turning on Cassian. "What's wrong with you?" he snarled. "Why don't you find yourself a tower to shout it from, man?"

Fortunately for him, the five of them were alone on the hilltop for the moment; Draco's men were still busy tending to the pyre they'd lit.

Cassian cast his friend an apologetic look but didn't defend himself.

Aila shared a glance with Gavina and Elizabeth. This all seemed unreal.

Lady Gavina then shifted her attention to Draco, understanding flickering across her face. "No wonder ye are so ruthless," she murmured. "Immortality has made ye so."

XXXII

NOT MY SECRET TO TELL

"YOU'VE GOT MUCK for brains."

"Clearly."

Draco and Cassian walked side-by-side over the last hill before Dunnottar. In front of them, the fortress rose against the morning sky. Gulls wheeled, screeching overhead. The two men led the way, a few yards ahead of Gavina, Elizabeth, and Aila, while the rest of Wallace's patrol brought up the rear.

"I don't understand," Draco continued, scowling. "All these years, you've been the most guarded of the three of us. What compelled you to tell those women?"

Cassian didn't reply immediately. Truthfully, he didn't feel like sharing anything with Draco at present. Nonetheless, he knew his friend wouldn't let the matter drop.

"Things got ... complicated," he murmured.

"What kind of fool answer is that?"

"Stop being an arse, Draco. I'll tell you when I'm ready."

Draco's dark brows knitted together as he continued to study Cassian. "You've fallen for one of them, haven't you?"

Cassian tensed. His pulse quickened as the full weight of Draco's accusation hit him.

He had.

"Please tell me it's not that haughty bitch ... I'd credit you with better taste than that."

"Lady Gavina rules Dunnottar now," Cassian replied, casting Draco a quelling look. "Try to be a little less insulting."

"Hades, you aren't in love with *her*?"

"No," Cassian snapped, his temper fraying. "It's ... Aila."

Draco stumbled, his eyes flying wide. A moment passed, and then a hard smile stretched his face. "So, you've started ravishing virgins now?" He glanced over his shoulder, looking back at the women, before turning his incredulous gaze on Cassian once more. "You horny hound!"

Cassian cast him a dark look, but Draco laughed, not remotely cowed. "Serves you right ... always preaching to us about how to behave with women. Max is going to love this."

Cassian drew in a deep, steadying breath in an attempt to rein in his quickening temper. "No doubt ... but he won't be as irritating as you."

Their gazes fused before Draco's mouth twitched once more. "I haven't seen any tender words or longing looks pass between you though ... things aren't going well?"

Cassian shook his head. He shifted his gaze back to Dunnottar's solid curtain wall. "I ended things before she found out about my immortality. Just as well ... I need to focus at the moment ... we all do. I imagine we can expect a visit from Edward soon."

Chaos reigned the moment they entered the lower ward bailey. Guards and residents of the keep rushed out to meet them. News that Lady Gavina had returned—but without her husband or escort—had raced through the keep. Rows of guards stationed high on the walls turned from their posts, their gazes sweeping over the ragged party that had just arrived.

Aila stood in the cobbled expanse while an excited crowd swirled around her. Legs, back, and feet aching, she looked for an escape. But, for the moment, she was hemmed in. Her belly was hollowed out in hunger, and she desperately needed to slake her thirst. However, she had to go to her parents and sister first.

Her attention shifted to the archway leading into the keep, where a huge man with wild dark hair emerged.

Wallace's heavy-featured face creased into a scowl as he surveyed the ragged party who'd returned with his men.

Behind him, a maid stepped out into the breezy morning, a bairn perched upon her hip. The lad—brown-haired and apple-cheeked—struggled to be let down. Even at three winters old, wee Robbie De Keith, was showing an independent spirit.

"Ma!" The lad had spotted Lady Elizabeth and was waving frantically to her. With a long-suffering grimace, the maid set the bairn onto his feet.

Elizabeth picked up her skirts and pushed her way through the fray, scooping Robbie up into her arms and spinning him around.

Aila's throat constricted when she saw that Elizabeth's cheeks were wet with tears. She'd risked never returning to her son. Not only that, but the disastrous turn of events had put her husband—Robbie's father—in grave danger.

Shifting her gaze to where Lady Gavina stood next to Cassian, Aila saw a weary expression settle over her mistress's face. This wasn't the return she'd envisaged. There would be a lot of explaining to do.

William Wallace approached now, his expression formidable. His gaze never wavered from Gavina. "What happened, My Lady?"

The Lady of Dunnottar swallowed before huffing a bitter laugh. Around her, the chattering crowd quietened. "Where to start, William?"

"Why didn't ye tell me?"

Heather stiffened at Aila's aggressive tone. "It wasn't my secret to tell."

Aila clenched her jaw. Part of her knew that Heather was right, but another part still stung with betrayal. "I thought we'd cleared the air after yer return to Dunnottar," she continued doggedly. "But still ye persist in keeping things from me."

Heather's eyes shadowed. "That's not true, Aila. I was trying to *protect* ye."

The pair of them stood in the tiny walled garden atop the castle's upper ward. A sheltered spot, it was usually the most peaceful corner of the keep. However, today, the chatter of excited voices echoed up from the lower ward, mingling with the ever-present hammering that drifted up from Galbraith's forge. The smith now had a group of lads working with him to keep up with the sheer volume of sword and dirk blades required to kit out the swelling number of warriors within the keep.

Aila had followed her sister outdoors after being reunited with her family. Iona had burst into tears when she'd heard what had befallen them in Stirling. Donnan was still trying to calm her.

A bee buzzed past the sisters, traveling from a pale-pink rose bush to a clump of lavender.

Aila folded her arms across her chest in an attempt to hold onto her anger. She didn't want to argue with her sister, not after the ordeal of the past few days.

Heather stepped close. "Now ye know why I was cautious when ye told me how ye felt about Cassian. He's a good man, Aila ... but the curse upon him is a heavy weight to bear." Her gaze narrowed. "Ye've lain with him, haven't ye?"

Aila nodded, not trusting herself to speak. Hot tears suddenly prickled the back of her eyelids. She hadn't wept since their flight from Stirling, but seeing Heather again made her defenses crumble.

Heather's features tightened. "When?"

"In Stirling ... before I learned his secret," Aila admitted, her voice hoarse now. "He ended things between us the following morning."

Heather's eyes deepened from grey-green to emerald, a sure sign she was angry. "He took advantage of ye?"

Aila shook her head. She knew what her sister thought, and she had to put her right. "No, Heather. It was me. On the journey to Stirling, I sensed that he was attracted to me but reluctant to act upon it. A woman at the castle, the steward's wife, gave me advice. She told me that if I wanted him, I had to take the initiative." Aila broke off there, her throat suddenly tight. "And so ... I did." Heather's eyes widened at this admission, yet Aila plowed on. It was best that Heather knew the whole embarrassing story; she wouldn't confide in anyone else. "I went to his door at night and gave myself to him."

Silence fell in the garden, the shouting of men on the surrounding walls now intruding. A sea breeze feathered through Heather's thick brown hair as she studied her younger sister. If Aila hadn't felt so miserable, she'd have smiled at her sister's flummoxed expression.

"Ye *seduced* him?" Heather asked finally, incredulous.

Aila's belly clenched. Put like that, it sounded awful, and yet it wasn't far from the truth. "I suppose so," she said weakly.

Heather raised an eyebrow, casting an assessing eye over her sister. She then favored Aila with a wide smile. "Don't look so worried. I'm hardly going to judge ye for yer boldness ... especially after my own behavior of late."

Heat flamed across Aila's cheeks. "Maybe not, but I judge myself. I acted like a right goose."

Heather's smile faded. Stepping closer still, she held out her hands and waited while her sister uncrossed her arms and took them. "Only an unlived life is absent of mistakes," she said softly. "Ye let yer passions rule ye for a short while." Heather's mouth curved. "And ye wouldn't be the first soul to do so."

Aila gazed back at her sister, her fingers tightening around Heather's. This was what she'd missed, this closeness between them. Ever since her return to Dunnottar, Heather had been guarding Maximus's secret, but now that Aila knew, there was no longer any reserve between them.

"I feel like such a fool," she whispered then, her vision misting. "I'm in love with an immortal—a man I can't have."

Heather's eyes glittered in response. She blinked furiously as her own tears welled. "Ye forget, I too fell for an immortal," she murmured back.

An ache rose in Aila's breast. "And Maximus risked all to be with ye ... despite that the curse isn't yet broken."

"Aye, but his story is different to Cassian's. Ye do know about his wife?"

Aila nodded. "She died a long time ago, Heather," she replied softly. It was time she faced the truth, as hurtful as it was. "He doesn't want me ... he never did."

"I didn't realize De Keith had it in him," William Wallace's deep voice rumbled across the laird's solar.

"De Keith wasn't a brave man," Cassian replied. "But he had an ambitious streak."

The Wallace turned from where he'd been staring out the window, fixing Cassian with an incredulous stare. "Ye think he did it for glory?"

Cassian pursed his lips. He stood by the hearth, with its glow warming the back of his legs. Frankly, he wanted only to escape to the solitude of his quarters, but this conversation couldn't wait. Lady Gavina had just left them after telling Wallace the story of their ill-fated visit to Stirling. Hollow-eyed from exhaustion, the lady had retired to her quarters, where servants had prepared a hot bath for her. "It's likely," he replied. "David felt overshadowed by his warrior brother ... he had something to prove."

Wallace snorted. His gaze fixed upon Cassian then. "Did ye manage to learn anything of Longshanks' plans ... or did De Keith ruin that too?"

"Our investigations were cut short. I'm afraid the mission was largely a failure ... but Comyn did reveal some things that might interest you," Cassian replied cautiously. He observed Wallace's expression as he said the Guardian of Scotland's name, but the outlaw's face gave nothing away. "Comyn says that Longshanks isn't planning to attack the north yet ... not for a while at least." Cassian paused there. "However, after David's act, I wouldn't be surprised if Edward's plans have changed." Of course, the riddle confirmed that the Hammer of the Scots would soon strike Dunnottar. Yet how could Cassian explain this to the Wallace?

Wallace listened, his gaze gleaming. "Aye, I'd say ye are right, Captain. Still, since we're already preparing for Irvine's 'Battle Hammer', we'll be ready for Longshanks as well when he does come. What else did Comyn tell ye?"

"The king's son, Edward, Prince of Wales, also has a taste for conquering ... and is doing a fine job of subduing the south-west. Scotland has more than Longshanks to worry about in the future." Wallace scowled at this, but Cassian continued. "Finally, Edward is as arrogant as the tales boast ... however, there are two Scots that concern him. He worries about the ambitions of Robert Bruce."

Wallace took this in with a shrug, before he grinned. "And the second bothersome Scot?" With a jolt, Cassian realized that he already knew the answer.

"Longshanks nurses a deep hatred for you, Wallace," Cassian confirmed. "He wants to see you hanged."

To his surprise, the big man laughed—a loud boom of mirth that rolled off the surrounding stone.

Cassian quirked an eyebrow. "Not many men laugh in the face of death," he observed.

"Every man dies ... not every man really lives," Wallace answered, sobering. "When I meet my maker, I'll do so knowing I gave my all to this life. I'd gladly die a thousand times over for Scotland."

Cassian stilled. *Brave words, Wallace ... but would you?* Moments passed, and then he cleared his throat. "All the same ... do you really want to be at Dunnottar when Edward of England arrives?"

The fleeting humor faded from Wallace's eyes, replaced with an iron look of resolve. "Aye," he replied roughly. "There's no place I'd rather be right now."

XXXIII

WORDS ON THE WALL

"I'M SO TIRED of this," Draco growled. "We'll never solve that damn riddle."

"We're *all* tired," Maximus replied frowning, "but we're so close now ... I can almost taste it." He glanced over at where Cassian leaned against the wall, his legs stretched out before him. "Aren't we, Cass?"

It was at this point that Cassian usually leaped in with some advice that would spur them on. He was the most optimistic of the three of them, but fatigue had lowered his defenses. Today despondency weighed upon him like a heavy mantle. He couldn't dredge up the words.

Cassian pinched the skin between his eyebrows. *Mithras, I need sleep.*

He'd just come from speaking to the Wallace, and been heading toward his quarters, when Maximus had intercepted him. Now the three of them sat around the small table in the center of their 'study', a windowless room at the back of Dunnottar dungeons.

"Max is right," Cassian said tonelessly when an uncomfortable silence settled in the chamber. "It might not seem like it ... but we *are* making progress." He lifted his cup to his lips once more and drained the rest of his ale. This conversation was giving him a headache. He really was tired after the journey, and longed to stretch out in his chamber and sleep the rest of the day away.

By rights, he should be jubilant, for they'd managed to get Gavina, Elizabeth, and Aila safely home. However, he felt empty. Even seeing Dunnottar rising against the eastern sky hadn't filled him with pride as it usually did. The mess with Aila had left a sour taste in his mouth, one that no amount of ale could wash away.

She knew his secret, but that only made things more strained between them. He'd been given a reprieve during the journey, for danger had brought them together for a spell. But things would be different back in Dunnottar. Shortly after they'd entered the lower ward bailey, she'd rushed off to see her family. He'd likely see very little of her from today forward. It was for the best, yet a hollow ache in the center of his chest plagued him whenever he thought of her.

Pushing the sensation aside, Cassian reached for the jug of ale and refilled his cup. "The board is set ... things are likely to move fast now," he said, avoiding his friends' penetrating gazes. "Maybe, we just need to stop searching for answers and let the game begin."

Loud voices boomed against the paneled walls of Dunnottar's hall, partially drowning out the conversation of those seated closest to Aila.

News of David De Keith's death had raced through the keep, and would have reached the nearby village of Stonehaven by now. Everyone would know how he'd tried to knife the English king and paid for it with his own life. Some would doubtless even consider him a hero for the act.

Steaming tureens of venison stew sat upon the table. The rich stew was served with oaten bread and wedges of aged sheep's cheese. Despite the knot that still sat under her ribcage, Aila ate hungrily. Although Iona had brought a hearty noon meal up to her earlier in the day, she still felt famished. Around Aila, the conversation eddied and flowed. Her sister sat next to her, but was kept busy placating their overwrought mother.

Relief settled over Aila. She was glad that few folk paid her much attention. She wished to be ignored this evening.

Farther down the table, William Wallace was deep in conversation with Cassian and her father, although Aila was careful not to look in their direction. She'd deliberately avoided glancing anywhere near Dunnottar's Captain of the Guard. Once or twice, she'd felt his gaze upon her, yet she'd refused to look his way.

Her conversation with Heather earlier in the day had made some things clear.

She'd made a mistake, one that she somehow needed to make peace with.

But she was home now, and with war looming on the horizon, she needed to focus on what had to be done to protect this stronghold. Many of the women currently spent their afternoons fletching arrows, and Aila would join them the following day. Lady Gavina had increased the number of guards keeping watch on the walls, and upped the frequency of patrols south of the fortress. Despite the word of Comyn, the consensus was that Longshanks would likely seek vengeance for De Keith's act. It was better to be safe than sorry. While Aila had helped her mistress dress for supper, Gavina informed her that Wallace intended to stay on in Dunnottar. Her brother wasn't the greatest immediate threat now, but sooner or later Shaw Irvine would likely have to be dealt with.

No, Aila's bruised and battered heart didn't matter. And neither did her shredded pride. She'd learned a valuable lesson, and although Heather had tried to soften the disappointment, she'd unwittingly just driven the blade in deeper.

After all, Maximus had bound himself to Heather *knowing* that there was a real risk he might never break the curse.

His love for her overcame his fears.

Obviously, Cassian didn't feel the same way about Aila. She couldn't blame him for it, for he'd made his position clear.

It was time to bury her broken heart.

All the same, it had been an effort to attend this supper. She'd wanted to avoid Cassian. Nonetheless, she couldn't skulk in the shadows now they'd returned to Dunnottar. This was her home too. In the end, she'd agreed to go just to keep her mother's nagging at bay.

Aila glanced up from her stew to see Lady Gavina was watching her. The Lady of Dunnottar had taken the laird's carven chair. It dwarfed her, although her mistress sat proudly upon it, her chin held high. Dressed in a charcoal-colored woolen kirtle, her pale hair tightly braided and wrapped around her crown, her mistress cut a regal, yet somber, figure. David and Gavina's relationship had been so strained it was sometimes easy to forget that the lady was now a widow in mourning.

"Are ye well, Aila?" Gavina asked, raising her voice to be heard over the clamor of nearby conversation.

Aila tensed. Was her unhappiness so easy to read upon her face? "Aye," she replied, forcing a bright smile. "I'm still reeling from it all, I suppose." She paused then, keen to turn the conversation away from herself. "Ye look like ye belong in that chair, My Lady."

Gavina cocked an eyebrow. "Really? I don't look like a bairn sitting in my father's seat?"

Aila gave a snort. "No." The two women's gazes held for a few moments before Aila continued. "I think ye'll make a fine laird. Ye rule these lands now, My Lady ... and I wager ye'll do a much better job of it than yer husband."

Gavina's gaze widened. It was a bold statement—the boldest Aila had ever made to the woman she served, but Aila meant every word. She dared her mistress to contradict her.

Gavina drew in a deep breath, a smile curving her lips. "I appreciate the faith ye have in me, Aila," she replied. "We live in dark times indeed ...but I swear to ye that I'll do my best to keep this castle and all living within its walls safe."

Cassian rose from the table, ignoring something that Draco had just said to him. Instead, his gaze was upon the young woman a few yards away.

Aila De Keith had studiously avoided his gaze all evening. Seated to the right of her mother and sister, eyes downcast, she had said little to anyone besides Lady Gavina. Her lovely face, which was usually so frank, was shuttered and strained.

He didn't like seeing her like this. Withdrawn. Detached.

This is my doing.

On the journey home, just before the English soldiers had caught up with them, he'd apologized. He couldn't let Aila shoulder the blame. She'd been gracious, yet reserved. He'd broken the trust between them.

Watching Aila now, as she exchanged a few words with her sister and raised her pewter goblet to her lips for a last sip, he tensed.

She'd changed since their trip to Stirling.

Gone was the shy smile and laughter that had once come so easily to her. Gone was the girlish enthusiasm. This evening—their first at home after the fraught journey—she was reserved and poised, yet aloof.

Tearing his attention from Aila, Cassian made for the door.

Enough of being sociable. He'd suffered through that supper, when he really just longed to be alone. But upon leaving the hall, he didn't go back to his chamber. He'd slept the afternoon away and now felt relatively rested. Instead, he made his way out into the upper ward bailey and then climbed the steps to the ramparts.

Dusk had just settled over the hills to the west. The North Sea was now flat and dark, and the first of the stars twinkled into existence in the sky. Finally, after a day of frenetic activity, the lower ward below had quietened. However, preparations for the anticipated conflict would begin again at dawn—Cassian intended to get the men out into the bailey for sword-practice. Thanks to the efforts of Galbraith and his lads, they now had plenty of new blades. They needed to make sure all the men knew how to wield them.

Staring out to sea, Cassian clenched his jaw. He'd thought to feel better once he was inside Dunnottar's sheltering walls again, that he'd be able to focus on breaking the curse. But tonight, he didn't care about any of it.

Tonight he felt alone—and far too old.

"There you are." Cassian tensed at the familiar voice behind him but didn't turn from the walls.

A moment later, Maximus stepped up next to him. Cassian glanced at his friend's face, his jaw clenching when he saw his expression.

Someone had told him.

"Why didn't you say something earlier?" Maximus asked.

"Because it's no one's business but mine," Cassian growled, before adding, "Draco has a flapping tongue. Sometimes I long to tie it in a knot."

Maximus snorted. "Don't we all. But Draco's not to blame for this particular indiscretion. Heather told me."

Cassian rolled his eyes. "Well, out with it then. Say your piece."

Maximus didn't say anything for a moment. He merely watched Cassian, his dark gaze now veiled. And when he spoke, his tone was guarded. "You're a man, Cassian ... not a god."

Cassian's mouth twisted. "I'm aware of that."

"Are you?" Maximus raised an eyebrow. "For centuries now, you've denied yourself. It was never going to end well for you. All of us could see that."

Cassian turned, fixing Maximus with a cool look. "You too shunned attachments for a very long time. Or do you forget?"

Maximus shook his head. "Things change, Cass," he murmured. "We have to change with them. Isn't it time to lay Lilla's ghost to rest?"

"And you're here to tell me how well everything worked out for you?" Cassian knew he sounded bitter, but he couldn't help it. He just wanted Maximus to leave him alone to his brooding.

Maximus frowned. "I didn't come up here to preach to you."

Cassian turned back to the wall, his gaze fixing upon the watery horizon. "Well, why then?"

"To check on you."

"As you can see, nothing ails me. Goodnight, Max."

Maximus went silent, and then a moment later, he stepped back from the wall, his boots scuffing on stone. "Wanting her doesn't make you weak," he said softly.

"I'll see you tomorrow," Cassian replied between gritted teeth.

Another pause followed, before Maximus moved away. However, he'd just gone a few steps when he stopped. "Oh, and by the way, I'd avoid Heather for the next few days. You're not her favorite person at present."

XXXIV

FULL-CIRCLE

CASSIAN STRODE ACROSS the lower ward bailey toward the armory. His gaze narrowed when he spied an unwelcome figure in the distance.

Blair Galbraith was standing near the steps to the chapel, looming over a woman who clutched a basket of flowers to her side.

Cassian's breathing hitched, his step faltering. He recognized the woman Galbraith was intimidating.

Aila De Keith.

Cassian slowed his pace, his attention riveted upon the pair. It was as if they'd just gone full circle.

Was it nearly a month since he'd happened upon them in the stairwell? It seemed much longer—so much had happened since then. Galbraith, maddened by a need for vengeance, would have surely raped Aila that day if he hadn't intervened.

Nearly two weeks had passed since their return to Dunnottar, and the whole keep was on tenterhooks. Surely, after De Keith's assassination attempt, Edward of England would attack the stronghold? But the Hammer of the Scots was strangely silent.

Just one more moon, at most, and the Broom-star would fade from the heavens, not to return for another seventy-five years. Time was running out.

And yet when he saw the hulking smith lean in close to Aila and murmur something to her, and watched her shoulders go rigid, Cassian ceased to care about the curse, or the riddle that still toyed with them.

Oblivious to the fact that he now had an audience, Blair Galbraith grabbed Aila's arm and hauled her against him.

Something shattered in Cassian, his tightly wound self-control snapping.

He broke into a run, a roar ripping from his chest. *This time, I'll kill the bastard.*

But before he reached them, Aila had already defended herself. The basket of flowers went flying, and she lashed out, punching the smithy in the throat. Choking, Galbraith released her and staggered back, his green eyes wide with shock.

Spitting out a curse, he lunged for her—but Cassian reached him first.

His fist collided with Galbraith's nose. Sinew and bone crunched under his knuckles.

The smith reeled back. He was a big man, but Cassian was of a similar size, and his weight carried them both onto the ground. Sprawled on his back on the cobbles, blood streaming from his nostrils, Blair Galbraith snarled up at Cassian. He then swung his meaty fists at his face.

Savage fury descended upon Cassian in a red haze.

He hit Galbraith in the face until the man stopped fighting back. He only paused when a woman's voice cut through the roaring in his ears.

"Cassian, stop! Ye'll murder him!"

Panting, Cassian straightened up, his gaze swiveling to where Aila stood a few feet away. Her face was ashen, her grey eyes huge. Behind her, a crowd of stable hands, servants, and warriors appeared. Father Finlay had joined them too. The chaplain stood on the top step below the chapel door. They'd all watched in morbid fascination while Cassian beat Galbraith's face into a pulp.

Looking down at the smith, Cassian saw that he was unconscious, his features a bloodied and swollen mess. "I warned him what would happen if he ever touched you again," he growled.

"We were out in the open," Aila countered, spots of color appearing on her cheeks. "He couldn't have gotten away with anything."

"He was about to drag you into his forge and plow you, woman!"

Muttering in the amassing crowd followed these words, and the blush on Aila's cheeks flushed a deep red.

She was angry, he realized—with him.

Cassian heaved himself off the prone blacksmith and shook out his stinging right hand. He turned and motioned to two of his men who'd joined the watching crowd. "Get him out of my sight." He then swept his gaze over the gaping faces. "Show's over. Return to your duties."

They did as he bid, leaving with lingering glances, both at him and Aila, for the tension between the two of them was palpable.

"Is there anything I can do, Captain?" The chaplain called down. The man wore a worried expression, his gaze flicking between Cassian and Aila.

"No, thank you, Father," Cassian replied with a nod. "The situation is dealt with."

Reluctantly, the chaplain turned away.

Cassian shifted his attention back to Aila then. She was watching him with a clenched jaw, fury smoldering in her eyes.

But anger also burned in *his* belly.

Cassian gestured to the armory behind him. "I need a word with you, Aila. In there."

Bristling at his tone, she held her ground. "Like you said, the situation is dealt with," she bit out the words. "I need to pick up the flowers and deliver them to the church."

"The flowers can wait," he growled. "This can't."

Aila's mouth compressed.

How dare he order me around?

But neither of them was going to back down. Staring back at her, Cassian's hazel eyes smoldered, and his jaw set. He didn't seem to notice or care about the fact that the smithy's blood stained his hands.

The urge to defy him rose up within her. Moments slid by, and she considered stalking off.

Don't be a coward, Aila De Keith. Her pride surfaced then, goading her. *Face him.* There were still a few lingering servants and guards about, all watching what she'd do next. She wouldn't give them the spectacle they craved.

Spine stiff, she picked up her skirts and marched past Cassian to the armory.

The tang of iron, leather, and oil enveloped her when she stepped inside. The armory was a low building with a thatched roof, its interior lit by a single oil lamp sitting upon a bench. Rows of spears, shields, and swords hung upon the walls.

Two of Cassian's men were in here, busy polishing helmets. They glanced up when Cassian and Aila entered, surprised by the intrusion.

Cassian entered the armory behind Aila. "Get out," he barked.

He didn't need to issue the order twice. Abandoning their work, the two warriors ducked their heads and hurried from the armory. The door thudded shut after them, the force of it shaking the walls.

Aila didn't look the men's way as they left. Instead, she turned to face the big man behind her. Aila folded her arms across her chest, creating a barrier between them.

"What were you doing?" Cassian demanded. "I told you to be wary of Galbraith ... and there you were carrying flowers to the chapel again. Are you really that goose-witted?"

His words stung, yet Aila didn't cower before them. Instead, she stood her ground, lifting her chin to keep eye contact.

"I was in the open ... and intended to return to the keep through a safer route than last time," she informed him coldly. "And I don't need ye to tell me what to do. I don't need yer protection, Captain."

"Yes, you plainly do." Cassian shifted over to the bench and picked up a cloth one of his men had abandoned. He then cleaned the blood off his hands in sharp, jerky movements.

Aila watched him, her lips thinning. "What's wrong with ye today, Cassian?"

"I could ask you the same thing," he snapped, his gaze spearing hers once more. "Did you think Blair Galbraith would ever forget? He was waiting for another chance to corner you."

"Ye overreacted," she shot back. "In future, let me fight my own battles."

His expression turned wintry. "Are you really so ungrateful?"

Fury descended over Aila, turning her reckless. "Aye, it appears so ... daft, ungrateful Aila. I'm nothing to ye, Cassian, so let's not pretend we're friends."

He went still, a nerve flickering on his cheek. The air inside the armory vibrated with tension, and Aila edged toward the door. She had to get out before the hurt and anger that still writhed in her belly broke free.

Before she said things they'd both regret.

However, he moved sideways and blocked her path. "We aren't friends, Aila," he said, his voice softening. "There lies too much between us now for that to ever be the case."

Aila's throat closed. "Then, I shall bid ye good day, Captain. Please move aside."

But he didn't.

Aila's breathing quickened.

Long moments passed before Cassian muttered an oath under his breath. His handsome features tightened, his mouth twisting as if he were in physical pain. "I'm a fool, Aila," he rasped.

Now it was Aila's turn to grow still. She watched him, her body tensing, her fists clenching at her sides.

His gaze found hers once more. For the first time ever, she saw raw pain there, vulnerability.

"When I lost Lilla, the agony almost drove me insane." His voice was rough, strained, as if he dredged each word up from his guts. "To lose my wits would have been a relief, I suppose ... but the curse didn't allow it. Instead, I took control of what I could."

Still Aila said nothing. She wouldn't interrupt him, for these were clearly things he needed to say.

"I've been alone for so long I forgot what it's like to crave a woman's touch, to live for the sound of her voice and the curve of her lips when she smiles," he pressed on, his voice growing hoarse now. "But then, you stepped under my guard, Aila De Keith, and I've been fighting a losing battle ever since."

XXXV

IN NO ONE'S SHADOW

AILA'S EARS STARTED to ring, and she realized that
she had forgotten to breathe.

Dragging in a deep breath, she stared up at Cassian.
The pain on his face was raw. She couldn't understand
why saying these things hurt him so much, and yet the
distress on his face wasn't feigned.

"I never meant to cause ye pain, Cassian," she
whispered. She paused then, gathering her courage
before she continued. "I've always been so timid, looking
on while others do things with their lives. I wanted to be
more like Heather ... to take risks. But I lacked the
courage ... and all the while I yearned for the handsome
Captain of Dunnottar Guard to notice me."

"I did notice you," he admitted, his eyes glittering
now. He then favored her with a sheepish smile. "I just
never intended to do anything about it."

"But I wouldn't leave ye alone," she cut in bitterly,
embarrassment stabbing through her. "I ... threw myself
at ye."

His smile turned rueful. "Painting yourself as a
cunning seductress doesn't work, Aila. It was your
gentleness, your shy smiles and innocent enthusiasm

that drew me to you. I was like a field of dry grass after a summer's drought ... all I needed was one tiny flame to be set alight."

He stepped forward, his hand catching hers. He then raised it, placing her palm over his heart.

Aila swallowed, her mouth going dry when she felt how fast it was beating.

"When you touched me that night in the hallway, I was undone," he murmured. His hand closed over hers, his fingers curling tightly. "And I still am."

Silence followed his words. Once again, Aila forgot to breathe. It suddenly felt overly warm inside the armory, and a wave of dizziness swept over her. "What are ye saying?" she whispered.

"That I am sick with love for you," he replied, reaching up with his free hand to stroke her face.

Aila shivered at his gentle touch. His fingertips sent ripples of pleasure down her neck and made her sweat. However, all she could think about was the declaration he'd just made. "Ye are?"

He nodded and stepped closer still, the heat of his body drawing her in. "I scorned Maximus when he fell for your sister, you know?"

Aila inclined her head, waiting for him to continue.

"We had an unspoken pact, and he broke it. I felt betrayed. I told him he was an idiot for taking such a risk when we haven't yet broken the curse."

"I'm sure Draco would have agreed with ye."

Cassian huffed a sigh, his thumb tracing the line of her jaw. "He does, but when I look at Draco these days, all I see is a bitter husk of a man. Do I really want to end up like him?"

Aila let out a shuddering breath. His touch was making it hard to concentrate. "I don't know," she replied weakly. "Do ye?"

"No."

He drew her against him then, his mouth covering hers for a deep, sensual kiss.

Aila trembled. His lips and tongue were achingly tender. He kissed her as if she was the most precious thing in the world. He'd said he loved her, but she didn't need to hear the words—for his kiss told it all.

Joy built in her chest until her ribs started to ache. Her hands slid up, and she linked them around his neck. She stood on tip-toe so that she could deepen the embrace.

With a groan deep in his throat, Cassian hauled her against him.

And in a heartbeat, the kiss went from tender to fierce.

Aila forgot everything except the man whose hard, muscular body now pressed against hers. She lost herself in his taste and the rasp of his stubble against her lips. He smelt of leather and tasted of warm, spicy, delicious male. She couldn't form one coherent thought.

All she wanted was him.

Cassian lifted her against him, spun her around, and pressed her up against the door. When his hands delved beneath her skirts, sliding up the naked skin of her thighs, Aila let out a soft whimper.

Memories of their night together crashed over her: the excitement, the hunger, the need to possess—and to be possessed. The disappointment that had followed that night had obliterated those memories, and she'd deliberately not dwelled upon them, for the pain that followed was almost unbearable.

But she could let it all go now.

Hands shaking with desperate need, she fumbled with the laces on his braies. Somehow though, she managed to release them, and his shaft sprang free. Her fingers closed around his hard, throbbing girth. The skin was so hot, so soft, in contrast to the iron strength beneath her fingers.

She stroked his engorged shaft while they kissed, thrilling at how he groaned against her mouth, how his hips bucked against her. Encouraged, she increased her tempo. An ache rose between her legs as she remembered just how good he'd felt inside her.

Cassian's agonized moan filled the armory. And then he was lifting her higher still, kneeing her trembling thighs apart.

He drove into her, sheathing himself fully in one deep thrust.

Aching pleasure shivered through Aila, radiating out from the cradle of her hips. The sensation was almost unbearable. She buried her face in his neck, biting down on his flesh to prevent herself from crying out.

Whispering something to her in a tongue she didn't understand, Cassian took hold of her hips, slowly withdrew, and then drove into her once more.

Now it was Aila's turn to buck against him. Their coupling that night in Stirling Castle had left her breathless, but she'd been a virgin then, and there had been a little pain at first. Not so now—this time her body sang from the moment he entered her.

Aila widened her thighs, welcoming him deeper still. Pleasure thrummed through her, turning her reckless and wild. When Cassian's lips found hers again, she thrust her tongue against his, urging him to take her harder still.

And he did. Their mouths fused, their cries smothered, they writhed together against the door.

Aila clung to him. Her vision speckled now, dizziness sweeping over her. The pleasure was almost too much, yet she didn't pull back from the brink. Instead, she let herself fall into him, let the last shreds of control unravel. And likewise, Cassian gave her everything.

He'd made passionate love to her in Stirling, yet a violent storm swept through the armory this afternoon. His strong body trembled, and his mouth on hers was a brand. He plunged into her as if nothing else in the world mattered, and when Aila arched against him, biting into his shoulder once more to smother a wild cry, he gasped her name, his voice breaking.

Cassian stirred upon the bed, stretching his limbs under the warm sun that filtered in through the open window. Eyes flickering open, he glanced over at where a naked woman lay on her side, facing him.

The sunlight played across her lithe limbs and milky skin. Her thick walnut-colored hair fanned out across the pillow, and her full lips—swollen from his kisses—were slightly parted.

Not wanting to wake her, and yet unable to resist touching her, Cassian reached out and brushed a lock of hair off her face.

Aila stretched like a she-cat, her eyes flickering open.

For a long moment, the pair of them just stared at each other, and then Aila wet her lips, an innocent-enough gesture that made his rod stiffen. Those lips had been wrapped around his shaft just a short while earlier, sucking and licking him into a frenzy.

"I should really get back," Aila said, her voice husky, breaking his reverie. "Lady Gavina will wonder what has become of me."

Cassian huffed, his hand trailing down her neck to the curve of her high, rosy breasts. "Let her wonder ... some things are more important."

Indeed, after their stormy coupling in the armory, he'd taken her by the hand and led her out into the lower ward bailey. He'd almost expected to find a crowd gathered there, to see his men smirking and servants giving them knowing looks. However, as he'd ordered, everyone had returned to their duties.

Wordlessly, Cassian had led Aila up to his quarters, high in the main guard tower, and with the door locked behind them, he'd undressed her before laying her down upon the bed and exploring her body at leisure.

Aila had watched him under lowered lids, her smoke-grey eyes dark.

Cassian had stared back at her, captivated. Since his announcement back in the armory, they'd barely spoken. A wildness had descended upon them both, a hunger that had to be satisfied.

But now, despite that his groin grew achingly hard at the sight of her, Cassian knew the time had come for him to speak once more.

"You're a feast, Aila," he murmured. "One that I will never tire of."

Her cheeks blushed prettily at that—despite all they'd done this afternoon, he still had the power to embarrass her.

Cassian moved closer, drawing Aila against him. Catching her under the chin, he gently raised it so their gazes fused. "It feels as if I've spent years trapped in a dungeon of my own making ... but am now a free man, Aila," he admitted. "Thanks to you."

She stared up at him, her eyes gleaming. "I love ye, Cassian," she whispered.

Swallowing the lump that rose in his throat, he smiled. "I'm scared," he admitted huskily. "Scared of losing you ... and scared we'll never break this curse. I can't promise you things will turn out as we both want ... but I can vow I will never leave your side."

A tear trickled down her cheek. "Ye must have loved yer wife very much," she said huskily, "to grieve for her as long as ye did ... I hope I can do her memory justice."

His mouth twisted, and he shook his head. "You don't need to. I did love Lilla ... but she's been gone a long while now. You stand in no one's shadow, Aila, remember that." His face relaxed a little then. "I need to stop trying to outrun things ... fate always catches up with me in the end. Lilla once said that love is always worth the pain of loss, and she was right. It's just taken me too long to realize."

Aila stared up at him, more tears flowing now. "But ye might break the curse ... ye are so close now."

"We are," he said softly, brushing away her tears with the back of his hand. "But there are no guarantees, love. I can only give you myself, as I am right now. Will you wed an immortal man, Aila?"

Aila's lips parted, and she inhaled sharply. Seeing her reaction, Cassian smiled. "Maximus will grin, and Draco will tell me I have the wits of a donkey, but I don't care. All I want is you." A shiver went through him as he said these words. In truth, he was terrified of what the future held, of what they were both risking, but he'd meant his words. He wouldn't use the fear of pain as a shield any longer.

Lilla had been right all those years ago—he wished he'd listened to her.

"Will you be my wife?" He heard the doubt in his own voice. "I can't give you children, but I will cherish you." He paused then, before favoring her with a wicked smile. "Unless of course we do manage to break the curse ... and if that happens I'll give you a brood of bairns, if that's what you wish for."

The smile was a brave front, for he worried that after what he'd put Aila through, she wouldn't want to bind herself to him. Would she want a man who couldn't give her a family? Lilla had insisted it didn't matter, but Cassian had always suspected she'd been disappointed.

However, the look on Aila's face made the tightness in his chest ease. Tears ran freely down her cheeks and glittered off her long eyelashes. "Gladly," she breathed.

Swallowing hard, as the urge to weep swept over him, Cassian pulled Aila against him, kissing her tenderly. When they broke apart, his own vision was blurred.

"Of course, that smooth bastard, Maximus, has shown me up, once again," he said huskily.

Aila choked a laugh. "And why's that?"

"He asked your father's permission *before* he proposed."

Aila gave a soft laugh. "Worry not, Da isn't an ogre."

Her words spurred Cassian into action. He released Aila, rolled off the bed, and reached for his clothing.

"Where are ye going?" Aila asked, sitting up and pushing her hair off her face.

The sight of her there, naked, hair mussed from their loving, made him want to return to the bed. But Cassian ignored his aching shaft and pulled on his braies. He then reached for his lèine. "I'm off to seek out Donnan," he replied with a grin. "I'll not let Maximus Cato best me."

XXXVI

BLESSED

THE CLANGING OF bells echoed across Dunnottar as a man and woman descended the steps of the chapel. The waiting crowd cheered, children rushing forward to throw rose petals over the happy couple.

Her arm linked through Cassian's, Aila was smiling so broadly that her face was starting to ache. She wore her prettiest lilac kirtle and had woven daisies through her hair. Next to her, Cassian had donned his best lèine and braies, with the De Keith sash proudly displayed across his chest.

Aila was breathless with joy. She didn't know such happiness was possible—that love could make one feel both weak and strong at the same time. For the first time, she understood why Cassian had been so reluctant to risk his heart again. Giving yourself up to love was braver than she'd thought.

She squeezed Cassian's arm tightly, tears prickling the backs of her eyes as emotion overwhelmed her.

Glancing down at Aila, Cassian smiled. His gaze was soft as it lingered upon her. "All is well, my love?"

Vision swimming, Aila nodded before smiling back at him.

Aila's parents, Heather, Maximus, Draco, Lady Elizabeth, and Lady Gavina all formed part of the crowd beneath them. William Wallace was there too. A wide smile split his bearded face; it appeared the Wallace loved a good wedding.

Aila's gaze swept the crowd. She caught Lady Gavina's eye before grinning at her. Dressed in 'mourning black', her mistress smiled back.

The night before, as Aila helped her mistress get ready for bed, she'd confided in Gavina about the riddle. However, Aila hadn't recited it to her. Truthfully, she couldn't remember half of the words. Gavina had assured her that she and Elizabeth would never speak a word of what they'd discovered to anyone. "But I hope for all yer sakes that ye manage to break the curse," Gavina had concluded.

Favoring the Lady of Dunnottar with a grateful smile, Aila had reached out and covered Gavina's hands with her own. "Aye, so do I ... but no matter what happens, I want to be Cassian's wife."

Gavina had answered her smile with a gentle one of her own. "I used to think ye and Heather were so different," she noted with a shake of her head. "But I see ye are both of the same mettle."

The Lady of Dunnottar hosted a banquet in honor of Cassian and Aila's wedding. Platters of roast mutton and venison, and tureens of boar stew—accompanied by braised kale, mashed turnip, and an assortment of breads—lined the long tables inside the hall. Servants had sprinkled rose petals everywhere, their scent blending with the rich aroma of the food.

Seated at the head of the table at Cassian's side—for Gavina had given up her place for this special day—Aila let her gaze roam around the busy hall. The rumble of happy voices and the strains of a harp flowed over her. She and Cassian had provided Lady Gavina with only a day's notice—but she'd managed to festoon the rafters with garlands of meadow flowers. Outdoors, the bell had stopped clanging, and instead, the crash of surf against the rocks drifted through the open window.

Aila took it all in, every last detail. She felt like pinching herself.

Is this really happening?

Sensing a gaze upon her, she glanced over at where her sister sat next to Maximus. Heather was watching her, an enigmatic smile curving her full lips. She'd been overjoyed when Aila and Cassian had visited her and Maximus with their news. The delight she'd found at her sister's happiness warmed Aila's heart.

Heather had only tried to protect her from being hurt earlier, and now that Cassian had revealed his feelings for her sister, she could be happy for them both.

Maximus leaned back in his seat, an arm slung possessively over his wife's shoulders. He was saying something to Draco across the table, although with the din of conversation, Aila couldn't make out the words.

The Moor replied, before he smirked. Draco had attended the wedding and congratulated them both. However, something in his manner had put Aila on edge. His gaze was sharp, despite the smile on his lips. Aila imagined he was sneering inwardly at the folly of his friends.

Let him, Aila thought, glancing back at her husband's handsome profile. Cassian was serving them slices of meat and spoonfuls of vegetables onto the platter they would both share. *Draco seems incapable of loving anyone.*

"It's time for a toast, I think." Aila's father rose to his feet, wincing as he favored his lame leg. He then held his silver goblet of wine aloft and waited as the conversation around them died.

"It's about time," Wallace boomed from farther down the table. "To the happy couple."

"Aye," Donnan De Keith raised his goblet to Wallace before twisting to face Aila and Cassian. When his gaze fell upon his younger daughter, a tender expression settled on his face. "Aila ... I do believe that ye are all grown up now." His grey eyes shadowed a moment then. "Time passes so quickly, lass. It seems only yesterday that ye and Heather were tiny, and Iona and I were newly wed." He paused, casting his wife a soft look. Iona smiled up at him. "Marriage can be life's best journey, or its worst," the steward of Dunnottar continued. "It all depends on whom ye choose to bind yerself to. I chose well. And I believe ye have too."

Aila glanced then at Lady Gavina. She was smiling, yet there was a stillness to her, a melancholy in her eyes that betrayed her. Of course, as a laird's daughter, Gavina hadn't been able to choose at all. Her and David's marriage was a cautionary tale.

"Not so long ago, I had two bonny daughters," Donnan continued. "I'm sad to lose them of course. But at least I know I don't have to worry about their safety and happiness." The steward paused there, his gaze flicking to Maximus and then Cassian, "because they are married to two of the bravest, most honorable men in this keep."

Aila's breathing caught at these words, while smiles stretched both Maximus and Cassian's faces. She knew how much his recognition would mean to them—more than her father would ever realize.

"May fortune and happiness shine upon ye both," Donnan concluded, raising his goblet higher still.

"Fortune and happiness!" The cry went up throughout the hall in a chorus, as all present raised their drinks. The force of their voices shook the rafters.

Aila's breathing quickened. Warmth filtered through her. These were her people, and this was her home. For years, she'd felt ignored, taken for granted. But she realized now that had never been the case.

In truth, she'd lacked the courage to live fully and blamed her circumstances for it.

Around them, the rumble of conversation and laughter resumed once more.

"Fill up your goblet, Cass," Maximus said with a wink. Leaning forward, he poured sloe wine into the silver goblet that Cassian held out to him. "Let's make another toast ... to the Broom-star ... may this be the last time the three of us set eyes upon it."

Both Cassian and Draco grinned. "I'll drink to that 'Great One'," Cassian replied, holding his goblet aloft.

The three men all raised their goblets and drank, and then Cassian turned to Aila. "Will ye take a sip of wine with me, my love?"

He was watching her with an intensity that caused butterflies to dance in her belly. How long had she wished for Cassian Gaius to look at her like this? It had seemed a dream, but somehow it had come true.

Nodding, she accepted the goblet he offered her and took a sip before passing it back to him. Holding her eye, he took a drink, a smile creasing his face.

"To fortune and happiness," he murmured, his eyes glinting, "Although I'd say we're already blessed with both."

Reaching out, she entwined her fingers with his. The rest of the hall faded as she gazed up at him. She could drown in the warmth of his hazel eyes. "We are," she whispered.

EPILOGUE

BLIND

BLAIR GALBRAITH crossed the lower ward, pausing as the sound of laughter and merriment drifted down from the open window of the hall above.

Mouth twisting into a sneer, he spat on the cobblestones before him.

"Curse ye all," he muttered. "Ye won't be making merry soon."

Blair winced. His face was a mess; he didn't need a looking glass to know it. Captain Gaius had pummeled it into a pulp. It hurt to talk, to eat, or drink—and even that sneer had cost him. He stifled a groan of pain and continued on his way across the bailey toward the gates.

And with each step, the heavy bag of silver pennies— all the coin he'd saved in the years he'd worked at Dunnottar—clinked against his hip.

He was leaving this fortress and taking nothing but the clothes on his back.

But he wasn't done with the De Keiths.

It was time to have his reckoning upon those who ruled this fortress.

Galbraith's belly cramped. He hated them all.

The only one he'd had any time for was dead—but even David De Keith had disappointed him in the end. He'd been useless after Iain went missing. He'd let Wallace bully him. Maximus Cato should have been strung up for killing his brother, but no one cared.

No one except Blair.

The guards at the gate greeted him. "Where are ye off to, Galbraith?" one of them enquired.

"To find myself a whore in Stonehaven," he growled. "My balls are tight."

They roared at that, pulling the gates open so he could pass through. "A wedding will do that to ye," another guard quipped. "Although the way yer face looks at the moment, ye'll frighten a woman off."

Galbraith muttered something crude in response, a comment that had them slapping their thighs with mirth, and made his way out onto the steep path that wound its way down from the gates.

As always, it was a lot windier out here. Briny sea air rushed past his face. It was bracing, a balm to the dull throb in his jaw and nose.

Gabraith made his way down the path to the bottom of the steep defile. Breathing hard, he then climbed to the cliff-top, reaching the edge of the wide green hills that stretched around Dunnottar. And then, casting one lingering look of spite over his shoulder, he strode away.

Stonehaven wasn't his destination though. He'd just said that to the guards so they wouldn't question him further. Instead, he was headed toward another fortress. For the moment though, he walked north—but would turn south as soon as the guards on the walls could no longer see him.

He was traveling to Stirling.

Edward of England was still there.

The news of how David De Keith had tried to plunge a dirk into Longshanks' neck continued to be the main topic at mealtimes in Dunnottar. Blair couldn't help but be impressed when he heard, but the castle's residents were now understandably nervous.

It wasn't a matter of *if* Edward's reckoning would come, but when. Two weeks had passed since the assassination attempt, yet there hadn't been a whisper from the south.

Blair Galbraith's swollen lips pressed together, and he flinched.

Maybe he needs a little extra persuasion.

How would the Hammer of the Scots react when he learned that William Wallace was sheltering at Dunnottar?

He'll march straight here without delay and smash down Dunnottar's walls.

Squaring his shoulders, Blair Galbraith lengthened his stride and didn't look back at the fortress again.

They watched the sun set over the sea in a blaze of red and gold, arms wrapped around each other. Below them, a man bellowed foul curses at the warriors sparring with wooden swords in the lower ward bailey.

"Sounds like Draco is making the lads work hard," Cassian murmured, his mouth quirking.

Aila huffed a laugh, snuggling close to him. She was glad Cassian wasn't overseeing sword practice this evening. Let Draco put the new members of the Guard through their drills instead for once. War was coming, but right now belonged to her and Cassian.

"I never tire of this view." Cassian spoke up once more, pointing south. "Look."

Following his gaze, Aila spied the boat on the horizon. Its large, single sail billowed as the vessel sailed north.

"I imagine it's a merchant's birlinn," he continued. "Bound for Inverness."

"It's hard to believe all of southern Scotland is under English rule now," Aila replied, her brow furrowing. "If I hadn't been to Stirling and seen it myself, I wouldn't believe it. Things seem so peaceful here."

"The calm before the storm," Cassian replied softly.

Aila shivered, pulling closer the woolen shawl she'd wrapped around her shoulders before coming up onto the walls. The prophetic edge to his voice cast a shadow over the day's joy. Yet at the same time, the knowledge that war was looming made every moment she shared with Cassian more precious.

The wedding festivities were over now. There would be no music and dancing late into the evening. The shortness of their celebrations was a reminder of the threat to Dunnottar. Of course, Edward of England wasn't their only foe. This fortress had already been preparing for an assault from Shaw Irvine. However, Longshanks had now eclipsed the danger Irvine posed.

"I've fought in so many wars over the centuries," Cassian continued, his gaze still tracking the merchant boat north. "I've lost count."

"I know ye can't die, but don't ye dread the fighting all the same?" she asked.

"I don't enjoy having a blade stab me through the guts ... but no, not really." He then glanced at Aila, and she saw his gaze was shadowed. "But I do worry for others."

He shifted closer still to Aila and wrapped an arm about her shoulders, drawing her against him. Aila sank into his warmth, his strength. When Cassian stood at her side, she felt as if she could face anything.

The pair of them lapsed into silence for a few moments, enjoying the moment of peace together here high up on the walls.

Eventually, Aila stirred. "It's been a wonderful day ... I'm sorry to see it end."

"So am I."

"The ceremony ... the banquet ... it was all perfect. It was great to see you, Maximus, and Draco relaxing together too." She paused there. "During the meal, ye called Maximus 'Great One' ... why?"

Their gazes met, and Cassian's mouth curved. "His name means 'the greatest', and since he's an arrogant bastard, Draco and I like to tease him about it."

"And what of *yer* name?" Aila asked, grinning now.

"I have no idea ... it was given to me when I enlisted in the imperial army and became a Roman citizen ... my old Spanish name was Barros."

"Really ... I think 'Cassian' suits ye better."

His smile widened. "Me too. I've had it for so long I can't imagine being called anything else."

"And Draco?"

"That's easy ... his name means 'dragon'."

Aila stiffened. "Dragon ... isn't that in yer riddle?"

Cassian inclined his head. "Yes ... 'when the White Hawk and Dragon wed, only then will the curse be broke'."

Aila pulled away from him, excitement quickening in her belly. "Maybe, Draco is part of the riddle?"

Cassian stared at her. "What?"

"Draco ... dragon ... it makes perfect sense."

"But I thought it might belong to one of the clans," he replied. The stunned expression he now wore was almost comical. "Part of a crest or a motto. Or maybe it refers to the name of a warlord or king."

Aila shook her head. "I think ye are casting yer net too broadly. It's made the three of ye blind. What if the person ye seek is right beneath yer nose?"

Cassian's big body went rigid. A beat passed, and then he threw back his head and laughed. The sound carried over the ramparts, causing the guards farther down the wall to turn and stare at them.

Cassian paid their bemused looks no mind. Still grinning, he turned back to Aila once more, his hazel eyes gleaming gold in the sunset. "Hades ... I knew there was a reason I wed you." And with that, he leaned in close and kissed her.

The End

FROM THE AUTHOR

I hope you enjoyed the second installment in THE IMMORTAL HIGHLAND CENTURIONS.

CASSIAN was an emotional book to write. I really felt for Cassian's situation, while at the same time wanting to give him a shake for being so guarded and stubborn. Aila was a fascinating heroine—a young woman full of contradictions. I loved seeing her blossom as the story progressed.

Unrequited love is one of my favorite romance tropes. Having said that, this is the first one I've done where the woman is the one who's hopelessly in love. It was a powerful theme to explore, as was the fact that pain is just part of love—and if we seek to avoid it at all costs, we avoid living. I found this story a real 'old-school' romance—there were so many fun scenes to write.

I'm afraid I've left you with a bit of a cliff-hanger at the end of Book #2 (insert evil author laugh here!), but fear not, dear reader, for Book #3 is already on preorder and due very soon!

Once again there's quite a bit of historical background that went into this novel (read my historical notes below for details on it), and it was great fun to bring Edward of England into the plot. As you might have guessed, we're not done with him yet either!

Get ready for Draco's story!

Jayne x

HISTORICAL NOTES

Once again, these notes are lengthy—but worth the read if you like a bit of historical background insight! Some of these are repeated from the notes at the back of Maximus (for those of you who haven't read Book 1), but there are also some additional details I think you'll enjoy learning about.

As those of you who've read Book #1 will know, this tale hinges around the story of the Ninth legion—a legion of five thousand men who marched into the wilds of Caledonia in around 118 AD and were never seen again.

The Ninth legion was also called 'the Hispana', or Spanish legion. The generals and commander would have all been Roman, but most of the legion was made up of soldiers from Hispania (Spain). Cassian comes from what is now northern Spain, and the Roman fort of Brigantium—now the town of A Coruña, in Galicia.

Halley's Comet is a prominent feature in the whole series. Back in the Dark Ages and Medieval period, it didn't go by that name (as it was named after the scientist who 'discovered' it in 1758). Instead, there are references to it being called 'the fire-tailed star'. Maximus calls it 'the Broom-star', which was actually a name that Chinese astronomers attached to the comet. Halley's Comet appears in our skies every 75-76 years, and in ancient times it was often heralded as an ill omen. The comet actually appeared in the night-sky in the months preceding the Norman invasion of England, something which the English blamed for their defeat. The Bayeux tapestry even shows the comet! The year in which this series takes place, 1301, was a year in which the comet was sighted.

Dunnottar does mean 'fort on the shelving slope' in Scottish Gaelic: Dùn Fhoithear. The castle is a mighty stronghold perched on cliffs on the north-eastern coast of Scotland. The castle was taken by the English in the final years of the 13th Century and then liberated by William Wallace and his men. When the English garrison realized they were doomed, they locked themselves inside the chapel, hoping to find sanctuary there. However, Wallace showed them no mercy and burned the lot of them to death inside it.

William Wallace, of course, is the famous Scottish freedom fighter. My depiction of Wallace isn't the Mel Gibson, *Braveheart* version. Instead, I followed the historical records of him as a giant of a man with thick dark hair and beard. He was also reputed to have had a terrible temper. Not a man to mess with!

Wallace was once in love with a woman called Marion Braidfute. Their story ended in tragedy when Marion was murdered in the Scottish town of Lanark. Fueled by rage and grief, Wallace attacked Lanark and took revenge by killing its English sheriff, Sir William Heselrig. And yes, it's true, Wallace did make the dried skin of Hugh de Cressingham—the hated English treasurer he'd killed at the Battle of Stirling Bridge—into a scabbard, hilt, and belt!

The year 1301, when our story starts in earnest, is also in the midst of the Scottish Wars of Independence (although they weren't called that at the time). When this series begins, there was a period of unstable peace although later that year Edward I of England resumes his campaign. The laird of Dunnottar, Robert De Keith, was an English prisoner as I describe, and he did have a wife named Elizabeth, and a son called Robert. However, his brother, David, is fictitious, as is Lady Gavina.

While it's true that Edward's son did occupy the south-west of Scotland while his father focused on the other territories, I couldn't find any mention of Edward residing in Stirling at this time.

However, that doesn't mean he couldn't have ...

I did a bit of research into Edward of England. Indeed, he went by the name of Longshanks (due to his considerable height), and did have the moniker: the Hammer of the Scots (something that ties nicely into our riddle). At the time of our series, he would have been sixty-two years old. He was tall with dark-blond hair and 'icy blue' eyes. He was also reputed to be quite handsome, although a drooping left eyelid marred his looks slightly. Edward was said to have a powerful voice, despite a slight lisp, and a terrible temper when riled. He was clever and a good fighter. With all this in mind, I had a lot of fun writing the scenes with him in them.

Of course, David De Keith (whom I made up!) did not try and assassinate King Edward, but who's to say a similar incident didn't occur during Edward's time in Scotland ... he was certainly hated by the Scots.

John 'The Red' Comyn also features in this novel. He was a leading Scottish baron and magnate who played an important role in the First War of Scottish Independence. He served as Guardian of Scotland after the forced abdication of his uncle, King John Balliol, in 1296, and for a time commanded the defense of Scotland against English attacks. I couldn't find out if he was actually in Stirling in 1301, but since he was Guardian, I thought it probable. Comyn stepped down from the role of Guardian in May 1301, so I played around with timelines just a little here!

You're probably wondering if Stirling Castle does have a secret gate in the Nether Bailey? It did once. If you visit that corner of Stirling Castle, you'll find an odd grassy mound by the wall walk. Long blocked up, this was the site of a postern gate. It acted as an emergency exit from

Stirling Castle in times of trouble. Later on, it may even have been the secret way out taken by a mischievous James V, disguised as 'the Guidman of Ballengeich'. Dressed as a farmer, James would allegedly sneak out to walk amongst his people incognito to hear what they thought of him.

Once again, we go back to the Kirk of the Holy Rude in Stirling. The kirk does exist, although (to my knowledge) there is no temple of Mithras underneath it!

I got the idea for the temple from a church in Rome, Italy. The Catholic church of San Clemente al Laterano (near the Colosseum) stands atop a 2nd Century mithraeum, a temple to the ancient Roman god, Mithras. I visited the church and temple many years ago (I lived in Rome for a decade in my twenties), but can still remember descending to the dark, damp, cave-like vault, and seeing the altar where a relief depicts Mithras slaying a bull. In the pre-Christian era of the Roman Empire, Mithras was a very popular god worshipped mainly by soldiers.

Of course, as with all my novels, I bend and shape historical fact to suit the story I'm telling. As much as I love research and incorporating fascinating details, they can never overshadow the love story.

CHARACTER GLOSSARY

The three immortal centurions:
Maximus—from Ostia, Italia
Cassian—from Brigantium, Hispania
Draco—from Valentia, Hispania

William Wallace—Scottish freedom fighter

The De Keiths
Robert De Keith (former laird of Dunnottar, currently imprisoned by the English)
Elizabeth De Keith (Robert's wife)
Robbie De Keith (Robert and Elizabeth's young son)
David De Keith (Robert's younger brother—current laird of Dunnottar Castle)
Gavina De Keith (David's wife, née Ivine)
Donnan De Keith (Steward of Dunnottar)
Iona De Keith (Donnan's wife)
Heather De Keith (Donnan and Iona's eldest daughter)
Aila De Keith (Heather's younger sister)

The Irvines
Shaw Irvine (laird of Drum Castle—brother to Gavina De Keith)

The Galbraiths
Logan Galbraith (laird of Culcreuch Castle)
Lena Galbraith (Logan's wife)
Cory Galbraith (Logan and Lena's son—the eldest of four sons: Rory, Aran, and Duglas)
Iain Galbraith (cousin to Cory, former blacksmith of Fintry)
Blair Galbraith (Iain's younger brother, smith at Dunnottar)

The English
Edward I, King of England
Hugh De Burgh (Edward's commander)

ACKNOWLEDGEMENTS

Thanks so much to my readers. I hope you're loving the series so far!

I'd also like to thank the wonderful Otago/Southland Chapter of RWNZ (Romance Writers of New Zealand), and the organization as a whole. I wouldn't have gotten this far without your amazing help and support.

And thanks to the love, assistance, and support of my husband, Tim, each book is the best we can make it. Thank you, my love.

ABOUT THE AUTHOR

Award-winning author Jayne Castel writes epic Historical and Fantasy Romance. Her vibrant characters, richly researched historical settings and action-packed adventure romance transport readers to forgotten times and imaginary worlds.

Jayne is the author of the Amazon bestselling BRIDES OF SKYE series—a Medieval Scottish Romance trilogy about three strong-willed sisters and the men who love them. An exciting spin-off series set in the same story-world, THE SISTERS OF KILBRIDE, is now available as well. In love with all things Scottish, Jayne also writes romances set in Dark Ages Scotland ... sexy Pict warriors anyone?

When she's not writing, Jayne is reading (and re-reading) her favorite authors, cooking Italian feasts, and taking her dog, Juno, for walks. She lives in New Zealand's beautiful South Island.

Connect with Jayne online:
www.jaynecastel.com
www.facebook.com/JayneCastelRomance/
Email: contact@jaynecastel.com